CHRISTMAS AT THE COVE

FIVE ISLAND COVE, BOOK 4

JESSIE NEWTON

COPYRIGHT

ISBN-13: 978-1-953506-29-0

CHAPTER ONE

AJ Proctor took off the red and white striped sweater with a muttered, "This makes you look like a chubby candy cane." She'd put on a few pounds since she'd quit her job at the sports network a couple of weeks ago.

Perhaps she'd left the station a month ago, but she really had only gained about five pounds. She was happier than she'd been in a long time, and she knew it was because of a trifecta of things all combining together to increase her overall mood.

One, she was now seriously dating Matt Hymas. Yes, he still lived in Five Island Cove, and she still lived in New York, but he came to see her every chance he got, and she'd been back to the cove several times in the past few months since they'd reconnected.

Two, AJ had started seeing a therapist. She wasn't sure

why she'd been so resistant to meeting with a mental health professional, only that she'd once believed that admitting she needed help was the worst form of weakness she could exhibit.

She now knew her father was wrong. All of the coaches she'd had over the years were wrong. She herself had been wrong. There was nothing wrong with getting the help she needed to be the best, most whole, and healthiest version of herself that she could be.

It was Dr. Genosie that had kept AJ in New York, actually. If not for the progress AJ had been making with her therapist, she strongly suspected she'd have already made the move back to the cove.

At the same time, AJ did not really want to move back to Five Island Cove. That was the topic of today's therapy session, and AJ pulled off her sweater and tossed it on her bed. She needed to make the right decisions for her about Five Island Cove, not because Matt lived there and she'd already fallen for him all over again.

He was precisely the kind of man she'd always wanted to look her way. Had she known he would respect her, show up on time, and hold her when she was uncertain, only providing suggestions if she asked for them, she'd have answered his telephone calls in the months following her departure from the cove.

Matt had gone to college too—right here in New York City—and he'd tried calling her in Miami a few times. She'd had her roommate screen those calls, because she'd been running from the first eighteen years of her life. She didn't know how sick she was. She truly didn't believe anyone could love her.

Sometimes she still felt like she was running and still trying to believe she had any worth to anyone.

AJ peered into her closet, which in the apartment she rented, was about the size of a kitchen cabinet and couldn't be called a closet at all, trying to find something else to wear. She reached for the same black, floral blouse she'd been wearing everywhere lately and tugged it over her head.

It at least lay so it wasn't obvious that she'd gained a few pounds. She needed to stop eating so much pasta, but she lived above The Noodle Factory, and it was so easy to stop there on her way back from the gym in the morning, and even easier at night when she finished writing her columns in the shared workspace she rented on the next block over.

That was the third reason she was so blissfully happy —her new career as a freelance sports columnist. She could finally get credit for all the contacts she had, all the stories she dug up, and all the knowledge of sports she'd acquired over the years. She'd had no problem selling her columns; as it was, she was booked out for the next three months, as the basketball regular season had just begun, and all football fans everywhere were gearing up for bowl games on the collegiate level, and then the Superbowl in just six weeks.

Everyone wanted to know everything about their favorite athlete's training schedule, and what they did to stay mentally strong through playoffs and stressful games, and their personal habits to rejuvenate in their off-season downtime.

AJ hadn't had to call in any personal favors yet, and she was making twice as much as she had writing the stories for the on-air talent at her network.

It's also a job you can do from the cove, she thought as she quickly stepped into her boots and reached for her coat. She wasn't sure why the thought was there; she had never wanted to return to the cove permanently. Just eight months ago, she'd only gone for Joel's funeral out of sheer obligation.

So much had changed since April, and AJ wasn't sorry about any of it. Down on the street, her stomach lurched as she lifted her arm to get a cab. She'd forgotten to eat again, but she reassured herself that Wendy, the woman who sat next to AJ in the shared workspace, would have snacks on her desk. She never minded sharing, and she even brought in the dried apricot and mango that AJ had sampled once and really enjoyed just to offer it to AJ.

She'd head to the creative commons after her session, and she'd be able to eat then. She watched the city go by, seeing images of her life on the windows and walls of the tall buildings. College, which had been one big disappointment, though she'd graduated.

Her failure to make the Olympic track team. Her

decline into more men for a year, until she cleaned herself up and got a job in sports broadcasting.

Her return to college, this time with an emphasis on broadcasting and journalism. Her graduation. Her long relationships that led to dead-ends.

Robin. Alice, Eloise. Kelli. The women who never truly left her, and who'd always accepted her for exactly who she was.

A smile touched her face, and AJ blinked. The images disappeared, and the city became just the city again.

"Lexington Building," the cab driver said, and AJ quickly tapped her watch to pay for the ride. Outside, she zipped her coat to her chin and started down the cleared sidewalk. Mother Nature had not been kind this first week of December, and she often felt like an insect bustling through paths with high walls of snow on either side.

Heat greeted her upon opening the door, bursting into her face with the scent of flames and vanilla. The receptionist at the front desk always burned candles, and AJ had started to purchase some of the brand for herself. They were all hand-created, with creative names and scents, from a female-owned business out of California.

"What's this variety?" she asked Raymond as she signed into the building.

"Take a chill," he said. "Vanilla bean ice cream, long naps, and marshmallow dreams." He grinned at her as he turned the jar toward her.

AJ read the same description, a smile crossing her face

too. "I got the Boyfriend's Sweater one. I love it."

"Darby loves that one too," Ray said, taking the check-in clipboard and pressing the button to let her into the building.

AJ didn't immediately move toward the door, though if she didn't pass through it in the next sixty seconds, Ray would have to open it for her again. "She does, huh? And you two are...? Engaged yet?"

"I'm working on it," Ray said, not meeting AJ's eye.

"Are you?" AJ had loved getting to know Ray, and he made it very easy to do that, as he could talk the ear off a deaf man. "What's the hold-up?" She was at least a decade older than Ray and his girlfriend, but she'd heard a lot about the two of them in the past three months since she'd been coming to the Lexington Building to meet with Dr. Genosie.

"The hold-up is Darby said she's not sure she wants to get married." Ray looked up then, and AJ's heart tore for him.

"Oh, no," she said. "Get on out here and hug me."

Ray shook his head, a small smile on his face as he did what AJ said. He was a sharp dresser, his hair always combed just-so. She'd thought him a good catch for someone lucky enough to find him, and she couldn't fathom why his girlfriend didn't want to marry him.

She wasn't going to be like Robin, though, and ask. A question did bounce through her mind, but she kept it silent. She'd been on the wrong end of it before, and she would not put another person through the emotional turmoil of wondering if Darby didn't want to get married in general, or if she simply didn't want to marry Raymond.

Nathan hadn't wanted to marry AJ, and that had been a painful, painful realization that she'd already worked through with her therapist.

"Thanks, AJ," Ray said, his voice muted and so unlike his own. He stepped back and kept his face turned away from hers as he returned to his desk. "Go on, so I don't have to open the door again."

"Okay," AJ said, stepping toward the door. She didn't move very fast, adding, "Ray, call me if you need to, okay?"

"Yep," he said, already back in his seat. AJ went through the door to the bank of elevators that led up to at least a dozen medical offices, knowing Ray wouldn't call her. They were friendly, and they had exchanged numbers, but she saw him once a week. She didn't really *know* him.

AJ thought about the people who she did know, and who knew her. If she needed help, she didn't need to call Ray or Wendy. She'd call Kelli first, who'd probably alert Eloise or Robin, and the entire Seafaring Girls group would know within minutes.

She swiped on her phone as the elevator took her to the sixteenth floor and checked the group text string the five of them had started months ago. Nothing new, and Eloise's message about how the inn would be ready for her holiday guests was the last one.

AJ had read it an hour ago, when it had come in, and she hadn't wanted to be the first to respond. Since no one else had either, she assumed she wasn't the only one who didn't want to be the first to confirm they'd be in the cove for Christmas and that she couldn't wait to see The Cliffside Inn in all its glory.

She had no hesitation about going; her plane ticket was already booked, and she'd already made several plans with Matt. She'd love to gush over the inn, too.

Last time the five of them had gotten together over the summer, they'd assigned meals and planned activities together. Someone would need to spearhead all of that, and it shouldn't have to be Eloise just because they would gather at the inn for a night or two. Or Alice, because she owned that huge house on Rocky Ridge.

AJ could see herself doing it, because her articles for the college bowl games were already outlined. All she had to do was wait to see who won, get a couple of quotes, make some minor adjustments, and they'd be done.

As the elevator dinged her arrival, she quickly sent, *Thank you, El. I'll put together a meal schedule, okay? Unless anyone has any objections, I can do activities too, since Matt and I already looked into everything happening around the cove during the holidays.*

She'd barely given her name and sat down to wait before a flurry of texts arrived. *Thanks, AJ*, Alice had said. *With the upcoming move, I'm so scattered.*

No objections, Kelli had said. *We'll be a day early to*

see the inn, Eloise, if that's okay.

Take it away, AJ! Robin had said, ever the cheerleader of the group.

AJ smiled at all of them, wondering why no one wanted to text first. She couldn't quite pinpoint why she hadn't wanted to either, and she looked up, trying to examine her feelings and make sense of them.

"AJ," Dr. Genosie said, and she looked toward the door where the woman stood. "I'm ready for you."

AJ smiled back at her, ready to do this too. She needed to determine whether or not she could return to the cove the way her other friends had, and if that was in her best interest and not because she felt left out.

A WEEK LATER, AJ DISEMBARKED FROM THE PLANE and hustled through the wind to get inside the airport on Diamond Island. *At least it's not raining*, she thought, because she'd been in the slanted, sideways rain that plagued Five Island Cove in the winter, and it wasn't pleasant. It could be as sharp as needles and as cold as ice, and a booming clap of thunder filled the sky as she stepped inside the airport.

Cries rose up, and AJ suspected the people in the waiting areas had been there for a while—and would be staying a little longer. Planes didn't take off in the driving rainstorms, and it was cold enough today to produce snow.

Sure enough, when she arrived at baggage claim, an announcement sounded through the whole airport. "All planes have been grounded for the next ninety minutes," a male voice said. He continued to talk over the groans of those who wanted to leave the cove, and the relieved conversations of those who'd made it in.

AJ wasn't sure how to feel. She'd come to the cove two weeks early, and not for a reason she wanted anyone to know about. She'd seen Dr. Genosie yesterday, but she'd already changed her plane ticket and packed her bag at that point. Meeting with the therapist had only confirmed what AJ knew to be right.

She hadn't told a single person she was coming today, not even the man she'd come to see. Her pulse fluttered in her throat, not strong enough to choke her. She'd been through that debilitating feeling of losing everything already, and it was time to do something about it.

After lifting her own bags from the belt, she went toward the RideShare line, hoping that wouldn't be too delayed, though she knew it would be.

Her mind raced, as it had been doing for the past three days, since she'd learned of her condition. She'd been working through so much since then. Flight changes. Laundry. Submitting a couple of articles early and pulling others. Packing. Flying.

"Ma'am," the attendant said, and she clued in. The man already stood at the back door of a sedan, waiting for her to take the RideShare.

"Thanks," she said.

He helped her with the bags, and gratitude filled AJ. She didn't want to lift them into the trunk, and she hoped the driver could help her once she arrived at her destination.

A woman sat behind the wheel, and AJ's hopes withered slightly. "Where to?" the driver asked, a pretty smile on her face. She eased away from the curb before AJ could comprehend the question.

"Oh, uh, seventy-four Hillshire Drive," she said, her stomach and chest rioting against what she was doing.

But it had to be done.

The drive didn't take long—or maybe AJ had zoned out again. She didn't need to take her luggage to the door, but she didn't have anywhere else to store it. She probably should've gone to the hotel first, but she hadn't allowed herself to even think of it. If she didn't just tell him, she was worried she'd chicken out.

The driver did help her with the bags, and then AJ faced the simple yet stylish house that sat only two blocks from the beach. The rain had definitely driven Matt indoors, and he'd told her once that he didn't stay at the clubhouse if he didn't have to.

"He'll be home," she whispered to herself as she towed her suitcases up his front sidewalk. She'd just stepped under the protection of the eaves when the rain started. She tugged her biggest suitcase out of the way and reached to knock.

He'd tried to replace the doorbell a month or so ago, but he'd ended up shorting out the whole assembly and hadn't gotten back to it yet, so she knew she couldn't press the button and get any results.

AJ's knuckles against the door sounded like gunshots to her own ears, and she only rapped four times. With all the rain and thunder, perhaps Matt wouldn't hear her.

Her fingers shook, as did her chin, and she told herself it was just because of the cold temperatures in Five Island Cove.

Matt didn't answer, and AJ's thoughts scattered again. She'd tried, right? She could just go get warm in the hotel now.

"No." She shook her head and knocked again.

Only a few seconds later, the door opened, and Matt stood there. Handsome, tall, refined, mature Matthew Hymas. "AJ," he said, clearly surprised. A smile touched his mouth as he stepped back. "Come in out of the rain. Come in."

He didn't ask what she was doing there. He reached to help her with her luggage. He closed the door behind her and drew her into a tight embrace, the fabric of his polo soft and slick against her skin.

"What a great surprise." His voice was soft and tender in her ear, his voice rumbling from his chest to hers. All of her fears evaporated, because he was so perfect. He could handle what she needed to tell him. "What are you doing here?"

AJ drew in a breath, realizing how shakily it entered her lungs. "I have to tell you something," she said. She stepped back, because she needed to see his face when she told him. All of her worries returned, because she and Matt had already spoken about this topic, and his desires were crystal clear.

"Uh, Matt, I don't know how to say this, so I guess I'll just say it." She looked him right in the eye and exhaled, the air sort of sounding like a nearly-silent machine gun. "I'm pregnant, Matt. The baby is yours."

A baby he'd told her he didn't want.

When he just stood there, saying nothing, doing nothing—barely even breathing and blinking—extreme foolishness filled AJ. After all, she was forty-five years old, and she knew how to make sure this particular brand of unexpectedness didn't happen.

"I'm sorry," she said, tears filling her eyes. Everything inside her broke, and she realized then that Dr. Genosie had been right to be cautious. AJ had somehow created a fantasy out of Matt's reaction, and he hadn't given her what she'd conjured in her mind.

Her tears spilled down her face, and that was finally when Matt wrapped her up in his arms again and let her cry against his shoulder. He still didn't say anything, though, and AJ really hated reality in that moment.

Finally, he whispered, "Shh, AvaJane. Don't be sorry," and those were the best words AJ had ever heard in her entire life.

CHAPTER TWO

Robin Grover added the red cooking dye to the chocolate cake batter and got the mixer going again. Her husband, Duke, loved red velvet cake, and it was his birthday today. The girls would be home from school in an hour, about the same time the cake came out of the oven.

Mandie, her oldest, would frost the cake once it cooled, and together, they'd decorate the house for the party they'd have when Duke came home from fishing.

He didn't go out every day in the winter, because the seas could be rough, and his boat was starting to get up there in age. He used her relentlessly, and she'd gone all the way to Alaska and back this summer.

Robin thought of Garrett Hall and his threats from a few months ago. He had a way of creeping into her mind at the most inopportune times, but she hadn't been able to shake him completely. To her knowledge, AJ had not been fired or lost her job. She'd quit of her own volition, and she claimed to be doing better with her freelance writing than her job at the station. She'd never gotten an on-air position, but Robin had no idea if Garrett had been responsible for that or not.

Duke's boat had not been sunk or vandalized. Kelli hadn't heard from or seen Zach again. Alice had not lost her home. Eloise was still engaged and finishing up all the finer details at the inn. The five Seafaring Girls and their families would be staying there for a few days before the holidays, to test out the rooms, the systems, the kitchen, all of it. It would be a good trial run for Eloise, and then she'd be ready to open the inn for Christmas.

Robin put her fears out of her mind, because there was nothing she could do about them anyway. She poured the cake batter into the greased and floured cake pans and slid them into the oven.

With a timer set, Robin got busy cleaning up the mess she'd made. She didn't work nearly as much in the winter either, though her spring wedding prep would start the moment the holidays ended. She had five brides who wanted the perfect wedding, Eloise being one of them. Robin would do everything in her power to make every event memorable and as easy as possible for the people who'd hired her.

But she still had time to bake a cake for her husband's birthday. The girls had picked out simple presents for him, and Robin had wrapped them after he'd taken them to school and continued on to the dock.

The gifts sat on the dining room table, and once the kitchen was clean, Robin went to get her present for him from her office. Mandie had bought his favorite candy—dark chocolate covered almonds—in bulk, and Jamie had used some of her babysitting money to get him a gift card from the Polish dog food truck that frequented the docks as the fishermen came in off their boats. Duke actually liked their breakfast dog the best, and his weakness was getting breakfast on the way out for a day of trawling.

Robin had purchased a new pair of gloves for him, along with a brand-new set of walkie talkies. He loved his radios to communicate with his friends on the other boats, as they usually went out in groups to the best fishing grounds. Bryan Reynolds and Duke were good friends, and Robin could always count on Bryan to have her husband's back.

She quickly wrapped the gloves and the walkie talkies, put them beside the other gifts, and got the cream cheese out of the fridge so it could start to soften.

Her phone rang, and her mother's name sat on the screen. Robin's heart dipped down to her stomach, but she answered the call anyway. "Mom, hey," she said, hoping she sounded reasonably normal.

"Robin, dear, I have a gift for Duke."

"Oh, of course." Robin had not invited her mother to their family celebration. She had been trying to improve things with her mother, and for the first time in her life, Robin had what she'd classify as a real relationship with her mom.

It certainly wasn't perfect, but they'd both been trying. There had been apologies and honest conversations, and while Robin didn't choose her mother as the person she wanted to spend the most time with, they definitely got along better.

"You can just bring it to the party on Sunday," she said.

"I'm not going to be here on Sunday," her mother said. "I'm just going to drop it by right now. I won't stay."

Robin had her doubts about that, but there was a bigger issue at play now. "Where will you be on Sunday?"

"Oh, there's a senior holiday cruise leaving from Rocky Ridge on Saturday morning." She gave a light laugh. "I bought myself a ticket on a whim."

Robin had fallen still, her mind trying to work through what her mother had said. "Senior holiday cruise?"

"Yes, for men and women above age sixty-five," her mother said, her voice full of forced importance. "It's going to Nantucket for a few days. Then over to the Hamptons, then down to New York City."

"You'll be gone for Christmas?"

"It's a fourteen-day cruise," her mother said. "So yes. I won't be back until the twenty-seventh."

"Wow." Robin exhaled, not quite sure what to think. "I can't believe I'm just hearing about this now."

"I just decided today," her mom said. "I'll be by in about ten minutes."

"Okay." Robin turned as the timer on the oven went off. "Bye, Mom." She set her phone on the counter and reached for the oven mitts.

The cake was done, and she slid it onto the stovetop just as the front door opened and Jamie's and Mandie's voices filled the air.

"...is all I mean," Mandie said. "You have to be careful with girls like that, Jamsey."

"Don't call me that," Jamie said. "I'm not a baby."

Robin held very still once more, listening to her daughters.

"I'm just saying," Mandie said, her voice purposefully quiet. "She's not a nice person, and she's probably using you."

"Whatever," Jamie said, and her footsteps went down the hall that led to the bedrooms in the house. Mandie came around the corner and met Robin's eye.

Robin's eyebrows lifted of their own accord. "What's going on?"

"Oh, there's this mean girl who's befriended Jamie." Mandie sighed as she put her backpack on the built-in desk and joined Robin in the kitchen. She opened a drawer and tied an apron around her neck and waist. "I tried to tell her to be careful. Sarah-Elizabeth is not anyone's friend."

"How do you know?" Robin got out of the kitchen as

Mandie started pulling together the rest of the frosting ingredients. Jamie was in eighth grade at the junior high, and Robin had just started her junior year at the high school.

"Everyone knows about those Phillips girls," Mandie said. "The queen bee at the high school is Carrie. She's the exact same way." She shrugged. "I just steer clear of her, but I've heard stories. Apparently Sarah-Elizabeth is twice as snobby, and twice as cruel."

Robin looked toward the hallway, hoping Jamie would reappear and they could talk. Her mama bear instincts wanted to keep Jamie safe from mean girls and boys and bad grades and anything disappointing at all.

In reality, she knew she couldn't do that. She didn't even want to do that. People learned a lot from the disappointing things in their lives, and she didn't want to rob her girls of those learning experiences. She just wanted them to have the softest consequences possible.

"Should I talk to her?"

"No," Mandie said. "I'll keep my eye on her." She put the cake in the fridge before she whipped up the frosting. "I'll get her to come help decorate."

"Oh, right." Robin jumped from the stool and went down the hall to her office. She took the huge bouquet of balloons she'd picked up that morning into the kitchen and returned to the office to get the streamers and tape.

Jamie had come into the kitchen, and the three of them worked together to turn the common area at the back of the house into party central. Mandie didn't say anything about Sarah-Elizabeth, and Robin followed her lead.

The time passed quickly, and Mandie had just finished the peaks in the cake frosting when the garage door opened. "He's here," Robin said, her heart beating faster now. "Come over here."

The girls hurried to her side, and the moment Duke appeared at the end of the hall, they started singing. He lifted his head, a smile spreading across his whole face. Robin could still tell something was wrong—terribly wrong.

She kept singing though, and when they finished, Duke clapped for them and stepped into all three of them to hug them. "Ah, my girls," he said, his voice not nearly as jovial as usual. "Thank you. What a great surprise."

Robin wasn't sure how he could be surprised, unless he'd forgotten it was his birthday. She made sure he had cake and dinner and decorations every year.

"Presents first," Jamie said, her normal, smiling self. She handed them out and Duke gave the proper performance for each one, even kissing Robin after he opened the walkie talkies.

"Okay, let's eat," she said. "We can have cake now or later. Doesn't matter to me." She met Duke's eye, and he'd sobered again already. He was usually so fun-loving, with bad jokes about the ocean and the types of fish it held, loud laughter, and serious-but-not-serious questions about Charlie, Mandie's boyfriend.

Tonight, there was none of that.

Robin pulled four plates from the cupboard and set them next to the slow cooker. "It's your favorite, baby," she said. "Barbecue meatball subs."

"Thanks, babe." His smile lit the house, and he perked up after that. The girls talked about school, and Robin spoke up about her weddings, and Duke said he saw a couple of whales that day.

Dinner ended quickly, and Mandie put the candles in the cake for her father. They sang *Happy Birthday* for a second time, and Duke actually paused, closed his eyes, and waited a moment before blowing out the candles.

Had he actually made a wish? And if so, what for?

Mandie served the cake, and Robin got out the vanilla ice cream. They spent the evening together, and finally, the girls went down the hall to finish their homework and go to bed.

"Come on, Mister Grover," Robin said, smiling at her husband. She stood and extended her hand to him. "It's time to put you to bed too."

Duke smiled at her, put his hand in hers, and let her lead him down the hall to their master suite. She hadn't cleaned up the dishes after dinner, something she always did. Tonight, though, she didn't care.

With the door locked, she turned toward her handsome husband. "What's wrong?"

Duke hung his head. "I didn't want to say anything during the party."

"You're not great at hiding how you feel," she said. "I knew something was wrong the moment you came into the house."

Duke nodded and started unbuttoning his jeans. "The boat got damaged in the storm today."

Robin paused in the middle of changing into her pajamas. "How bad is it?" His boat had been damaged before, and he'd come home with a positive attitude. He'd been working on a fishing boat for decades, and the man could fix almost anything.

"I couldn't stay to see how bad," he said. "It was dark already, and we barely made it back to the dock."

"Barely made it back?" That didn't sound good at all.

"Bryan said he'd help me tomorrow if he can't go out. The weather is supposed to be wicked for the next couple of days." He stripped his shirt off and, wearing only his boxer shorts, went into the bathroom.

Robin slipped into her silk pajamas and sat up in bed, waiting for him to return.

He did only a few minutes later, and he looked a decade older instead of just one year. He ran one hand down his face and crawled into bed with her. He laid his head in her lap, and Robin liked the way such a simple gesture made her feel powerful and strong.

She stroked his hair, wondering if he wanted to be intimate that night. He sure seemed to be in a bad place, and perhaps he was too tired though it was his birthday, and he'd always told her she was the best and only present he needed each year.

Duke rarely worried, and that made Robin's concern double. She was the one who obsessed over every little thing. It made her a great wedding and event planner but brought a lot of stress into other aspects of her life.

"Duke?" she finally asked.

"Hmm?"

"How bad is it?"

"Bad, babe," he said.

"Like, so bad we need a new boat? So bad we can't afford to fix it?"

"I won't know until tomorrow." He lifted his head and looked at her with those dark, deep, delicious eyes she'd fallen in love with the very moment she'd seen them.

"We need a Christmas miracle then," Robin said, thinking she better start praying for exactly that.

"I just need you," he whispered, lifting himself up so he could kiss her. Robin felt his usual passion for her in his touch, and as they made love, she tried to be as present as possible.

But really, the worry about how they'd pay for a new boat if the damage was really that bad lingered in the back of her mind.

Please, please, she thought as she lay in her husband's embrace. The one thing she'd feared Garrett Hall would do seemed to be coming true, and Robin told herself that even Garrett, though he'd seemed all-powerful last fall, couldn't influence the weather in the Atlantic.

She simply needed a Christmas miracle, and she pressed her eyes closed, inhaled the scent of her husband's skin, and prayed for that miracle.

CHAPTER THREE

"Grab that other garbage bag, bud," Kelli Thompson said to her son. Parker did so without complaint, which meant a lot to her. He was normally a pretty agreeable child, but there had been so many changes in his life lately, and Kelli had seen him getting upset at seemingly simple things.

She knew everyone dealt with trauma in different ways, and having his father come to the cove with a pledge to make things work only to have him leave ten weeks later had definitely been hard on Parker.

Kelli could admit that she was still having a hard time letting go of her marriage to Julian. She had no problem hauling out three bags of trash and tossing them in the can she'd gotten just this month. Once Julian had finally admitted that he wasn't happy in Five Island Cove, and that his "quick trip" to Jersey to oversee a few things for his courier business would be a permanent relocation for him, Kelli had decided she needed to do something to move forward.

Living in limbo simply wasn't fun, and while she did like the cottage on the beach, and it was more than sufficient for just her and Parker, she owned a home on Bell Island which didn't require a mortgage payment.

As she lifted the lid on the garbage can and hefted her bags inside it, Kelli's lungs burned with the chill in the air. The weather had turned in the past couple of days, and Kelli felt a shift in her life as well.

She'd brought Parker to visit her mother, spent a great day with her and her boyfriend, Devon, and then they'd ended up at the house on Seabreeze Shore.

She'd told him that she'd grown up in the house with her two sisters, and then she'd said, "I own it, Parker. It needs some work, but if we fix it up, we can live here." She'd looked at him, the light of the day quickly fading, and Parker had simply stared up at the house with the pillars on the front porch, the crooked shutters, and the faded front door. Everything about the house needed to be spruced up, but Kelli had watched Eloise dig into a house four times this big and at least five times as messy.

She'd cleaned up The Cliffside Inn, and that had inspired Kelli in ways she couldn't name.

"I got it," Kelli said, throwing out her hand to help Parker as he tried to lift his garbage bag into the trashcan. "We got so much done today." She dropped the bag in the can and let the lid bang closed. "Should we stop by Kaleidoscope and get one of those chocolate cakes?"

"Yes," Parker said with a smile. He looked like the little boy her whole world revolved around in that moment, and she drew him into a hug.

"Thanks for working hard today," she whispered into his hair. It used to be the same color as hers, and she'd waited so long to get this boy in her life, she'd thought God had blessed her with the most beautiful child on the planet. Now, Parker's hair was darkening into a tone very much like his father's, but Kelli would love him until her dying day.

"I think if we come a couple of times each week and work hard," she said. "We can move in once the weather turns warm again." A springtime goal of moving from the beach house on Sanctuary Island to this one on Bell felt fast to her, but Kelli needed to do things without thinking about them until she knew the precise solution, all of the steps, and exactly how the outcome would look.

Life was simply too messy for that, and the worst part was, Kelli hadn't even known it until Julian had called to say he just couldn't come back to the cove.

Her life had not been perfect up until that point, but once she'd left Five Island Cove behind her, it had been simple. She'd found a great guy, and she'd fallen in love. It had taken a while for her to get pregnant, but she just readjusted her plans and made new ones.

That was all she had to do now too. The difference

was, she wasn't going to take a year to decide. She had a job at the junior high on Diamond Island, and she and Parker rode the ferry together each morning. He sat in the teacher's office until he had to walk the half-mile to the elementary school, and she finished before him, so she was always waiting in a RideShare when his final bell rang.

Lately, Duke Glover had been waiting out front at the junior high to drive Parker to the elementary school, as he brought his youngest to school and didn't mind waiting for Parker. He didn't get out on the boat as much in the winter, and he apparently had time.

Kelli was grateful for every person who came into her life and offered her some assistance. Even just a friendly text meant the world to her.

"We're not coming next week, though, right?" Parker asked, and Kelli finally led him back toward the garage.

"No," she said. "We'll be at the inn next weekend." She smiled at her son. "Grandma and Devon are coming too. It's going to be a big party."

"Charlie and Jamie will be there too," Parker said, and Kelli smiled at the way he worshipped the older kids.

"Yep." Kelli went up the steps and into the house. They'd spent the morning on the first floor, filling garbage bags with anything in the house that she didn't want there anymore. Old things that had been left in the house, or trash that had blown in somehow.

She took a deep breath and continued through the kitchen and into the living room. Three-quarters of the house was one big, open area on this floor, and the kitchen flowed into the living room, which melded into a den or office of sorts. In the back corner sat the master suite, and while the bathroom and closet weren't anything to write home about, Kelli adored every corner of this house.

The popcorn nook under the steps still held the bean-bags she and AJ had lounged in last time they'd come to the house together, and she'd only managed to mop one room while Parker dusted all the blinds and windowsills.

The house sat empty, without much furniture in it. Just the beanbags under the steps and a rickety dining room table in the kitchen.

Kelli sighed as she looked around and saw how much she needed to be able to live here. All of it cost money, something Kelli didn't have a lot of. Worry and doubt started to gnaw at her hopes of moving into the house in only three or four months, but she straightened her shoulders.

She wasn't going to let anything slow her down or stop her. Not this time.

When she got home, she'd go over her budget again, and she'd see if she could squeeze out a few more dollars. The island always had estate sales and yard sales in the spring and early summer, and perhaps she could find some decent furniture at a reduced price.

Satisfied with that idea of a plan, she walked over to the railing, where she and Parker had draped their coats.

"Here you go, bud." She handed Parker's dark blue coat to him, and then she shrugged into her red one.

"Mom?" Parker asked as they left the house. They could get a RideShare to the ferry station, but it was only a ten-minute walk, and it would take that long just to get a car to her house. This was definitely one way she could save a few dollars.

"Yeah, baby?" She reached over and tugged his beanie over his ear.

"Is Dad coming for Christmas?"

Kelli's lungs seized. "I don't think so." Julian hadn't said anything about the holidays. He hadn't asked to see Parker for Thanksgiving, which was a couple of weeks ago, and Kelli hadn't spoken to him about custody at all.

She had called the state of New Jersey to find out how to get divorced, and she had a green file folder in a drawer in her kitchen at the beach house. If she filed, it would cost three hundred dollars, she'd have to take a parenting class —which also cost money—and she'd have to be the one to appear in court.

Julian could skip the hearing if he wanted to, and he wouldn't have to pay a dime. He also hadn't been sending her any money since she and Parker had come to the cove in the middle of August, and they'd lived here for about a month before he came with the claims that he wanted to try again.

He'd left five weeks ago now, and Kelli's pulse felt heavy in her chest and loud in her ears. He hadn't removed her from their joint checking account either, so she supposed he was still willing to help her with things.

Kelli hated logging onto their bank account though, because then she saw transactions at the gourmet cheese shop she'd told Julian about that he'd never wanted to visit because everything was too expensive. She saw money flying out of the account with nail salon names attached to it. She saw utility bills getting paid doubly, for different amounts.

All of it told her that Tiffany was back in his life, and that he was paying for a large portion of her life.

Her throat narrowed as the wind picked up, and Kelli turned her face fully into the salty, stiff air. So many things gave way to the wind, but she would not. She was going to see her way through this, no matter what.

The ferry station came into view, and she and Parker hurried inside as the return ferry was already at the dock. They had monthly passes they scanned and they were two of the last people onto the ferry. They'd barely had time to find a spot inside the enclosed section of the ferry before it pulled away from the dock, and Kelli pressed her eyes closed, trying to quiet her pulse and her thoughts.

She hadn't told her mother about the house where she and Parker had been working for the past two weekends. She hadn't told Alice, Eloise, Robin, or Kristen. For a long time, Kelli wasn't sure she could ever live in the house again, though she certainly didn't want anyone else to live there.

You're ready now, she told herself. Being there these past few weeks had been very therapeutic, and Kelli felt herself taking a big step forward. A smile touched her lips, and Kelli just let her body sway with the movement of the boat, maybe liking the sea for the first time in her life.

"Ma'am?" a man said, and Kelli's eyes flew open. She blinked a couple of times before she could truly see the person standing there.

"Sorry," she said.

The man smiled, and he looked really familiar to Kelli. A lot of people in Five Island Cove did, and eight months ago, she hadn't wanted to run into anyone she knew. Now, though, she could handle meeting someone she'd known as a teenager.

"It's fine." He narrowed his eyes at her. "Do I know you?"

"I grew up here," she said. "If you did too, it's likely."

He touched his jacket, where the name tag read *Billy*. "I'm William Bridge."

"Billy Bridge," she said, her smile widening. "Kelli Watkins." She put her arm around Parker. "Well, Thompson now." *At least for a little while longer*. She needed to talk to Julian about him filing for divorce. If he could pay for his mistress to get a manicure and a pedicure, he could foot the cost to file for divorce. He was the one choosing another woman over his current wife and son.

"So good to see you." Billy gave her a quick handshake.

"You hung around with AJ Proctor, right?"

Of course he'd be interested in AJ. Men always were, and that was absolutely nothing new.

"That's right," she said. "And Eloise Hall, Robin Golden, and Alice Williams. You surely remember Robin."

"I remember," he said, still grinning. "I knew Alice the best. We rode the ferry over from Rocky Ridge together for a while before I moved to Diamond."

"Oh, right," Kelli said, though she hadn't known that. Alice had rarely spoken of her home life out on Rocky Ridge, and she was almost two different people in Kelli's head.

"Anyway," Billy said. "We're doing a survey on the ferry system." He handed her a small, square card. "You just scan that with your phone and answer the questions. It'll take less than five minutes, and anyone who does it is entered to win a free monthly pass." He gave her a professional smile, and Kelli returned it.

She took the card, and he moved over to the next patron. Kelli scanned the card, listening to him give the same spiel to a couple down the row.

On his way by again, he paused as he was almost past Kelli. "You don't happen to have Alice's number, do you?" he asked.

Kelli looked up from her phone, surprise darting through her. "I do," she said slowly.

"Let me give you mine," he said. "If you talk to her,

and it's okay that I have her number, maybe you could pass my number to her. She can text me herself." He cleared his throat. "If she wants to."

Kelli twisted more fully toward him, trying to read his expression. Those dark blue eyes simply held a hint of hope, and Kelli wondered just how good of friends he and Alice had been three decades ago.

He wore his sandy hair a little bit long, and Alice would probably like that after her polished and buttoned-up, lawyer husband. Billy's hair curled along the ends, and he sported a little bit of stubble on his face too.

He'd aged just like the rest of them, but he was still tall, tan, and trim, and Kelli had no doubt he could get a date any time he wanted.

"All right," she said, tapping away from his survey to a fresh note. "I'm ready."

"It's Will now," he said as she tapped out the wrong name. "I left behind Billy when we graduated."

"Okay." Kelli erased what she'd typed and put in Will Bridge. "Go."

He recited the number, and she tapped it in. She turned her phone toward him so he could double-check it, and after he'd nodded and continued on with his survey cards, Kelli stared at the number.

All thoughts of the survey gone now, though she could use the free ferry pass, Kelli quickly tapped and held to copy everything she'd just typed into her phone.

She couldn't get a text off to Alice fast enough.

CHAPTER FOUR

Alice Williams said, "Thank you," in a calm voice as she finished up her transaction with the RideShare driver. She opened the back door and stepped out of the car, only to have her breath stolen by the freezing temperature of the air.

Her phone buzzed, but she ignored it. She was late for her weekly lunch with Robin, Kristen, and Eloise, and it was likely one of them. While she and Eloise had planned to meet up on the ferry, Alice had been late leaving home, and now she was twenty minutes behind schedule.

Inside one of the only chain restaurants that had come to the cove, Alice finally took a breath deeper than a gasp and pulled out her phone. There was a line of people just to check in with the hostess, and if her friends were already here, she wouldn't have to wait.

Robin had texted ten minutes ago to say they'd gone

back to a table without her, and she quickly sent a reply to let her friends know she'd arrived.

The most recent text had come from Will Bridge, and Alice's smile came instantly. She'd been texting with him for a few days now, and she hadn't told anyone yet. She held her head high, though, because she had to have something to say during today's Good News Minute, something she and her friends had implemented into their lunches in the past few months.

Eloise almost always said something about the progress of her inn. If it wasn't that, she spoke of Aaron and their upcoming wedding. She and Robin tried very hard not to discuss the wedding much at lunch, as it left the others out, and Robin didn't want to work at their midweek lunches.

Robin often spoke of her family or Duke's fishing, and Kristen's news was almost always something about Rueben, Kelli, or AJ.

Alice loved them all fiercely, so when Robin said, "Alice," she lifted her eyes from Will's text—*What's your favorite meal these days? Like, last meal type of stuff*—and moved effortlessly through the crowd.

She'd gained fifteen pounds since the most stressful summer of her life, and Alice was very happy where she was right now. She didn't feel like only bone and skin, and no one looked at her like she was one breath away from collapsing.

"Hey." She reached Robin and hugged her. "Sorry I'm

late." She sighed like someone else was to blame for her tardiness, but she really only had herself to pin the problem to. "I set a timer, but I just couldn't stop in the middle of what I was doing."

"The Tacoma estate?"

"Yes," she said. Alice didn't speak of her cases often—or at all—but the ones where the most unusual things happened sometimes got a mention. The Tacoma estate had been in probate for over three years, and the siblings were still fighting as if their father had died yesterday. Alice had met with each of the four siblings twice now, and she was the third lawyer they'd hired to try to sort out the mess their dad had left behind.

If Thomas Tacoma hadn't been loaded, with three separate homes scattered up and down the East Coast, the fact that he hadn't prepared his estate or final will and testament wouldn't have mattered at all.

He'd died here in the cove, and two of his children still lived here. They'd been using the big city lawyers until her, and Alice was determined to prove that she could do a better job than anyone in any city.

Kristen and Eloise grinned at each other as Alice and Robin approached, and Alice took the only seat where nothing had been disturbed. She deftly spread her napkin across her lap as Eloise and Kristen finished their conversation, and sudden gladness moved through Alice that she hadn't canceled today.

She probably should have, as she'd signed another

client on Monday, and she needed to get through the initial paperwork by next Monday. That was her policy—she'd review all documents the client brought her within seven days.

Alice reminded herself she had plenty of time, as the estate and this new client were the only two cases she had at the moment. When she thought like that, her heart skipped a beat, reminding her that she had bills to pay, groceries to buy, and children to provide for.

She drew in a deep breath and pushed it out, something the trio of other women at the table all saw.

"What's wrong?" Robin asked.

"Nothing," Alice said. They all knew about Frank. They all knew that he wasn't sending money anymore. "I have two things for Good News Minute." She smiled at Robin to get the worry to leave her best friend's eyes. "Should I go first?"

Robin looked down at her drink and said, "I don't have anything this week, so you can have my spot."

"Nothing?" Kristen asked. "It was Duke's birthday recently, wasn't it?"

"What's so great about being one year older?" Robin asked, and that so wasn't like her. She looked at Kristen with an edge in her eyes that said, *How dare you try to make me feel better?* and Alice wondered what had happened in the past week.

She spoke to all of her friends regularly, and no one

more than Robin. She'd said nothing about anything, and her foul mood came at Alice out of left field.

"Sorry," Kristen said at the same time Robin said the word too.

"I'm just stressed," Robin continued. "Duke's boat is not repairable." She reached up and swiped at her eyes, and that sent tremors through Alice. It took something huge and heavy to bring tears to Robin's eyes. "My mother's off on some single's cruise and won't be here for Christmas, and someone called me this morning to put together a wedding for a December twenty-eighth date. Apparently their planner bailed on them, and they heard I was good."

"You are good," Eloise said quietly.

"The twenty-eighth is in eleven days," Robin said. "No one is that good."

"What do you always say?" Kristen asked, glancing at Alice. "Find a venue. Everything else after that is just gravy."

"I think she says icing," Eloise said, her dark eyes glinting with joy.

"*Chocolate* icing," Alice said, piling her voice onto those trying to help Robin feel better. She looked around at all of them, and it was clear she was trying to stay mad. In the end, she broke. Her shoulders slumped, and Alice reached over to put her arm around her.

"I'll take the wedding," Robin said. "But I'm going to have to work at the inn." She looked hopefully at Eloise, as if El would tell her to forget about booking a wedding if she had to actually work to plan it.

"There's downtime," Eloise said. "That's the whole point of the inn."

"You don't like the pressure of the holidays with your mother anyway," Kristen said, and Alice wished she'd jumped in with that reassurance.

"True," Robin mused.

Kristen and Eloise looked at Alice as if she would have a perfect solution for the fishing boat that Duke needed to support his family. Alice had no idea what to say, and she silently begged her friends for help.

No one said anything, and Alice finally opened her mouth. "I'm sure you and Duke will figure out what to do about his boat. He really can't fix it?"

Robin had texted last week to say Duke's boat had been damaged on his birthday, when the storm that had officially brought winter weather to the cove had blown across the islands. She'd asked for their prayers and good thoughts, and Alice had given them both to Robin and Duke.

Charlie was still dating Robin's daughter, and Alice didn't stop worrying about her son for a single moment. The two teens seemed to get along really well, and with Mandie as mature as she was, she helped to keep Charlie's hormones in check.

Alice reminded herself that her son was a good boy too, and that he wasn't his father. It was Alice's entire goal to get him to adulthood with a new vision for how he could live his life that didn't involve taking advantage of women.

"My good news is that The Cliffside Inn is completely full from Christmas Eve to January sixteenth," Eloise said, her face one glowing ray of light.

"Eloise," Alice said, her smile forming quickly. "That's so great." She reached across the table and squeezed her friend's hand. "You're ready."

"I hope," Eloise said. "You guys will help me with that this Saturday. Check-in starts at three." She drew a deep breath and looked at Kristen. "I've texted all of you the times I want you to come, so I can see how it goes when we have a rush, and when people are coming in late."

Alice nodded and flipped her phone over when another text from Will came in. "Robin and I will be there at our appointed time."

"Oh, that's right," Eloise said. "You're moving on Saturday."

"Well, kind of," Alice said. "We're moving a lot of stuff so we can enjoy our time at the inn, and then our last Christmas in the big house." Alice refused to let her emotions get the best of her. She did love the house on Rocky Ridge, but when she'd first bought it, it was a status symbol. It has been a safe haven for her and the children for the past six months, but Alice wanted to keep a roof over her head, and it didn't need to cover eight thousand square feet.

She'd found a house here on Diamond Island, which

would be easier for the twins to get to school. She'd also get more clients by being more centrally located, and Alice was actually excited for yet another change in her life.

"That's actually part of my news," she said. "I got an offer on the house on Monday, and I accepted it."

A moment of silence pressed down on the table, and then all three of them broke into various exclamations of congratulations. Alice grinned at them, basking in their love and friendship, and she did let her emotions shake her chin then.

A waitress appeared, and Alice glanced up and said, "I'd love a raspberry gin and tonic," she said.

"What in the world?" Robin asked, waving away a refill on her soda. Eloise had likewise quieted, and only Kristen continued to look around.

"I'm missing something."

"Alice doesn't drink," Robin said. "Unless she has something huge to celebrate."

"She just got an offer on her house," Kristen said. "That's huge, right? It's been on the market for six weeks."

"It's huge," Robin said. "But not drinking huge." She hadn't taken her eyes from Alice for a single second. "Alice, you better start talking."

Alice reached for her water glass, her fingers shaking slightly. She loved holding a secret—a good one, at least—over Robin's head. "Kristen, do you have anything for Good News Minute?"

"I guess I better say my thing before you tell us why you're drinking today."

"Ooh, sometimes drinking is bad," Eloise said. "It's not bad, is it, Alice?"

"It's *Good* News Minute, El," Robin said, finally moving her gaze to someone besides Alice.

"Sometimes good news is actually something bad happening," Eloise said. "Like my divorce."

"And Kelli's," Alice said.

"Did she file?"

Alice shook her head as she took a sip of her water. "No, but she she said she was getting ready to do it."

"I worry about her," Robin said with a sigh. "Though, I suppose she can't simply stay married to him. I just don't want her to have to go through anything hard."

Alice had only met Julian once, when he'd come to the cove at the end of the summer. He'd seemed distracted and overwhelmed, but he did seem to want to make things work with his wife. At least for a few weeks.

If there was anything Alice had learned in the past nine months, it was that she couldn't do it all. While it seemed like Julian could move here, keep his wife and son, and run his business in New Jersey, Alice knew there were limits to a person's energy, time, and patience.

She knew, because she'd never expected to be where she was, sitting at a table with her friends from her childhood, having lost everything that had been ultra-important only a few months ago.

The house in the Hamptons—gone. The vacation home overlooking the beach—sold. The PTA Presidency —given up.

All she had were her twins and her friends, and Alice had learned she didn't need anything more than that.

"My good news is that Jean and I have started sewing together in the afternoons," Kristen said, her voice as quiet as her smile. "She's getting more comfortable here, and I'm so enjoying getting to know her."

"That's great," Alice said genuinely. Kristen's daughter-in-law had really struggled to come to the cove and make her life as a lighthouse keeper's wife, something Alice understood on a fundamental level.

"Yes," Robin said. "I'm so glad, Kristen. I wish I liked to sew. I'd come over."

"Like you have time to sew," Eloise said. "My mother tried to teach me, and I just can't seem to get the thread to obey me."

"Oh, I should invite your mother," Kristen said. "Do you think she'd like that?"

"I honestly don't know," Eloise said. "It's not like she's sewing for enjoyment. But she might come once a week or something." A bit of anxiety had come into Eloise's dark eyes, though, and Alice shot a look in Kristen's direction.

Robin had obviously picked up on Eloise's nerves too, because she said, "You don't want to invite someone else anyway. It's your special time with Jean."

Kristen nodded, and the message had gotten through. "All right, Alice. Go ahead."

Alice's fingers automatically inched toward her phone. "The reason I'm celebrating with a drink today is because —" She cut off as the waitress set her perfectly pink drink on the table in front of her. "Look how pretty it is." She smiled at the drink, her mouth watering already.

She told herself to take three sips and be done. She hadn't had alcohol for a long time, and even a few sips could make her tipsy despite her increased weight.

"Alice, I swear, if you don't start talking," Robin warned.

Alice picked up her phone and swiped it on. Will had texted her a couple more times, and Alice scanned them quickly. *I like to cook after riding the ferry all day.*

If you'd like, I'd love to cook for you sometime. Or we can go to dinner. Whichever you prefer.

Alice grinned at the words, but she didn't take the time to answer right now, not with Robin's glare boring holes in the side of her face. Instead, Alice handed the phone to her and said, "Will Bridge and I have been chatting, and he just asked me out."

"Will Bridge?" Eloise asked, her eyebrows bunched down. "Who is that?"

"Billy Bridge," Robin said, the words almost a hiss. She looked up from the phone. "You're going to go out with Billy Bridge?" Her blue eyes looked like dinner plates, and Alice sure did enjoy that.

She lifted her drink to her lips and took a sip. Oh, she liked that too. The tang of the raspberries made her smile, and the alcohol warmed her from the inside out.

"Yes," she said with a giggle. "I looked him up online, and he is very good-looking."

"*Billy* Bridge," Eloise said. "How do you know him? He grew up on the Ridge too, right?"

"Yes," Alice said, exchanging a glance with Robin. Her dinner plates turned hopeful, and Alice gave her a nod.

She squealed and faced Kristen and Eloise. "Alice used to sneak out of our cabin in summer camp and go over to the boys' side to see one Billy Bridge."

"He goes by Will now," Alice said. "Can I have my phone back so I can confirm that I'd *love* to go to dinner with him?"

Robin handed her the phone while Eloise started to ask more questions. Alice took another sip of her drink and started tapping out a reply.

CHAPTER FIVE

Kristen Shields walked beneath the foaming, nearly black sky, her luggage bumping over the rough sidewalk behind her. If she didn't get on the ferry in the next half-hour, she didn't think she'd make it to Sanctuary Island.

A half an hour remained before she needed to leave to arrive at her assigned check-in time at The Cliffside Inn, but Mother Nature had a way of disrupting the most well-laid plans. Kristen quickly put her luggage in the back of her car and turned back to the lighthouse.

Though the afternoon still had hours of light left in it, Rueben had already turned on the beam. Worry hit her as she moved as quickly as she dared toward the navy blue door on the back of the lighthouse.

The rain hadn't started to fall yet, but it was imminent. Kristen had lived for decades in the cove, and she could feel the weather down in her bones. She knocked on the door and twisted the knob as a gust of wind kicked up off the water.

The crashing of waves against the rocks on the other side of the lighthouse could be plainly heard, and she needed to send a text to all of her girls, too. No one should be traveling this afternoon or evening.

"Reuben," she said, barely able to push the door closed behind her. She managed it, the windows above her in the stairwell rattling with the force of the wind outside, angry as it was that anything dared to defy it.

She went up instead of down, because if Rueben was doing his job, he'd be up in the office on the upper level of the lighthouse. It was three flights of uneven stairs, and Kristen took them one step at a time.

"Reuben," she said when she reached the top landing. She glanced out the huge windows that overlooked the ocean beyond, and all she could see was a wall of blackness coming toward the cove. She suddenly wished she'd brought her bag into the lighthouse instead of putting it in her backseat.

"Mother." Reuben appeared in the doorway, concern in his eyes. "What are you doing here?"

"I was just getting ready to go to The Cliffside Inn," she said. "I saw the storm."

"You shouldn't go," he said, turning back and gesturing to her at the same time. "Come look at the radar." He retreated into the office, and Kristen hurried after him.

All of the screens shone in the small space, and she'd read them for years alongside her husband. She knew what they showed before her son said a word. "There's a huge storm in the Atlantic," he said. "It's finally been named a hurricane as of nine o'clock this morning, but it's just sitting out there."

"Obviously not," Kristen said as the wind attacked the front windows again.

"This is something else," Rueben said. "I've never seen anything like it." He indicated the middle monitor. "Look at that. It's like there's just...nothing. There's just nothing. I can't see the meteorology. I don't see any of the wind or rain or anything."

Kristen sucked in a breath. "Rueben—"

"It's like it's just open water, but I feel like I could see something there a few minutes ago."

"Check the Richter scale readings," she said, her pulse pounding. "I'm calling the mayor."

"The Richter scale readings?" Reuben tore his eyes from the screen. "The mayor?"

"That's a tsunami," Kristen said. "And it's coming this way." She put the call on speaker so she could text her Seafaring Girls.

Tsunami coming toward the cove. Get somewhere high and safe right now. I'm at the lighthouse with Reuben and Jean. Please check in so I know you're safe.

She'd likely lose cell phone service when the wall of water slammed into the East coast of the cove, but Kristen couldn't control everything. She couldn't control anything, as Joel's death had taught her.

"Kristen?" Connie Adams asked. "To what do I owe this honor?"

"There's a tsunami coming toward the cove," she said, bending down to peer at the screen. "It's moving fairly slowly; definitely not as fast as the only other one I've seen, and Reuben is checking the Richter scale readings right now."

"There was a seven-point-five magnitude earthquake right about halfway between here and Europe a little over two hours ago," Rueben said, and Connie started barking orders at someone in her office.

"When is it going to hit us?" Connie asked, adding, "Yes, get the National Geological Survey on the line to confirm this. Send out the emergency texts."

Kristen met Rueben's eyes. "We'll sound the siren," Kristen said, and Rueben's eyes widened. He straightened, his shoulders pulling back as he drew in a deep breath. He left, and he'd have to go down a level to start the siren. He was big, fast, and strong, and Kristen was so glad she wasn't running this place anymore.

"Yes, the calls too," Connie said. "Everything. Kristen," she said, her voice louder. "How long do we have?"

"If it's been moving for two hours," Kristen said. "I don't know...Connie."

The first whine of the siren started, and it would grow to an earsplitting volume in a matter of seconds, making conversation nearly impossible. Kristen studied the screen. "I think it'll be here by nightfall."

Some of the most powerful tsunamis in the world could cross whole oceans in a day, but this one clearly wasn't moving as fast as ones generated by stronger earthquakes. "It probably has to travel two thousand miles," Kristen said, crossing to the door and closing it to buy herself a few more seconds. "Even at two or three hundred miles per hour, it might be halfway here."

"So two or three more hours."

"Probably," Kristen said. "And it's going to run straight into the hurricane brewing out there. Reuben said they just named it this morning."

"Get somewhere safe," Connie said. "Thank you, Kristen."

"You get somewhere safe too," Kristen said, and the call ended. Her phone lit up with text notifications, several of them from her girls.

How long? Alice had asked.

The Cliffside Inn is open for anyone, Eloise said. *It's one of the highest places on the cove. If you can get here, Kristen, get here.*

We're heading to the ferry now, Robin said.

Parker and I are on the ferry from Bell, Kelli said. *Arrival on Sanctuary in thirty-seven minutes. Do we have time, Kristen?*

Matt and I are already at the inn, AJ said. *What can we do to help the rest of you get here?*

I called Aaron, Eloise said. *He's on his way here too, and he's going to get my mother. Kelli, he's probably going to arrive at the same time as you. He'll look for you before he leaves.*

Kristen read through the texts as quickly as she could, glad she could warn those she loved. She sent a text to her church knitting group, though the siren was going strong now. It was so loud, it could be heard on all five islands in the cove, and the next text that came in was from the city of Five Island Cove.

A confirmed 7.7 magnitude earthquake struck at 12:24 PM this afternoon, about 2100 miles from Five Island Cove. A tsunami has spread in all directions, and the wall of water is currently making its way toward the cove.

All flights have been grounded, and no flights will be outgoing.

Her phone rang, and Kristen swiped on the local area code number. A recording of the text message she'd been reading started. She let it run so it would register, otherwise their system would call her again.

The ferry system will close immediately. No more ferries will be leaving any of the stations around the cove, and any ferries in transit will dock at the nearest station. All hotels are open for anyone who needs them, and anyone who can should get to the highest location possible. Anyone on the outer islands should not attempt to come to Diamond, though the majority of the hotels are here.

There are several options on all of the islands with

upper-level floors, and we urge all businesses to open their doors to anyone in need.

For more information, visit the Five Island Cove website, where all information will be updated in real time.

Rueben bustled back into the room and sat in front of the middle screen. "I've never seen a tsunami on the radar. I didn't know. I saw this forty minute ago." He scoffed and shook his head. "I feel like an idiot."

"I've only seen it once," she said. "You have nothing to feel bad about. There's time."

"How much time?" he asked.

"At least three hours," Kristen said. "Mark where the earthquake was, and then where the tsunami is now, and chart it."

Reuben began doing that, and Kristen went back to her texts. Her girls kept messaging, and she hated that almost all of them were currently on ferries on the water. At the same time, she wanted to rush to the ferry station and get on the next one headed to Sanctuary. The Cliffside Inn would be ten times safer than this lighthouse on the edge of the ocean.

Yes, it sat up on a cliff, but it was the first thing the waves would hit.

It doesn't matter, she thought. *The waves are going to cover the entire island.* They might not be big enough to reach the upper cliffs on Sanctuary, where Eloise's inn sat, and Kristen closed her eyes and thanked the Lord that all of her girls would be there soon.

"It's moving at two hundred and fifty-seven miles per hour," Rueben said. "It's only a third of the way here." He spun in his chair. "We have about six hours before it'll be here."

"I'll text Connie that we've done more precise calculations," Kristen said. "But the professionals at the NGS will have figured it out by now." She sent the text anyway, because she wanted the mayor to know they were still there and still working on the problem.

Kristen almost wished the tsunami would hit sooner. In six hours, it would be after nine-thirty, with a night as dark as pitch.

CHAPTER SIX

Laurel Baker blew her whistle and gestured at the blue sedan. It was times like these that she'd rather be anything but a police officer. Technically, she was a detective, but in an island crisis, it was all hands on deck.

The last ferry had arrived on Sanctuary twenty minutes ago, and almost all of the cars were off the streets now.

When the first texts had come in from Chief Sherman and then the government about the tsunami, Laurel's first thought was to get home and make sure she had everything essential. Her birth certificate and passport. The photo albums with her grandmother's pictures.

She needed to board her windows and doors. She needed to make sure her younger sister got somewhere safe. She'd called Jenny, and she was headed to her boyfriend's house on the southwest side of Diamond. With any luck, they wouldn't be washed away.

Laurel hadn't had time to check on the tsunami's progress in the past forty minutes since the warnings had gone out. She and her partner, Connor, had been assigned to clear the traffic from the streets and then get up to The Cliffside Inn, where Eloise was expecting them.

She blew a bit harder on her whistle to make a white truck stop while Connor waved someone else out of the lot. Her stomach churned, because she hadn't spoken to Eloise in months—since the night she'd accused Aaron of cheating on her with Laurel.

She'd smiled at her at the station a couple of times, and Eloise had been cordial. They hadn't spent any time of any significance together, despite having a holiday party over Thanksgiving at the station they'd both attended.

The last place Laurel wanted to ride out a tsunami was at The Cliffside Inn, but as her house was on Diamond Island and the ferries weren't running anymore, Laurel's choices were very limited.

The last car pulled out of the parking lot, and Laurel turned toward Connor. "That's it," she called, letting her whistle fall down onto her chest. She shivered in the cold, though she wore gloves, a hat, and a heavy winter coat.

She got in the passenger seat while Connor got behind the wheel, and neither of them said a word. He adjusted the heater as Laurel pulled off her gloves and hat. Her own sweat had made her hat a bit wet, and she was warmer without it on.

Connor picked up the radio. "Traffic cleared at the ferry, boss," he said. "We'll do a circuit and make sure everything's closed and no one's doing anything stupid."

"Don't take long," Teresa said. "The Chief doesn't want anyone on staff to risk themselves. Everyone can hear the sirens and everyone got the texts. There's only so much we can do."

"Roger that," Connor said as he turned down the road that led right along the coast, where the majority of shops and restaurants were on the island. They'd all closed, and the street looked like a ghost town.

"It's almost eerie," Laurel said.

"Have you ever been through a tsunami?" Connor asked, looking at her.

"No," she said. "You?"

He shook his head. "I've only been here for twelve years. There's just been the one hurricane that came this way, and it mostly blew out by the time it made it this far north. Still super windy, though." He glanced at her.

"It's the wind that's the worst," she said. "Are you going to head up the cliffs now?"

"Yeah," he said. "Did you get ahold of your sister?"

"Yes, she's going to Cory's." She looked at him. "What about your mother?"

"She's at the Cove Hiatt," Connor said. "Dad's going

to the Atlantic Building on Pearl. It's twelve stories, and apparently, that whole top floor is full already."

"Wow," she said, swallowing. "Would you mind if I called Paul?"

"Of course not," he said.

Laurel switched the channel on the radio and said, "Come back, Paul. It's Laurel." She released the button, hoping he was in the car, as the signal was so much better there than if he was out on the street.

She waited in silence as Connor navigated the quiet streets. Finally, Paul said, "I'm here, Laurel."

"Where are you?"

"In the line of cars heading up the cliff," he said. "On Sanctuary. I just heard your report to the Chief. You on your way up?"

Relief filled her that he was headed up to safety too, and she pressed her eyes closed. "Yes," she said. "We haven't quite made it to the road going up to Cliffside Drive."

"Oh, no," Connor moaned, and Laurel looked over to see what he'd noticed. The street to the left was lined with cars, both lanes with vehicles heading in the same direction. "I knew it would be packed."

"Wow," Laurel said. "Paul, where are you on the road?"

"Almost up," he said. "It moves faster than you think it will. We've only been on the road for about twenty minutes."

"So we might make it," Laurel said as the first drops of rain splashed the windshield. At least she and Connor weren't standing out in the street directing traffic anymore. "Okay, I'll see you up there."

"We're going to be okay, Laurel," Paul said, and Laurel nodded, her chest tight with worry. She'd never been in a tsunami before, and she had no idea what to expect. It was going to hit the island after dark, and she couldn't imagine being able to fall asleep tonight. She didn't want to be caught unaware when the water came gushing in through the windows.

That's not going to happen, she told herself, but the truth was, no one knew what was going to happen.

"I'll see you when you get here," Paul said. "Okay, peanut?"

"Okay," Laurel said. "Thanks, Paul." She switched the radio back to the public channels connected to the home base, only to hear Chief Sherman's voice calling for all units to report where they were.

Connor quickly pressed the button on the radio and relayed where they were, and it certainly seemed like they were the last partnership heading in for the day. The radio went silent after that, and Laurel had a hard time keeping her fingernails out of her mouth. She always chewed her nails when she was stressed or worried, and she tucked her hands under her thighs in an attempt to control her nervous habits.

Eventually, they did make their way up and up the

road, but there wasn't anywhere to park at The Cliffside Inn. Thankfully, there were a few other cop cars there, one with lights flashing.

"Pull in right there," she said. "There's Paul and the Chief." Both men got out of the car with the lights, and Laurel had the distinct thought that they'd been waiting for her.

The Chief lifted one hand, and Connor brought the car to a stop. He and Laurel got out, and Aaron said, "I need to take your car back down to get Eloise's mother."

"You're going to go back down?" Connor asked as Laurel's eyes sought out Paul's. Their gazes met, and she wanted to run to him and let him hold her in his strong arms. They'd been dating for four months now, and it was a relationship Laurel really enjoyed. He'd been very patient with her, and she'd been very honest with him.

"I have to get Eloise's mother," Aaron said. "And Kelli and Parker aren't here yet. I'm going to get them all and bring them here."

"I'll go with you," Connor said.

"I'm going to have three people with me and two cats," Aaron said. "I'm okay. I need you guys to keep an eye on Eloise and help her out any way you can." He stepped around the open driver's door and added, "Okay?"

"Okay, Chief," Connor said, stepping out of the way. Laurel migrated over to Paul's side and slipped her fingers into his, the idea of Aaron going down into danger sitting strangely in her stomach.

The Chief backed into the street and went back the way she and Connor had painstakingly come. Paul gently turned her, and Laurel faced The Cliffside Inn, a place she literally never thought she'd visit.

She took a deep breath as a gust of wind picked up, driving the rain into her back.

"Let's get inside," Paul said, and Laurel told herself she didn't have anything to worry about. She could talk to Eloise; she hadn't done anything wrong by doing the work Aaron had assigned her to do.

She let Connor lead the way, and when it was time to go inside, she went last. Eloise already stood there, talking to and then hugging Connor.

"Paul, thank goodness," Eloise said, taking him into a hug and holding him tight. They parted, and Laurel came face-to-face with Eloise.

The other woman didn't even hesitate. She stepped forward and grabbed onto her. "I'm so glad you made it."

"Thank you, Eloise." Laurel hugged her back, and it sure did feel nice. "How many people are here?"

They stepped back, and Eloise pressed her lips together. "Maybe fifty? I feel bad, but I've had to start turning people away."

Laurel rubbed her hand hands up her arms. "Tell us how to help you. Paul's good in the kitchen, and Connor can boss people like nobody's business." She grinned at her partner, who simply shook his head without denying it.

Laurel fumbled for the whistle around her neck and lifted it. "And we have whistles. Anyone steps out of line, and we'll get them back in."

Eloise blinked at her and then started laughing. "I could use some help in the kitchen, and Connor, if you could go over this list of room assignments to make sure I haven't made a mistake, I'd appreciate it." She handed him a clipboard. "Aaron says you're good at details."

"Sure thing, Eloise." Connor took the clipboard and studied it.

"Paul, Laurel, you're with me in the kitchen. I hope you're ready to deal with my friend Alice, though. She knows nothing about cooking, but I can't get her to leave the kitchen."

Laurel exchanged a glance with Paul, stepped back to his side, and said, "I'm glad we're together at least."

"Me too." He swept his lips along her hairline. "Your family is okay?"

"Nantucket sounded their siren too, and they're running every ferry they have back to Hyannis. It's only an hour-long trip, and in the same direction as the tsunami. Then they have a hotel in town, with hopefully a high-floor room. They said they'd call as soon as they were on the mainland."

"Good," Paul said. He squeezed her hand as they stepped into a beautiful, industrial kitchen. Paul pulled in a breath. "Oh, wow."

Laurel was in shock about cooking for fifty, but Paul

was obviously excited about it. Another woman stood there, bent over another clipboard. She looked up and said, "I have no idea, Eloise. Do you even have enough food to feed fifty people?"

"Go," Laurel said. "Go now, Paul," and she watched with pride and a smile as her boyfriend strode further into the kitchen to see what he could do to help.

CHAPTER SEVEN

Eloise glared at Alice. "There's plenty of food here," she said. Maybe she didn't know how to make it into meals to feed everyone at the inn, but there was enough food. The full-time chef she'd hired to serve breakfast and dinner hadn't been able to make it off of Bell Island before the tsunami warning went out, and the worry inside Eloise started to intertwine with the irritation.

"Did you have a menu?" Paul Lehye asked, and Eloise turned toward him. He worked for Aaron, and Eloise had met him on several previous occasions. She gave him a quick smile and cut a glance at his girlfriend, Laurel. They both wore their uniforms, as they'd been on duty when the warnings had gone out.

Eloise really wished it was Aaron standing next to her, wearing his uniform and offering help. Her stomach lurched, and she pressed one palm into the cool, stainless steel counter beside her.

Aaron was going to be fine. He knew how to drive in the rain, and their cell phone service still worked. He had a radio besides, and if Eloise didn't hear from him in an hour, she'd sit in one of the three other police cars that were parked int front of The Cliffside Inn.

"Yes," she said. "Meghan and I went over a menu so I could order all the groceries." She pulled her phone out of the pocket of her black slacks. She'd dressed up today so she could show her friends how professional she could be, a fact she was now regretting as the loafers she wore weren't quite wide enough for her feet, and her pinky toes existed in a constant state of getting smashed.

"Let's see," she muttered as she navigated to her email. The seconds seemed to stretch into long threads, and surely Paul would rescind his offer to help if Eloise took much longer to find the email from Meghan.

"I know I have it," she said, her heart starting to pound. This was not the way she'd wanted to kick off having guests in The Cliffside Inn. When it was just going to be her girlfriends and their families, Eloise had been out of her head with nerves.

Now she had over four dozen people, most of whom she barely knew. Aaron knew them all, and if she could hide behind him, Eloise would be fine. He was gone now, though, and the clock had just ticked to five o'clock.

"Here it is," she finally said, landing on the right email.

She scanned the message quickly and handed the phone to Paul. "It was just going to be me and my friends, though. Maybe we don't have enough food."

"I think the Chief was going to be here through Christmas, though, right?" Paul asked, flicking his eyes at her for a moment. "You surely have enough for tonight and tomorrow morning. Everyone won't stay forever."

"Right," Eloise said, though it felt like she couldn't see past the next minute. She'd never experienced a tsunami before, and she simply needed to focus on the moment, deal with whatever came up, and look back after it was all done.

Looking back at a crisis was always easier than trying to see through it, and Eloise blinked, trying to focus.

Dinner, she told herself. She needed to offer people dinner.

Robin and AJ had taken over the front desk and placing people in rooms. Eloise quickly sent a text to the group. *Robin and AJ, I asked Connor, one of Aaron's cops, to help with the organization of people, just in case he says anything.*

Okay, Robin said. *People seem to be settling in just fine.*

"All right," Paul said with a heavy exhale. "She was going to make a pumpkin curry soup tonight. Let's get these ingredients out and see how much we can make. Perhaps there's enough to double or triple. Soup goes a long way."

"Not everyone will eat besides," Laurel said.

Eloise turned toward her, as the woman had come up beside her. "You're right." She took a deep breath. "Okay. Tell us what to find, Paul."

He started naming ingredients, and Eloise, Alice, and Laurel claimed it and bustled off to find it. Within minutes, a pile of cans, cream, spices, and three rotisserie chickens sat on the cooking station.

Paul looked at the recipe and then the ingredients. "We can feed people with this. Eloise, it says she was going to serve rolls and salad too."

"Right," Eloise said. "The rolls are store-bought, and I got three dozen. That's not enough for everyone."

"We can cut some in half," Laurel said. "Perhaps some of the children won't need a full roll."

"They're going to have soup and salad too," Paul said. "It's going to be fine.

"Cutting them in half is a good idea," Alice said. "I'll find the rolls."

Eloise started toward the big walk-in refrigerator. "We got two kinds of salad," she said over her shoulder. "A broccoli kale one, and a classic green salad." She retrieved the bagged salads from the fridge, and she had four of each.

"This is a lot," Paul said, smiling at her. "I'm going to get started on the soup. It seems straightforward enough, and I think it'll be done in about forty-five minutes."

Eloise bent to get out a couple of the big, industrial

bowls she'd bought. With her hands busy, her mind couldn't linger on Aaron and where he was. She couldn't dial her mother for a fourth time. She couldn't text Kelli or Kristen to find out where they were.

She'd never heard back from Kristen, but with the ferry system closing immediately, Eloise didn't think she'd be coming to the inn. Her chest felt like someone had knocked her down, stomped on her breastbone, and refused to let her stand.

She reminded herself that Kristen had lived through some terrible storms here in Five Island Cove. The physical kind, with wind, rain, sleet, and waves as tall as the lighthouse. She'd also survived some of the worst personal and emotional storms a person had to go through, and Eloise told herself not to worry about Kristen.

It was so very hard, though, because worrying was something Eloise did best. Not only that, but she loved Kristen, and she didn't want anything bad to happen to her. She let her mind roam free as she piled the bags into separate bowls. She'd cut them open, dump them out, and mix everything up closer to when the salads would be eaten.

Meanwhile, she got out the pot Paul needed, and she found the can opener, opened the cans of pumpkin, and measured out the half-and-half they'd add very last.

Eloise could do a lot in the kitchen, even if it wasn't putting together a meal for fifty. She knew how to make rice, and she set another pot on the stove and measured water, salt, and the white rice into it.

She knew how to dice up the meat on a rotisserie chicken, and she did that while Paul sautéed onions and measured spices.

Only ten minutes later, he said, "That's it. This boils for fifteen minutes, and we add the cream and rice."

"Wow," Alice said. "That's fast."

"Paul's a good cook," Laurel said. "We took a class once, and he put me to shame." She smiled at him, and it was obvious to Eloise that she really liked Paul. A slip of foolishness moved through Eloise for her behavior toward Laurel.

She started toward Alice, who'd been slicing rolls and talking quietly with Laurel. They'd gotten out butter to go with the rolls, found bowls and spoons, as well as small plates for salad and rolls, and as Eloise joined them, Alice asked, "How long have you and Paul been seeing each other?" She wore such a friendly smile, and Eloise wanted to be more like that.

"Uh, since August," Laurel said, shooting a look at Eloise. "They do those cooking classes down by the beach on Diamond. Have you ever done those?"

"No," Alice said, still smiling as she piled rolls into a basket Eloise didn't know she owned. "I just moved here permanently in June, and my divorce was final at the end of August." She spoke in the same smooth, professional voice Eloise had heard her use with clients. "I'm not so sure I'm ready to get back on the dating bandwagon."

Eloise stared at her in surprise. She'd literally accepted a dinner invitation with Will Bridge only a few days ago. Alice ignored her though, and Eloise kept her mouth shut. It wasn't her place to make Alice tell Laurel—who was a complete stranger to Alice—about her first date after her divorce.

"It took me a while," Laurel said with a faint smile. She turned away from the other two. "Should I find some napkins or paper towels?"

"I have napkins in the pantry," Eloise said, pointing her in the right direction.

Alice let her walk away before she said, "Thanks for not saying anything about Will."

"Why didn't *you* say anything about Will?"

Alice shrugged. "I don't know. Maybe because I haven't told the twins about him yet, and I don't want them to hear it from someone else."

"Did you tell Robin that?" Eloise asked, catching Laurel headed back their way.

"Yes," Alice said. "Now, where are we going to have everyone eat?"

"I kept a dining area," Eloise said. "But we're putting people in it as a bedroom."

"But not right now," Laurel said. "Should I go check on it?"

"Yes," Eloise said. "I'll show you where it is." She

gestured for Laurel to come with her. "Alice, would you check on the rice?"

"I don't know anything about rice," Alice said, a look of panic crossing her face.

"Then open the salads," Eloise said. "Paul, would you check the rice?"

"On it," he called from the stove, and Eloise could see what Laurel liked about him.

She exited the kitchen to more noise than she anticipated, which only accelerated her anxiety. The kitchen sat behind the dining room, but Eloise remembered putting someone's luggage against that door.

Down the hall, past the chest-high podium she'd installed herself, painted, and decorated with a traditional poinsettia flower for the holidays, she turned into the dining area. Several people milled about here, as this was the inn's official lobby. Eloise had envisioned serving cookies during check-in, breakfast every day of the week, and dinner for an added charge per person.

She needed to say something to Laurel, as there was a five-hundred-pound gorilla between them. "There's a closet over here," she said, stepping past a couple facing one another. Eloise pulled out her keys and fitted the right one into the knob. It twisted easily, as all fixtures in the inn were brand new.

She opened the door and stepped into the storage closet, feeling for the light switch on the wall just inside. It snapped on, and Eloise made room for Laurel. Once she'd taken a step inside, Eloise said, "Listen, Laurel, I wanted to apologize for my behavior in the fall."

"Oh, no, Eloise. You don't need to do that."

Eloise looked right into the other woman's eyes. "Yes, I do. It was...not my finest moment, and I hope you know I have no ill feelings for you." She smiled at Laurel, and surprisingly, she meant her words.

Laurel nodded, her mouth tight. "It was difficult for me as well," she said. "I didn't know how to tell my boss no."

"He shouldn't have put you in that situation," Eloise said. "If he does again, you just come tell me, okay? I'll set him straight." She smiled at Laurel, the sudden urge to hug her coming over Eloise. She grabbed onto Laurel, who sucked in a breath.

A moment later, though, she eased into Eloise's hug. "Thank you for being so forgiving," she whispered.

"Nothing to forgive," Laurel said quietly. She stepped away a moment later. "Are the Chief's children here? If you need help with them until he gets back, Paul and I can help. We both know them, and they know us."

"They're in my apartment," she said. "Robin's youngest is hanging out with them."

"Oh, you have an apartment here?"

"It's a tiny, one-bedroom area behind the inn," she said. "Just enough for the caretaker. I think I'm going to have my chef live in it, actually. I haven't decided yet." She didn't like thinking about all the details she hadn't worked out yet, and this trial by fire wouldn't help her make them.

This situation was so unique, and Eloise hoped she never had to relive it.

"I don't know if I have enough tables and chairs for everyone." She turned to face the folded tables.

"They can eat in shifts," Laurel said. "Let's get out what you have." They started pulling out the first table when Charlie and Mandie joined them.

"My mother sent us to help," Charlie said, taking Laurel's end of the table.

"I'll get the chairs," Mandie said.

Together, the four of them got the tables and chairs set up. Eloise moved the luggage in front of the door leading into the kitchen, and she opened that door and called to Alice.

She brought out the rolls, and Eloise and Laurel went to get the plates, utensils, and salads. Charlie and Mandie asked everyone to please move out of the lobby area so there was room for people to form a line, and Charlie stood at the head of the line.

"Now we just need to let people know it's ready," Paul said as he brought out a giant pot of soup. It was pale orange and smelled liked garlic, pumpkin, and curry, and Eloise's mouth watered.

She didn't think she'd be able to eat much, as tight at her nerves were, but she hoped someone would.

"Oh, I have a speaker system," Eloise said, turning to

run off to the public address system she'd had installed just three weeks ago.

"Put a basket at the end of the table," Alice said before Eloise got too far. "She should collect donations for meals like this. The food isn't free."

Eloise wanted to disagree, but she let Alice do what she wanted, because she was right. The food wasn't free, and while Eloise hadn't planned on charging her friends for the next several nights they'd stay at the inn, she was sure she'd have gotten offers from all of them to help with the food.

She bustled to the back of the inn, to the system just inside the back door the led out to the patio and the pool. The sun was completely gone now, though darkness hadn't stolen all the light from twilight yet. Eloise took a moment to look out into the soupy atmosphere.

Once, she'd stood out back here and looked down at the house she'd hated. She wondered if she'd be able to see it tonight.

Shaking herself, she picked up the phone and dialed star-nine. "Good evening," she said, channeling her inner Alice. "For anyone who's hungry, we have a delicious pumpkin curry soup downstairs in the dining room. There are two types of salad, and rolls with butter. We ask that you only take what you can actually eat, so that we have enough for all who desire to eat tonight."

She drew in a deep breath as the door to her apartment opened and Billie and Grace appeared with Jamie.

Her heart expanded, as she loved those girls so much. "We ask that rooms one through seven come eat first, while those of you in eight trough fourteen wait about twenty minutes to allow room in the dining room. If you are not assigned a room, please come at your convenience. There is enough food for all."

She nodded as if anyone could see her and hung up. She immediately moved outside and gathered her soon-to-be stepdaughters into a double hug. "How are you guys? Hungry?"

"Yes," Grace said, gripping Eloise tightly. Even Billie clung to her, and Eloise pressed her eyes closed.

"Did you tell Jamie thanks for staying with you?"

"Thank you," Grace said as she stepped back from Eloise.

Eloise straightened and kept her arm around Billie, who looked up at her. She was getting taller, and she was so beautiful and so wise. "Where's my dad?" she asked.

Eloise swallowed, as she wouldn't be able to live with herself if anything happened to Aaron. "He went down to my mother's to help her," she said. "He's going to meet Kelli and Parker there too. Then they'll be back." She put a smile on her face, but it felt all wrong. She let it slip away as they went inside, and Eloise paused on the threshold of the inn.

"I'm going to grab something from my apartment," she said. "You guys go ahead. I'll be right there." She watched the three girls go around the corner, and then she turned back to the patio.

She crossed it and went past the pool too. To the very edge of the yard she went, and Eloise folded her arms across her chest as she looked down the cliffs to the rest of Sanctuary Island. She'd stood here before, and she'd been able to see all the way to the beaches, watch the ferries come in and go out, and gaze across the ocean toward Boston.

Tonight, she didn't try to see any of those things. All she wanted to see was her mother's house, and she wished Aaron would turn on the flashing red and blue lights on the top of the car.

She pulled out her phone and called him, relieved when the call went through. The line just rang and rang and rang though, which did nothing to soothe the flurry of bat wings flapping in Eloise's stomach.

"Please stay safe," she whispered into the night, unable to find her mother's house in the soupy atmosphere in front of her. "Please."

CHAPTER EIGHT

AJ lay in Matt's arms on the couch in one of the rooms inside the Cliffside Inn. Robin and Alice lay in the same bed, only Robin's face illuminated by the bright blue-white light of her phone. Every so often, she'd turn her face toward Alice and whisper something, to which Alice would respond.

No one was sleeping, and AJ couldn't even get herself to swallow.

Their room was on the ground floor, and if the waves of the tsunami reached this high, they'd get wet before anyone on the second or third floor.

She shifted, and Matt's arms around her tightened. "Scared?" he whispered, and AJ could only nod.

"Me too," he said. "I've never been through anything like this.

"I had to hunker down during a hurricane a couple of

time," AJ said. "In Miami. We knew it was coming though, and we boarded everything up. We gathered in the middle of the dorms, which were made of cinderblocks. We were fairly far inland, too, and while our apartment complex had downed trees and a few broken windows, we barely even knew the storm had come and gone."

"I've been through one hurricane in New York City," he said. "It was so strange not to see people on the streets. The whole building swayed, and the five of us huddled in a coat closet with flashlights and Go Fish."

"Your children must've been young," she said, leaning back into his chest a little further. He'd been nothing but loving and kind since she'd shown up on his doorstep with her luggage and the news of their pregnancy.

He'd told her she could stay with him, and she'd spent the next few days researching doctors and then making her first appointment. She'd been told her pregnancy was automatically high-risk because of her age, and AJ didn't quite know how to cope with the stress that had been added to her plate.

This tsunami certainly wasn't helping her to relax.

She'd also had to go off her anti-depressants and her ADD medication, and she felt like she was currently on a child's swing set. One moment, she was fine, and all of her thoughts were aligned and working together. The next, she was swooping downward, unable to remember what she was working on, or even saying sometimes.

Matt had finally asked her what was going on, and

she'd admitted to going off her anti-anxiety medication, as well as the pills that helped her focus and kept her attention in a normal sphere. She didn't feel like herself without the meds, and she didn't know what that said about her. What she knew was that she could hardly sleep, tsunami notwithstanding, and that the past nine days since she'd landed in the cove with the news of the life inside her had been some of the hardest of her life.

She didn't want to risk her pregnancy, and she didn't want to give birth to an underweight, possibly lethargic infant that could go through some major withdrawal symptoms. She could weather this personal storm for nine months.

You can, she told herself again. She had to remind herself of that every few minutes, it seemed, and tears pressed behind AJ's eyes.

"The children were very young," Matt said. "Justin was only three."

"That makes Derrick...six?" AJ guessed.

"Yes," Matt said.

"And Lisa would've been eight."

"She was almost nine, but yes," Matt said, placing his lips right against AJ's neck. She pressed into the touch, almost desperate for him to keep kissing her. She could get lost inside the physicality of making love in a way that quieted her mind like nothing else ever had.

That was why she'd let boys into her life as much as she had. If she could just get her thoughts to settle down, then she'd know what to do next. She knew how to kiss a man and where to put her hands. She knew exactly what to do in bed, and that didn't require her mind to work at all. It somehow freed her up to be able to make better decisions in other areas of her life.

Someone shifted in the bed across the room, and AJ heard Alice talking to Charlie. All of the other teens and kids were staying in Eloise's apartment with her and a couple of Aaron's cops. The three of them would absolutely be awake, as Aaron Sherman had not returned to the inn yet.

He'd been gone for almost five hours now, and Eloise had been in tears when she'd hugged Alice, Robin, and then AJ and gone with three of his cops and all the kids.

Because Aaron wasn't back, Eloise's mother wasn't in the inn either, and Kelli and Parker also hadn't arrived yet.

AJ pulled her phone from under her hip and looked at it. Her last ten messages to Kelli had gone unanswered, and her own worry felt like a boulder in the back of her throat.

"AJ?" Matt whispered.

"Mm?"

"I'm in love with you." His breath wafted hotly across her shoulder, and she imagined him ducking his head shyly as he made his confession.

AJ stilled, all of the scattered pieces of her life suddenly coming together. "Really?"

He chuckled almost silently against the back of her

neck. "I've been in love with you for almost thirty years. You can't be that surprised."

"I'm..." She twisted in his arms to face him, placing the bright screen of her phone against his shoulder blade. It was too dark to see all the fine features of his face, but she searched anyway. She'd been in love before, and as she tried to define her own feelings, she realized she loved him too.

"I love you, too," she said.

"Do you want to get married?" he asked. "We can make a life right here in the cove and raise our baby together."

AJ had once scoffed at anyone who wanted to settle down and have a quiet life in Five Island Cove. She had never wanted that, and she'd done everything she could to set her life here in the cove on fire.

She'd been in town for eight days and still not even called her father. Amelia likewise lived on Pearl Island, and they'd probably both like to see AJ and find out how she was doing. She hadn't texted them when the tsunami warning went out, and sudden regret reached right around her throat and squeezed.

Matt kissed her, but AJ already couldn't breathe, and she pulled away. "Don't cry," he whispered.

AJ had a lot to cry about though, and she buried her face in his chest. His hands ran up and down her back, and he started to hum. She wasn't sure how much time had gone by before Alice said, "Is she okay? Maybe she should get up for a second."

Strong hands lifted her, and Matt said, "AJ, baby, can you stand up?"

She rolled, glad Alice and Charlie were there to help her. "I'm okay," she said. "Sorry, I just...I didn't even text my father. What if he's still in that stupid cottage on the beach? Why can't I call and face him?"

She hadn't been the nicest to her father once she'd left the islands; she knew that. She'd wanted nothing to do with Five Island Cove, and that included all the people who still lived here.

The real problem lay in her genes, and AJ didn't want to admit that she was more like her mother than she should be. Her mom had abandoned her and her siblings when AJ was just ten years old, and she barely remembered the woman.

She had taught AJ how easy it was to walk away from anything unpleasant in her life, and a fresh set of tears rolled down her face.

"AJ." Alice took her into a strong grip. Low voices spoke around her, and AJ knew they were talking about her. Fear gripped her heart, because she didn't want Alice to know she was pregnant. She hadn't told anyone except Matt, and she wanted to talk to her friends when she was ready and not a moment sooner.

"Mom," Charlie said, and that single word broke the

haze in AJ's mind. She turned toward the teenager. "Did you feel that?"

AJ hadn't felt anything, but all five of them moved over to the window. Only darkness stretched beyond them, with a burst of light to the right, where an outside spotlight shone onto the front lawn of the inn.

Robin looked at her phone. "It's nine-twenty-four. It could be here."

Charlie reached down and opened the window a couple of inches, and a horrible chill came inside. A low, rushing, hissing sound filled the air, and it sounded very much like the roar of the ocean waves.

"It's here," AJ said, her voice deathly quiet and hollow. She reached for Matt at the same time he wove his arm around her waist. Alice took her hand, and AJ squeezed her fingers. They all stood there, gathered around the window, waiting for their fate to arrive.

"Dear Lord," Robin whispered. "Hear our pleas for safety and the preservation of our lives. Bless my children with Eloise. Bless Eloise and this beautiful inn. Bless my husband who is on lower ground."

She continued to pray for every person she knew, and AJ found herself mentally adding her own prayers for her sister and her father to Robin's vocalized prayer.

Robin had not finished speaking and had not said "Amen," when a horrible, terrible, crunching and crackling sound filled the air.

All five of them made some sort of noise, and AJ's

mind went wild. She imagined the very earth itself cracking and shedding off into the dark, dangerous waters below, and she had no recourse but to go with it.

The ground beneath her feet trembled, and she shrieked, though it wasn't a violent enough shake to even make her sway. It stopped only a second later, but AJ could still imagine the whole island sinking into the sea.

"Dear Lord," Alice said, her voice shaking as much as the earth just had. "Keep Aaron Sherman safe."

"Where is he?" AJ asked. "Why isn't he back?" She gripped her phone and lifted it to her face. She jabbed at Kelli's name. "We have to get in touch with Kelli." Panic gripped her lungs, and AJ struggled to breathe against the tension there.

The phone connected, but it just rang and rang and rang.

Beside her, Matt muttered something that sounded very much like a plea to God to keep his parents safe if at all possible, and AJ lowered her phone while it continued to ring, adding her voice to the four people already praying as they stood in front of the window.

It felt like the whole world was holding its breath, and all anyone could do was wait to see where they'd land on the other side of the tsunami.

Pray, and wait.

CHAPTER NINE

Kelli gripped Parker's hand as Aaron kept going up the road. It had taken her a very long time to get to Sanctuary Island—much longer than the thirty-seven minutes it should've taken. The ferry was one that bypassed Diamond and went from Bell to Sanctuary. There had almost been an uprising when the conductor had stuck to the route instead of going to the nearest ferry station, as the emergency information had said they would.

Kelli had been secretly glad, but the ferry had floated in the water for a very long time while the conductor was on the radio with his manager. By the time they'd reached Sanctuary, the sun was all the way down and the Ride-Share station was closed.

She and countless others had stood there for a long

time, all of them requesting rides on their apps and getting denied.

Kelli pulled back on the tears for at least the tenth time since those texts had gone out, over five hours ago. She couldn't believe the waves hadn't doused the cove yet, and she wondered if the tsunami was real. The anxiety and tension in her body told her it was, but Kelli had been known to worry about nothing in the past.

She'd stayed in contact with Aaron Sherman, because if she missed him, she'd never get up to the inn, and she couldn't hunker down in her beach house—the one only a hundred yards from the ocean as it was.

Her chest constricted, and she couldn't wait to tell her friends what she'd done at the ferry station. She could barely believe it, and AJ would fall down dead when Kelli told her she'd legitimately picked up a rock from the frozen landscaping at the ferry station and thrown it through a window.

A sense of pride touched her soul, though, because Kelli was done playing the weak link. She wasn't going to be a woman who stood on the sidelines of her life anymore, and as she'd looked down the line of people who needed a ride, she'd determined to make sure they got one.

She could see herself stepping out of line and calling down it: *Who here knows how to hot wire a car?*

Who here has a car we can borrow?

One man had stepped out of the line, towing his little girl with him. She hadn't been bigger than a kindergartener, and he'd never let go of her while Kelli gave her backpack and purse to Parker and broken that window.

She'd gotten the passenger van unlocked, and her new friend Ted had gotten it started. They filled it with as many people as possible, and Kelli drove them around Sanctuary Island to the safety of their homes.

She'd dropped Parker off at Dawn Hall's house, where Aaron joined her in the quest to get everyone away from the ferry station and into a better position of safety.

They'd finished after a couple of hours, and then Aaron's car had run out of gas. *Challenge after challenge* had run through Kelli's mind, and she wasn't going to let a little thing like gasoline prevent her from achieving her goals.

She'd gone to a closed convenience store and broken another window. She'd confessed everything to Aaron, and he'd assured her he wouldn't let anything bad happen to her. She was willing to pay for the windows and repairs for the damage she'd caused.

She still couldn't believe she'd broken two windows that night, and she flexed her fingers in the darkness as Aaron took a corner a little bit too fast. Dawn sat in the front passenger seat, and Parker's thigh pressed into Kelli's right one, both of them huddled behind the Chief as he drove toward the inn.

After she'd filled a gas can with gas, helped the Chief get it in the police car, and they'd picked up Dawn and

Parker, they'd finally started their exodus up the mountain.

Exhaustion filled Kelli once and then twice, but the night wasn't over yet. Her phone had died hours ago, and the only reason she'd been able to find Aaron and help him was because the passenger van belonged to a senior citizen center and had a radio.

A blessing, she thought as they passed a house that had all the lights on. She caught a shadow in the window, and she understood the sheer anxiety she could feel in the scene. She could see herself standing at a window, peering out, wondering when disaster was going to strike.

Kelli felt like it had struck her life several times, and she pressed her eyes closed and prayed for a miracle. Her father had lost his business. Their family had fallen apart. Kelli had dealt with infertility, mental unrest, and feelings of unworthiness. She'd endured first a cheating husband, and then one who wanted an open relationship with two women.

It was said that lightning didn't strike the same place twice, but she'd felt its hot torch of disappointment and despair in her life several times. She wasn't sure if she could handle another disaster.

Yes, you can, she told herself, feeling her spine straighten and strengthen. She could do anything—she'd broken a window in a van tonight and driven over two dozen people to safety. She was going to weather whatever this storm brought her way.

The car swayed and something beneath it rumbled, and she and Aaron said, "Whoa," at the same time. In the next moment, he gunned the engine, adding, "We have to make it past this."

She couldn't see out the window to know what "this" was, but she reached up to grab onto the handle above the window as the car started to slide.

A shriek came out of her mouth, and Parker started to cry as the car turned sideways and slid. Kelli's mind raced. Small, short thoughts hit her mind.

We're going over the side.

We're literally going to fall off the cliff.

This is it.

I love you, Parker.

Everything slowed down but moved so fast at the same time. She tried to keep her body upright, but it was useless, and she felt like she was on one of those carnival rides where the centrifugal force forced everyone to the outside edge of the car.

Parker smashed into her, and she leaned her whole body weight into the car door.

"Aaron," Dawn yelled, and then she screamed as something heavy slammed into the side of the car.

The car spun.

Kelli closed her eyes and let her body's involuntary functions take over.

She couldn't think.

Only a moment later, the police cruiser came to a stop,

and all Kelli could hear was the labored breathing of the four people in the car. Dawn whimpered, and Aaron said, "Talk to me, Dawn." He spoke in an authoritative tone, but his voice was made mostly of air.

"It's my leg," she said. "It's—it got smashed when that boulder hit us."

"Boulder?" Kelli asked.

"It was a landslide," Aaron said, his voice still somewhat breathless. "We're not getting up to the inn tonight." He reached for the radio and pressed the button. "Paul, this is Aaron. Come back."

Silence filled the car.

"Paul, this is Aaron. Come back."

He tried again and then again, and no one answered him.

"I think the radio is out," Parker said. "There's not even static coming through, Aaron."

"You're right," Aaron said, finally replacing the mouthpiece. "I don't think we can stay here. Let's see if I can get us back to Dawn's."

He put the car in gear, and it shuddered, but it moved. Kelli finally took a breath that was more than a gasp, but her worry hadn't gone anywhere.

Aaron swore right out loud, and she didn't have time to reprimand him to watch his language in front of her son. His next words were, "The water is coming right at us."

Kelli strained to see over the seat and past the metal mesh that separated the front seat from the back, where criminals usually rode. She couldn't see much, and she couldn't believe Aaron was going to drive into that.

"There was a house right there," Kelli said, remembering the shadow in the window. "Maybe they'll let us hunker down with them."

"Where?" Aaron asked, pressing on the brake.

"It was right here somewhere," Kelli said, her confidence for the night shot. "Maybe right around the corner. How fast is the water rising?"

"Fast enough," Aaron said, easing the car forward. They bumped over debris in the road, and the lights from the house Kelli had seen came into view.

It was honestly like a mirage in a desert, or manna from heaven.

Aaron pulled right up onto the lawn and jumped from the car. He opened Kelli's door and said, "You're okay? You can get Parker inside?"

"Yes," she said, spilling out of the cruiser. "Get Dawn."

Kelli turned back to grab her son, and they ran up the few steps to the door and pounded on it. "Help!" she yelled. "We need help!"

The door opened a moment later, as if the watcher at the window had been waiting just for them. "Come in," a woman said, reaching for Parker. Kelli passed her son over and turned around.

Behind her, Kelli saw the lights from the house

glinting on dark water, and she darted down the steps to help Aaron with Dawn.

Kelli was not going to let anything happen to Eloise's mother or fiancé, that was for dang sure. "I'll get the cats." She yanked open the back door and grabbed the cat carriers, both cats yowling their displeasure of the last twenty minutes.

Aaron had Dawn out now, and Kelli swept to her right side and buoyed her up as they all shuffled up the steps in a painfully slow way.

"Parker," she barked. "Come get the cats."

Her son did as she asked, and a man had joined the woman on the porch. He took over Kelli's spot in helping Dawn, and the woman said, "Hurry. The water is coming."

They made it inside, and she closed the door behind them. "Stacy," she said. "Help me seal it." Another adult woman came forward, and they both knelt on the floor while Kelli tried to catch her breath, and they pressed a thick, black plastic along the seams of the door.

Kelli glanced around, seeing the black plastic everywhere. She wondered if that worked, but she didn't have time to fully consider it right now.

"Second floor?" Aaron asked. "I need a first aid kit too. Any painkiller you've got. She needs somewhere to sit and put her leg up."

"Upstairs, Chief," the man said. "We have a lounger in the loft she can sit in."

"She's bleeding," Aaron said. "I'll pay for whatever I have to."

"It's no problem," he said. "I'm Malcolm, and we're glad to help."

That started the introductions, and Kelli met Malcolm and Tara Bent, their daughter Stacy, and her husband Jake. They had a baby, who was blissfully asleep in a crib on the second floor.

Kelli herded Parker in front of her as she told them all of their names, including Aaron's and Dawn's. When she made it upstairs, she found Dawn lowering herself into a recliner, a wince of extreme pain on her face.

Aaron and Malcom adjusted the foot rest, and Dawn's leg shook as it lay there. Kelli saw the blood above her knee, and then she turned Parker away.

"You can go into the extra bedroom there," Tara said. "There are blankets and everything."

"Thank you," Kelli murmured, wishing she'd thought to grab her backpack or purse from the car. She needed to charge her phone. She needed to text her friends. She needed to find out if the tsunami was going to hit Boston or New York, and if the water would get all the way to Newark.

She couldn't believe she was thinking about and concerned for Julian's safety, but she was. He was the father of her son, and she did love him on some level.

She turned toward Parker and said, "You can crawl right into bed there, buddy."

"Should I change?" he asked.

"No," she said. "I left my backpack—" She cut off as he lifted it up. A smile touched her face despite the events of that night. "You smart boy."

She hugged him tightly, barely able to hold back her tears. She was about to collapse, and she told herself to hang on for just a little bit longer. Just a little bit longer. Five minutes. Then five more.

"No," she finally said. "Stay dressed, bud. We have no idea if this is over yet."

He nodded, and Kelli took precious moments to dig through the bag to find her phone charger. She did, and she plugged in her phone before she stepped over to the window to check on the depth of the water.

If it reached all the way to The Cliffside Inn, this house would be completely submerged underwater.

She looked out the window, the headlights of the police car flickering as the water started to reach the engine. It was at least twenty feet below where she stood, and as she watched, it didn't seem to be getting much higher than it already was.

Beyond the doorway, she heard Dawn suck in a breath through her teeth, and Kelli's motherly instincts told her to go check on Eloise's mother. Then she could make a proper report when her phone had enough charge to make a call.

Out in the loft, Aaron knelt at Dawn's right side, focused on her injury. He worked swiftly and with steady hands. He finished cleaning the wound, and that addition of alcohol had probably been why she'd gasped.

"All clean," he said in a calm, soothing voice. "I'm going to put this antibacterial cream on it, and cover it up."

"Okay," Dawn said, her voice high-pitched.

Aaron did that and stood, pure exhaustion on his face.

"Here are some of my looser pants," Tara said, and Aaron took them from her, a bit of apprehension in those eyes now.

"I'll help her," Kelli said, moving forward. "Will you go see if you can get in touch with anyone up at the inn and let them know what's happening with us?"

"Yes," Aaron said, handing her the pants. "Thank you, Kelli." He took her into a hug and held her tight. "You've been so amazing tonight."

"So have you," she said, surprised at the level of emotion and relief in the usually strong, stoic Chief's voice.

"I'll go see if I can get in touch with Eloise." He bent down and hugged Dawn too. "Okay? I know she'll be worried."

"She's strong too," Dawn said. "Thank you, Aaron. I'm so glad she found you."

"Oh, I'm the lucky one," Aaron said as he straightened, a smile on his face. It disappeared quickly as he turned toward the steps. "I'm going to run down and see if—"

"The water is on the porch," Malcolm said, blocking

his way. "You're not going outside, and you're not going downstairs."

Aaron blinked at him, but he didn't argue with Malcolm. "I'll try my phone. Thank you so much, Malcolm." He reached out and shook the man's hand, then retreated to a corner of the loft.

"Come on, Dawn," Kelli said. "Let's get you up and into this bedroom."

CHAPTER TEN

The sun rose slowly but steadily. Robin stood on the front porch at the inn and watched it crest the horizon. The ocean to the east rippled slightly, but otherwise didn't show any signs of a wall of water having moved through the cove only ten hours ago.

No water had come up to the inn, a fact that had allowed Robin to get a few hours of sleep in the quietest parts of the night.

She hadn't been able to get in touch with Duke yet, but she kept her phone under her arm. He'd stayed at their house, as he'd been planning to come to the inn on Monday, after a weekend of fishing with Bryan.

All of the boats had probably been damaged beyond repair after last night's wall of water had hit the cove. Robin had woken to a world without power, and it had been off for hours now. Her phone had charged most of the night, but she couldn't help thinking any calls or texts she tried to get through would simply fail.

She clung to a tiny thread of hope that the tsunami hadn't been too bad. After all, it hadn't even reached the inn.

"Then where's Aaron?" she asked herself, looking automatically to the two police cars sitting in the driveway of the inn. Paul, Laurel, and Connor had been inside the cars for most of the night, trying to get in touch with him—or anyone else on the force.

They hadn't been able to, and the logical conclusion—at least to Robin—was that their radio system was down. That, or else the station had been wiped out, all the other cars in the entire fleet were damaged or underwater, and they'd entered the apocalypse.

The walkie talkie in her back pocket beeped, and Robin jumped as she hurried to reach for it. "Robin," Duke's voice said. "Are you—in the morning?"

He sounded somewhat upbeat, but the most important thing was that he was still alive. Pure relief rushed through her, and she depressed the button as she brought the walkie to her mouth. "I'm here," she said. "Tell me everything."

"The house is okay," he said. "We've got some standing water in the back yard, and some has seeped into the kitchen and living room. I swept it all out, and I have fans blowing to get it dry."

"Wow," Robin said. "That's all?"

"The carpet is probably ruined," Duke said. "It's not like the water was clean."

Robin pressed her lips together and added *living room carpet* to their growing list of things they needed to replace. She felt like the heavens had opened up and the rain streamed down. While that happened, a hurricane approached. And then, an earthquake threw another wrench into Robin's life.

"Bryan and I just got to the dock. It looks like a giant reached down and picked up every boat, crushed them in his fist, and dropped all the timber in a pile."

"*The Lady Hawk*?" Robin asked, part of her heart dying a little bit, because she already knew what Duke was going to say.

"She's gone, Robin," Duke said.

"Why do you sound so happy about it?" Robin asked as someone stepped out onto the porch with her. She turned toward Alice, wishing she didn't have to have this conversation in front of anyone.

It's Alice, she told herself. She'd put her house up for sale so she could support herself and her children with her own income. She'd gotten rid of her car, and she'd only kept the sensible sedan her kids used from time to time.

"I'm not happy about it," Duke said. "But the insurance will pay out now, no questions asked."

Robin met Alice's eyes, and she raised her eyebrows as if to say, *He's got a point.*

"You always see the silver lining," Robin said.

Duke chuckled. "How did you fare over there?"

"The water didn't reach us here," she said. "The biggest issue right now is locating Aaron, Kelli and Parker, and Eloise's mother. We haven't heard from or seen them since last night."

"Oh, no," Duke said, and he sounded genuinely upset. "What can I do?"

"I don't know," Robin said. "I think the ferries will be down for at least today."

Alice nodded and gestured to her phone. Robin had no idea what she was saying, and she held up her hand to get her to stop. "The girls and I are fine. We arrived without any issues, and we have plenty to eat here. We've got a bed and it's decently warm, though the power is out."

"I'm glad," Duke said. "We still have power here, but—is the—so I'll do that—tomorrow."

"I'm losing you," Robin said. "I can't hear everything." When she released the button, she expected to hear Duke's voice again, but she didn't. Only dead air came through the line. A crackle of static, where she thought she'd get him again, but she didn't.

She lowered the walkie talkie as she admitted defeat. "What were you trying to say?" she asked Alice.

"They updated the webpage," she said. "The ferries won't reopen until tomorrow morning." She faced the sun as the golden rays of light rose higher into the sky, and Robin turned her face into the light and warmth too.

"What else did they say?"

"The wall of water was twenty-one feet."

"That's not too bad," Robin said. "The lighthouse is taller than that, right?"

"Right," Alice murmured. She hugged herself and drew in a deep breath. "They say it slowed because the cove has a shallow rim of water around it. That usually makes the water rise higher, but it didn't have time."

They stood together in silence for a minute, and Robin was glad they were together. "Have you heard from Kristen?"

"No." Robin shook her head. "I'm sure she's okay. Instead of going high, they go underground. I think they'll be okay."

"It's going to get cold in the inn," Alice said. "If we can't get the power on."

"Mm." Robin had bigger problems than the power being out. "Duke lost his boat."

"I figured." Alice put her arm around Robin. "I'm so sorry, Robin. What will you do?"

"He'll file with the insurance company, but they're not fast, Alice. We have no money to buy a replacement boat until the insurance comes through, and by then, we'll have nothing."

Alice said nothing, and that same feeling filled Robin. She hated feeling nothing. Nothing didn't spur action. Nothing didn't help her find a solution. Nothing literally did nothing for her.

At the same time, she couldn't get herself to care about the boat right now.

"Where do you think Kelli and Parker are?" she whispered, leaning into Alice's embrace a little further.

"I don't know," Alice murmured back. "Last I heard, she was on the ferry."

"Yeah." Robin let her imagination run away with her, and she couldn't stand the thought of one of her best friends being swept out to sea on a ferry. "I bet she's so scared." Kelli was a wonderful woman, but she was quite a bit more fragile than any of the rest of them—and terrified of the water.

"Probably," Alice said. "Like the rest of us standing at that window last night."

"Even AJ said a prayer," Robin said, and she straightened to meet Alice's eyes. They grinned at one another, and their laughter spilled out of their mouths at the same time.

Once they'd sobered, Robin twisted to look at the door behind her. "There's something going on with her and Matt."

"I'm sure there is," Alice said. "When have you known AJ to not have something going on with the man she's seeing?"

"I don't mean sex," Robin said quietly. "Something else."

"You think so?" Alice asked, looking toward the police cars as Paul got out of the nearest one.

"Yes," Robin said as he called to them.

"Where's Eloise? I have the Chief on the radio."

Robin's breath hitched in her chest again. Her pulse kicked into high gear, and she practically flew down the steps. "I'll get her." She jogged around the inn to the back apartment. "Eloise," she called. She and the officers had taken all of the kids, as they could sleep anywhere, and Eloise had a lot of floor just not a lot of bedrooms.

"Eloise," she said, barging into the apartment. She stood in the kitchen, a spatula in one hand and holding the handle of a pan in the other as she fried eggs. "Paul has Aaron on the radio."

Eloise's eyes widened, and she dropped the spatula and rushed toward Robin, her expression filed with hope and horror at the same time.

CHAPTER ELEVEN

Eloise hadn't realized she'd be getting a big, huge family of officers when she'd started dating Aaron. He'd already given her two beautiful daughters, and a set of parents that didn't scream at each other or hit one another.

He'd given her an entirely new reason to keep living her life and doing the best she could, and her heartbeat hadn't been right since he'd left last night.

As she slid into the front passenger seat of the police car where Paul Lehye sat behind the wheel, Eloise knew she'd gained more than she even knew. Paul loved and cared about Aaron, as did Laurel Baker and Connor Moon, and every single cop currently standing around the car. Despite the cold temperatures, all the windows were down, and Eloise knew it was so everyone could hear

Aaron's report. Robin, Alice, and AJ crowded around, and Grace and Billie climbed into the back with Laurel.

"Go ahead, Chief," Paul said into the radio. "Eloise and the girls just got in the car."

"Everyone's there, right?" Aaron asked, and just hearing his voice made Eloise's eyes fill with tears. He was all right enough to speak. He could supposedly walk well enough to get to a car.

"Yep," Paul said. "You have the whole force assigned to Sanctuary, so maybe don't say anything you don't want us all to hear." He grinned at Eloise, and she smiled back at him, her heart opening to him in a whole new way.

All of these people loved Aaron as much as she did, and that bonded them in a way she hadn't anticipated or even thought about.

"Hey, sweetheart," Aaron said, and the line clicked.

Paul handed her the mouthpiece. "You just hold that button in as you speak."

Eloise nodded and pressed the button, her throat so dry. "Hey, Aaron. I'm here," she said, quickly letting go of the button.

His chuckle came through the car, and Eloise warmed from the inside out. "It's so good to hear your voice. I love you, and I can't wait to marry you."

Paul started to chuckle too, and Eloise couldn't stop smiling.

"I suppose you want an update on what happened," he said.

Eloise nodded, but she didn't need to take precious seconds to press the button and say so.

"It was one of the craziest nights ever," he said. "Kelli came in on another ferry, after all the others. It apparently didn't go to Diamond the way it was supposed to, and there was suddenly another hundred people or so right there on the beach."

"After we cleared the lot?" Laurel asked, and Eloise tried to hand her the radio, but she forgot about the protective guard between the front seat and the back, and she knocked her knuckles against the metal mesh.

"It's fine," Laurel said as Aaron started to talk again.

"They waited in the RideShare line, and they were all using the app to call for a ride, and no one came."

"Oh, my," Eloise said, trying to imagine herself in that situation.

"You'll never believe this," Aaron said, laughing again. "But Kelli took charge. She broke into a van, and she and another man drove everyone in the line to where they needed to go."

Eloise's eyes widened, and she turned to look at Alice, Robin, and AJ. They all looked equally stunned, especially Robin. AJ started to laugh a moment later, and she shook her head as she did.

"She was very late getting to your mother's, but she'd texted me, and I went to help."

"Of course he did," Eloise said.

"With the two of us, we got everyone home. Then I ran out of gas, if you can believe it."

"I believe it," Robin said. "Seems like everything bad that could happen, did happen."

Eloise agreed, but she didn't press the button to talk. She didn't want to miss a word of Aaron's story. He went on to say they'd then gone back to her mother's to get Parker and her mom, and they'd started up the road.

"It was dark," Aaron said, his voice lower now. "About nine-thirty."

Eloise pulled in a breath and held it. She'd been awake when the island had shaken right down to the foundation. It had happened just after nine-thirty.

"What's it like up there?" he asked without continuing.

Eloise lifted the radio to her mouth and pushed the button. "Normal," she said. "The water didn't come this high. The inn is fine. No damage." Eloise had been outside checking on everything from the empty pool to the shingles on the roof to the fenced volleyball court and grassy area down the steps from the patio. "It almost seems like nothing happened at all."

She'd stood at the top of the hill, though, and she'd been able to locate her childhood home. It looked different in the winter, with the trees leafless and a cold steel color against the weak, blue sky.

"Once I looked down toward the beach, though, I could tell something happened."

"What did it look like?" Aaron asked.

"I don't know," Eloise said quietly. "I could tell there'd been a storm surge. The water's foamy, and—" She swallowed, because she couldn't even imagine having to clean up after a disaster like this.

"It seemed like there were some fresh wounds on the Earth," she said. "Places that normally didn't see the sun, because a house or barn used to be there but wasn't anymore. The road was black in places where the water had touched, and the parking lot at the ferry station is still covered in water."

Eloise became aware of how articulately she'd spoken, and what horror her words had conveyed. She hadn't been able to see Kelli's row of beach bungalows from her vantage point on the cliff, but she didn't have much hope for them. Not with the ferry station as it was.

She released the button to hear Aaron saying, "—wanted to stay in the station. I'm so glad they didn't." He sighed, and continued with, "I'm glad there's no damage at the inn, baby. That's so great." He wore a smile in the words, and Eloise fell a little bit more in love with him.

"Anyway," he said, clearing his throat. "We obviously didn't make it back to the inn. We got hit in the landslide."

Eloise's ears started to ring, blurring Aaron's story of seeing the landslide and trying to turn into it so he could go back down. The car had been hit; they slid; he'd finally gotten the cruiser to limp along.

"But we couldn't get back to your mother's either," he

said, his voice haunted and hardly his own. "The water was coming up."

Eloise pressed her eyes closed and let the darkness of last night fill her mind. Rocks coming down at her from one side. Water rising on the other. A cliff against the third.

"Kelli had spotted a house, and we made it there. The Bents took us in, gave us food and medical supplies, somewhere to sleep on the second floor."

Eloise wanted him to continue, but she pressed the button and said, "Medical supplies?"

"Baby, don't freak out, okay?"

Eloise was already freaking out. Starting a story like that only caused a person to freak out, and she wished she had Billie or Grace next to her so she could squeeze their hands.

"Your mother was on the side of the car that got hit. I'm fairly sure her leg is broken, but I'm no medical doctor. She can't put any weight on it. Kelli and I dressed the outside wound, gave her painkillers, and sat with her all night. She doesn't have a fever, and there's no infection. But wow, the swelling. I'm almost sure it's broken."

A sob had gathered in Eloise's throat while he spoke, and she held it back as long as she could. As it came out, Paul reached over and squeezed her shoulder.

"It's okay, Eloise," Robin said, leaning into the window. "She'll come up here, and we'll take care of her."

Eloise nodded as Alice affirmed that. Of course her

friends would step in and help her. In the grand scheme of things, a broken leg wasn't that big of a deal. The landslide could've pushed the whole car off the cliff, and she'd have lost her fiancé and her mother in a single breath.

She drew in a breath and pressed the button. "Thank goodness you were with her, Aaron."

"It was Kelli who said her leg was broken. I guess she's saw a woman at the gym once with a broken leg, and it looked just like your mom's."

"What are the chances of getting her to the clinic?" Eloise asked. She couldn't see the emergency care clinic from the inn either, and Five Island Cove only had a full-blown hospital on Diamond Island.

"I'm trying to get her to go now,' Aaron said. "Not sure if you're aware, sweetheart, but your mother is really stubborn."

Eloise giggled, especially when Aaron said, "Now I see where you get it."

She sobered quickly though, because her mom's stubbornness wasn't what was keeping her from going to the clinic. She hated that she had her friends and a large portion of Aaron's cops milling about, listening to the story, but some things couldn't be helped.

"Baby," she said quietly, lowering her head as if that would save some of her mother's pride. Some of hers, too. "Mom doesn't like the clinic, because when she took me there after my dad beat me, they didn't believe her that we were in danger."

She lifted her head, refusing to be ashamed of what her father had done. That wasn't her burden to bear, not anymore.

"They actually investigated her for child abuse, and my father got to keep hitting both of us."

The door opened, and Eloise looked over to find Alice squeezing her way into the car. Eloise scooted over, glad for her friend's presence. She'd thought she was fine, but her lungs vibrated with nerves, and as she blew out, she felt stronger than before.

Alice put her arm around her, and Eloise leaned into her, the way they'd always done for one another.

"It was years ago," Eloise said. "Tell her that, okay, Aaron? Surely the same nurses aren't there, and she needs to get her leg set or it won't heal right."

"I didn't know," Aaron said over the radio, and Eloise felt the comforting embrace of his warm, strong arms around her. He'd hug her if he was there, she knew. "I'm sorry, El."

"It was a long time ago," she said again. "But that's why she won't go. I suppose she's good at carrying a grudge too."

Aaron blew out his breath and said, "I guess she's entitled to that. Are the girls close enough to the radio? Can I hear their voices too?"

"I'm offended he doesn't want to hear my voice," Paul joked as he got out of the car. "Come up here, girls."

Billie and Grace piled behind the wheel, and Eloise gazed at them with fondness as they spoke to their dad.

Finally, Eloise said, "I know your people are dying for you to tell them what to do now. We'll clear out so you can be the boss."

"I love you," Aaron said. "You girls too."

"We love you, Daddy," Grace chirped into the radio before Billie had the button all the way depressed. She got it and said, "I love you too, Dad. We'll help Eloise and everyone here until you can get here, okay?'

"I know you will, Bills."

Billie handed the radio to Eloise, who pressed the button and said, "I love you, Aaron Sherman. You be careful out there, because I need you." Her throat tightened, and her grip on the radio did too. "I need you."

"—need you too, El. Love you."

With that, he was gone. Eloise replaced the radio on the clip and followed Alice out of the car. Billie and Grace came around the front of it, and she embraced them, holding them right to her chest the way she had last night. They'd all slept in the same bed last night, with Billie telling them stories of the crazy things Aaron had done with his brothers growing up. Eloise had told them that she'd known their dad in high school, and while they were all scared and worried, it had been a powerful few hours before Grace and Billie couldn't stay awake for another moment.

Eloise straightened, and Robin put her hand on her shoulder. "He's okay, Eloise."

"Yes." She took a deep breath. "He is." She looked at the three women watching her, her eyes flitting over to where Laurel stood a few feet away, clearly not wanting to intrude. Eloise gestured her over and they formed a group as they hugged.

"Thank you," Eloise said. "Thank you all, for all your help last night and this morning."

"I'm thinking of stealing that Officer Leyhe," Alice said with a giggle. "Did you guys *taste* those omelets this morning?" She stepped back and smiled at Laurel. "You better hold onto him."

"I'm trying," Laurel said. "Sometimes he feels...slippery." She glanced over to him and then to Eloise. "I was a victim of domestic abuse too, Eloise. I work with the Five Island Cove women's support center, if you or your mother ever need anything."

Surprise darted through Eloise, and she felt another plank in the bridge between her and Laurel cementing in place. "Thank you," she said. She met AJ's eyes, and the woman seemed different.

Softer, somehow. She had one hand pressed against her heart and one resting against her flat stomach.

"What about Kelli breaking into a van?" Eloise asked, her eyes going wide again. "I can't wait until she gets here so we can hear *that* story."

"Right?" AJ laughed and looked at her phone. "She

still hasn't answered me. I wonder if something happened to her phone."

"Kristen won't respond either," Robin said. "I think radios are the only way to communicate right now."

"The lighthouse has a radio," Alice said.

"Maybe we can tune one of ours to it," Laurel suggested, her eyebrows lifting. "When they're done with the Chief, I'll see what I can figure out."

CHAPTER TWELVE

AJ's head ached in such a way that she'd never experienced before. Her stomach existed in a pinched state she couldn't quite get rid of. First she'd thought she was hungry, but eating only made her feel sicker. Not eating made her feel light-headed.

She found herself back in the kitchen with everyone else, helping to clean up the breakfast dishes. Robin, Alice, and Laurel talked easily, as if they'd known each other for years. AJ supposed they might have, as she hadn't been in the cove for a while. Alice had always made friends easily, and everyone loved Robin on sight. She had a special way of making everyone feel like they belonged right where they were.

AJ just listened to Laurel tell the story of her and Paul's first date as she picked up washing the dishes she'd left to go listen to Eloise talk to Aaron. The inn had a homey, welcoming feeling about it, and AJ felt like she could spend a lot of time here and be very happy.

Matt had gone upstairs to help others get packed up and loaded up, and he'd been trying to get in touch with his parents for a couple of hours to find out how their house and the golf course on Diamond Island had fared.

AJ hated this quiet, seething feeling just beneath her skin. She didn't like being disconnected from those she wanted to speak with. She'd grown so accustomed to having everyone and everything only a tap or a swipe away, and she found herself reaching to check her phone, though it hadn't buzzed, chimed, or rung for over twelve hours now.

Eloise came bustling back into the kitchen, and she came to stand next to AJ. "Thank you so much, AJ." She put her arm around AJ and squeezed.

AJ grinned as a little grunt came out of her mouth. "Of course, Eloise. I'm so glad you got to talk to Aaron."

"Me too." Eloise pulled in a big breath and exhaled it right back out. "I don't want to ever go through worry like that again." She started drying the plates AJ washed clean. "I've been meaning to ask you how the freelancing is going. You haven't said much lately on the group chat."

"Oh, well, that's because I haven't been doing much lately," AJ said. How could she tell her friends she'd been in the cove for over a week now? She hated feeling like she'd done something wrong when she'd just needed the time with Matt as they sorted through some complicated things.

Do you want to get married?

He'd asked her that question last night, only a few moments before she'd gone through a full-blown panic attack about being a wife and mother, right here in the cove. She'd been working through a lot with her therapist, but they hadn't even touched the subject of her mother yet. Her father either.

"No jobs out there?" Eloise asked. "You were so busy when you first started."

"There's been jobs," AJ said, glancing at Eloise. "Do you think...? Did you ever just come to the cove and not tell anyone?"

Eloise stopped drying, but AJ kept her focus on the plate, not able to bear the full weight of Eloise's eyes.

"Sometimes," she said. "When I'd come to see Aaron, I wouldn't tell my mother." She leaned a little closer and lowered her voice. "Sometimes I wouldn't even tell Robin." She smiled and gave a light laugh.

"What secrets are you two sharing?" Robin asked.

"See what I mean?" Eloise muttered under her breath, and AJ handed Robin the next clean, dripping wet plate. "Nothing," Eloise said in a chirpy, louder voice. "What are you, Alice, and Laurel talking about?"

"The first time we met our significant other," Robin said. "We want to hear your stories too." She grinned at

Eloise and then AJ. "I think you ran into Matt at the grocery store, right?"

"Yes," AJ said, her smile genuine for perhaps the first time that day. She related the story of their reconnection in the produce section of all places, and as she said, "And he wouldn't let me leave without giving him my number. Said he didn't want to let me get away for a second time," she knew she wanted to marry him.

She turned away from the sink. "I need to tell you guys something," she said, swallowing a moment later. "I wish Kelli were here."

As if summoned by her wish, every device in the kitchen started making noise. Bleeps and snaps and crackles sounded for several seconds, and as AJ looked around, surprised, Alice said, "I guess the cellular network is back."

She plucked her phone from the pocket of her wide-leg beachcombers and looked at it. AJ did the same, though she was wearing a pair of elastic waistband pants that had plenty of breathing room in the leg and hip. She'd never be able to pull off Alice's classy-without-trying look. Whatever AJ did, it looked like she'd tried dang hard to achieve it.

"I have a bunch of texts from Aaron and my mother," Eloise said.

"My dad is okay," Alice said, exhaling heavily. "They're up on the cliff, but they had water surge up to four feet in their house."

"Oh, my word," Robin said. She looked from Alice back to her phone. "Duke's at my mother's house. She's on that cruise, you know? Look." She turned her device so they could all see.

The lawn held puddles in plenty of places, and the front porch sagged heavily to the right, because the pillar there was broken.

Robin scrolled, and the pictures just got worse and worse. "She lives at sea level," Robin said. "It looks like a total loss." She sniffled, and that stole AJ's attention from the phone to her friend's face. "Just like Duke's boat." Her eyes crinkled as her face crumpled, and AJ stepped right into her to hold her up.

Robin clung to her in a most un-Robin-like way. AJ always considered Robin to be the most put together of all of them, even if Alice looked like it on the outside. On the inside, and in real life, it was Robin who had all the right pieces in all the right places.

Alice hugged her from the other side, and AJ met her eyes. No, she didn't know what to do. She hadn't done any articles recently, and she didn't have the money to replace a fishing boat. They were terribly expensive—and Robin and Duke's best means of supporting their family.

"My father is going to check on the house for me," Alice said. "I'm sure the one on Diamond is in ruins too."

"Kelli probably lost her place," Eloise said. "Look, anyone can just stay here. There's probably going to be a million cancelations because of the airports and ferries anyway. Maybe I should just delay the opening overall."

"No," Robin said, pulling away from AJ's embrace. "Don't do that, El. We're going to get this place put back together for you, and it's going to be an amazing Christmas." She nodded like that was that, and AJ had seen Robin make such things come true in the past. "When everyone gets here, we're going to hang all those Christmas balls on the gutters, and we're going to put up the tree. You'll see. It's going to be the best Christmas the cove has ever seen."

AJ looked at her phone again, most of her messages from Kelli. Sharp guilt gutted her once more, and AJ actually tapped to start a new text to her father. She needed to find some measure of relief in her familial relationships, especially if she was going to do what Matt had suggested—move back to the cove and raise their baby with him.

"I'm pregnant," she blurted out, pausing Alice, who'd started to say something about how she wasn't going to climb any ladders to decorate the inn for the holidays.

Every eye zeroed in on AJ, whose heart danced through her chest in a strange triple-beat waltz.

"Excuse me?" Alice asked, one hand fluttering near her throat. She wore an expression AJ knew well—it showed the shock and fear that had flowed through AJ when she'd gotten the phone call from her doctor.

"Is the baby...?" Robin didn't finish, and AJ hated that the unsaid question even needed to be asked.

AJ swallowed back her irritation. She couldn't live her life one way and expect a completely opposite reaction to certain news items. "Matt and I are talking about getting married," she said. "Living here and raising the baby."

She couldn't swallow back the rising panic, at least not physically. She did look away from everyone and press her eyes closed. She could breathe in through her nose and out through her mouth, trying to find the center of her mind and focus on the good things there.

A light touch on her forearm had her opening her eyes. "Congratulations, AJ," Laurel said. "What great news for you and Matt." She wore a warm, friendly smile that somehow had AJ in tears.

It was exactly the kind of gesture Kelli would've said and done, and AJ missed her best friend so powerfully in that moment.

"Thank you," she murmured.

"Yes," Alice said. "Congratulations, AJ. I'm thrilled for you."

"Me too," Robin said.

"As am I," Eloise said, but she didn't turn from the sink. "Congrats." The word came flying over her shoulder, and AJ knew the news of her pregnancy had caused turmoil for Eloise.

She disliked that, just like she disliked the false smile on Robin's face and the sympathetic one on Alice's.

Instant fury spiked through her. This wasn't the reaction she'd expected from her best friends. This was why she'd hunkered down inside Matt's house, drifted aimlessly online, and hadn't told anyone she'd come to the cove early.

"What?" AJ asked. "I'm not allowed to have a baby because my mother was so terrible?"

"AJ," Alice said, her eyes widening. "Of course not."

"That's what you're all thinking, isn't it? My mother abandoned me and my siblings, and I'm going to do the same to this baby. Well, I'm not."

"I don't think that," Robin said, actually puffing her chest out. "Why would any of us think that?"

AJ looked around at Alice, Robin, and Eloise, who had turned from the sink now. She felt like a wild animal who'd been caged after experiencing life on the savannah, and she needed to get out. She needed to get out now.

"Excuse me," she said, her stomach lurching and her chest tightening so much the last word sounded choked in her throat.

She turned to leave just as the door opened. Kelli walked in, and she looked tired, yet fierce and strong and absolutely beautiful.

AJ burst into tears and ran toward her, saying, "Kelli, I'm so glad you're okay." She engulfed the shorter, petite woman in a hug and clung to her while she cried. "I'm just a mess right now, because I'm pregnant, and I don't know how to be a mother, and everything is going to fall apart, and then I'm going to be left alone again, but this time I'll have a baby I don't know how to take care of."

Perhaps that was how her mother had felt. Inadequate. Broken. A failure. AJ felt all three of those keenly, and she added, "And I had to go off all of my medications, and for the love of all that's holy, I just need a drink and a fist full of pills."

Kelli stepped back, but she didn't let go of AJ's shoulders. She searched her face, which was surely a mess, and asked, "You're pregnant?"

AJ nodded, her chin quivering all over again.

A smile filled Kelli's face, and it was like watching the sun rise over calm water. It was glorious and filled with light and acceptance. "Oh, congratulations, AJ. What an amazing thing." She hugged her again, and AJ started to believe that her pregnancy was an amazing thing, because Kelli had said it was.

Someone pressed in behind her, and AJ didn't mind the sandwich hug. It reminded her of her younger days when she'd score a goal and her teammates would pile in for a celebratory hug.

"You're going to be an amazing mother," Alice said, her voice soft and absolutely genuine. "And when you struggle, because we all do, you'll have all of us right here to help you."

"We're thrilled for you," Robin said, and the group jostled as she added herself to the huddle-hug. "Please don't think we're not, even for a moment."

"I've always wanted a baby," Laurel said. "I don't

know you super well yet, AJ, but I think you're going to do just fine."

"Yes," Eloise said. "Sorry I reacted so strangely, AJ. I didn't mean to make you feel bad. I just..."

AJ was taller than all the other women in the kitchen, and she twisted to look at Eloise. Something warred in her expression, and AJ knew exactly how she felt.

It was the exact same turbulent, unsettling, unnamed feeling AJ had experienced several times in her life. Whenever a girlfriend got engaged, AJ was beyond happy for her. She simply wanted the same thing for herself, and it had always felt unattainable and just out of her reach.

For Eloise, motherhood probably was completely out of her reach.

"You have Grace and Billie," Laurel said. "Those girls are lucky to have you, let me tell you."

"Did you know their mother?" Robin asked.

Laurel nodded, a hard-as-flint glint in her eye. "Trust me, Eloise. Aaron hit the jackpot when he sicced his dog on you."

"Wait," AJ said. "Aaron sicced his dog on you?"

Eloise started to giggle, and that set off a chain reaction that moved through all six of them like wildfire. Before she knew it, AJ was laughing so hard, her stomach hurt for an entirely new reason.

Movement by the door caught her eye, and she found Matt standing there with Paul and Aaron. She grinned at them, well-aware of how she was now up on the swing, which meant down was the only way to go.

Right now, it didn't matter. She nodded toward the doorway, and said, "El, Aaron's here."

Eloise sucked in a breath. "Oh." She ran her hands through her hair and practically danced over to Aaron, who took her straight into his arms and kissed her.

AJ sighed, a content little sigh, because she was so happy for Eloise, who had waited as long as she had to find her one true love. Matt grinned as he came toward her. "What's so funny, AvaJane?"

"Nothing," she said, smiling up at him as he wrapped one arm around her waist. They swayed together, and he put his hand flat against her stomach, a look of adoration that AJ had never seen on a man's face before—at least when they were looking at her.

"I want to marry you," she said, the moment sobering. "I love you, and I want to marry you, live here in the cove, and raise our baby together." Plenty of fear ran through her veins, but AJ was tired of giving in to it.

She wasn't her mother, and it was time to stop thinking her future only held sadness and misery.

CHAPTER THIRTEEN

Alice's phone rang with the shrill, old-fashioned ring she'd assigned to her business number just as she put a bite of the lemon doughnut in her mouth. She breathed in, which was a big mistake, as the outside of the doughnut had a healthy amount of powdered sugar on it—which was now floating in her lungs.

She coughed and choked, the ringing so loud it hurt her ears.

"Mom," Charlie moaned from the bed where he still slept, but Alice wasn't focused on letting him sleep at nearly eleven o'clock in the morning. Breathing was more important. Staying alive trumped his sleep schedule.

Ginny said, "I'll get you a drink," and she bustled into the bathroom in their suite at The Cliffside Inn. They'd been amazing over the past day, as everyone had to pitch in and help to get all the extra guests out the door. Some had family and friends they could stay with, but the large majority had gone to see what had become of their homes, cottages, bungalows, and apartments.

The ferry system was operational now, but only on a holiday schedule, as Will had lost several boats, with many more which needed repairs. Alice had finally spoken to him last night, and he'd told her all about it.

She sure did like talking to him, and while she'd agreed to go to dinner with him, she didn't see that happening in the immediate future. She'd spoken to Eloise and Robin, and they'd both agreed that she could invite him to their dinner on the last night they'd be at the inn.

She'd done that, and he'd said he'd do "whatever was necessary" to be there.

Alice's eyes watered as she finally got the powdered sugar out of her lungs. The phone stopped ringing as Ginny returned with the water, and Alice gulped it.

"Sorry," she finally said, her voice sounding rusted and overused at the same time. "Time to get up anyway, Charlie. I want to talk to you two about something."

Ginny crossed the room and pulled open the curtains, and Alice squinted into the bright sunlight. It wouldn't be that warm outside, but it was nice to be reminded she didn't live in a cave.

"Fine," Charlie grumbled, sitting up and kicking off his blankets.

Alice checked the number on her phone, but it wasn't one of her known clients. She got calls from numbers she didn't know all the time, though, and she wished she'd been able to answer, as she needed the work.

She didn't know the state of her house yet, but Will lived on Diamond, and he'd said he'd be going by this afternoon to get some pictures for her. Her blood buzzed in her veins, and she looked up from her phone.

"I've..." She couldn't say, "met a man," to her teenagers. Alice had no idea how to do this, and worse, she didn't have anyone she could ask. Robin was happily married, and Eloise didn't have children she had to tell about her new possible-boyfriend.

"Mom?" Ginny asked, always the more serious twin. She worried too much too, and Alice didn't want to add to that.

"I reconnected with someone I knew in high school," Alice said. "He asked me to dinner, and I..." She looked away from Ginny to Charlie, who would likely take the news harder. A smile spread across his face slowly, and Alice didn't understand the meaning of it.

"You said yes," Charlie said.

Alice nodded. "I said yes. We haven't been out yet or anything," she added quickly. "With the tsunami, he'll be very busy. He owns the ferry system here in Five Island Cove, and he's got a tremendous amount of work on his plate." She took a breath and squared her shoulders. "So I invited him to our dinner here, on the last night."

Ginny blinked rapidly. "Is he coming?"

"He said he would."

"Wait a second," Charlie said. "He owns the ferry system?" He glanced at Ginny, and they clearly knew something she didn't. Alice used to love their twin connection, and how they could have entire conversations with one another without saying a word.

Right now, she didn't love it all that much. "Yes," Alice said cautiously. "Why?"

"His daughter is Tori?" Charlie asked, stopping next to Ginny and folding his arms. He cocked one hip, and that was his aggressive stance.

"I believe so," Alice said. "He hasn't said much about her, obviously. I—" She cleared her throat. "I haven't actually seen him yet. We've just been texting or talking on the phone." A slip of embarrassment moved through her that she'd gotten his number from Kelli, who'd run into him on the ferry.

"What do you know about him?" Charlie asked, and Alice didn't like it.

She turned away from her children and focused on her laptop. "I don't have to answer to you, Charlie. I was merely letting you know. I'm single, and I'm not doing anything wrong by going on a date with a man."

"Of course not, Mom," Ginny said, ever the peacemaker between Alice and Charlie. "It's great. I mean, good, that you're dating. It's not that."

Alice removed her hands from the keyboard and worked very hard not to sigh. "Then what is it?" She twisted back to the twins, only to find them silently communicating again. Ginny nodded toward Alice, but Charlie shook his head.

"Tori is a brat," Ginny finally said, the words practically bursting from her. "She's a year younger than us, but everyone knows who she is. She's on the drill team as a freshman, and boy, does she make sure everyone knows it." Ginny rolled her eyes. "She's always talking about how rich she is, and how she can get her dad to buy her anything."

Ginny stopped and took a deep breath, her eyes round and wide. She pressed her fingertips together, a nervous tell that Alice hated. Whenever she'd done it as a little girl, Alice had smoothed her hands away from each other and told her she could always confide in Alice. Always.

"Oh," Alice said. "I...don't know what to say." She hadn't asked Will a whole lot about his daughter, and she'd suspected he'd be well-off, because he owned the entire ferry system in Five Island Cove. That didn't happen for free.

"Maybe you won't like him," Charlie said, some measure of hope in his voice.

Alice already liked Will, but she didn't want to be quite so explicit with her kids. "Maybe," she conceded. "I don't know if he's bringing Tori to dinner. He didn't mention it."

"She's in Hawaii with her mom," Ginny said.

Surprise wove through Alice. "Oh."

"That's right. She said it on the morning announcements at least forty times," Charlie said, rolling his eyes.

Ginny glared at him. "Probably only once or twice," she said, quickly looking back at Alice. "I have, uh, something to tell you too." She sat down on the bed she and Alice had shared last night. "There's this boy..."

"Oh, dear," Alice said, though a smile quickened her soul and curved her mouth. "Go on."

"His name is Cameron," Ginny said. "He's in my chemistry class, and he's *so* cute, Mom."

"Cameron Heights?" Charlie asked. "Uh uh. No way. No *way*, Ginny."

"He asked me to the Spring Fling," Ginny said, glaring at Charlie with a stronger edge in her eyes. "You don't get any say in who I go out with."

Charlie turned to Alice. "Mom, he's a total douche."

"Language," Alice said, trying to maintain a balance between the two of them. She knew Ginny sometimes felt left out, because Alice spent so much time talking to Charlie one-on-one. He had always needed more attention from Alice. More reassurances, more help with his homework, and more affection. Alice wanted to keep the lines of communication open between her and Charlie, and that took time and energy.

On the other hand, Charlie sometimes felt left out, because Alice and Ginny both loved girly things. They loved getting pedicures and buying fancy dresses. They loved parties and dances and going shopping together.

She looked back and forth between them. "Why is he a douche?" she asked.

Charlie sat on the bed next to Ginny. "He goes out with a different girl like, every week, Mom." He reached for Ginny's hand and took it in his. "You know he does, Gin."

"So what?" Ginny asked. "The Spring Fling isn't until March, and he's *already* asked me."

"Yeah, so he can sleep with you after the dance," Charlie said, his eyes trained on the floor. "I have PE with him, Ginny. He is *not* a nice guy."

Ginny looked at Alice, anger and pleading in her expression. Alice wanted to protect her daughter, but she couldn't take Charlie's side straightaway.

"Maybe you should go out with him at least once or twice before the dance," Alice said. "Just to see if you really like him. Men can be cute and not worth your time."

"He's not even that cute," Charlie muttered, and Alice couldn't help the beat of laughter that sprung from her throat.

"Mom," Ginny said, tearing her hand away from Charlie's. "I knew you'd take his side." She got up from the bed and stomped toward the door. "I'm going to see if I can get a ride down to the disaster zone and help out for the day."

"Ginny," Alice called after her, but her daughter didn't slow or stop.

"I have my phone," she said, and with that, she exited

the suite, the door practically slamming behind her she pulled it so hard.

Alice sighed then and looked at Charlie. He wore a fierce look of determination on his face. "He's a total and complete douche, Mom. She *can't* go out with him."

Alice thought of Frank, and how she probably should've known what kind of man he was too. She thought of Eloise's first husband, and how everyone but her could see he was no good for her. She thought of Nathan, and how AJ had clung to him for years.

"Yes, well, every woman has to decide for themselves what they can tolerate and what they can't," she said quietly, her own hands weaving patterns around one another now. "How are things with Mandie? Are you going to take her to the Spring Fling?"

"I haven't even thought about it."

"I guarantee she has."

Charlie sighed, clearly irritated by the thought of going to a dance at all. He'd never been into those kinds of high school things. "I guess I'll have to take her."

"You make it sound akin to torture," Alice said with a smile. When he returned it, she swallowed and braced herself for her next question. "You guys aren't having sex, are you?"

"Gross, Mom," Charlie said, standing up. "I'm going to take a shower."

"It's not gross," she called after him. "You still shouldn't be doing it, but it's not gross."

"Whatever," Charlie said before he went into the bathroom and definitely slammed the door behind him.

"You didn't answer me satisfactorily," Alice muttered as she picked up her phone. "I would've liked an 'absolutely not, Mom. I would never do that. I don't even *think* about having sex with my girlfriend.'"

She sighed, because she knew he did. Thinking about it and acting on those thoughts were two totally different things, and Alice tapped to dial back the number that had called before the conversation that had both of her kids walking away from her angry.

"Hello?" a cool female voice answered the line.

Alice immediately sat up straighter and donned her professional demeanor. "Yes," she said pleasant. "Hello. I'm returning a call from this number that I missed. This is Alice Kelton." She had not changed her name after the divorce, because she wanted the same last name as her children. She'd been married to Frank for almost twenty years. Just because they weren't together anymore didn't mean she couldn't use the name.

"Ah, of course. Let me put you through to Ms. Summers."

"Thank you," Alice said as if she knew who Miss Summers was. Fancy elevator music actually came on the line, and Alice's eyes widened.

She quickly navigated to a new document on her laptop, and she'd just typed Miss Summers at the top of it when another female voice said, "Alice Kelton. Thank you for calling me back."

She sounded pleasant enough, and it was so hard to assign age to a voice. Alice estimated her to be middle-aged—at least in her forties, if not older—though she did have a somewhat high tone that didn't sound too nasally or whiny.

"Of course," Alice said. "What can I do for you?"

"I run a charitable foundation out of Halifax," she said smoothly. "We've seen all the devastation there on the island, and when I searched online for who to contact there, you're one of the first names that comes up."

Alice smiled at that, but she hadn't typed in any notes. "That's great," she said. "But I'm a lawyer, ma'am. I'm not organizing anything charitable."

"You're not?"

"No, ma'am." She cocked her head to the side. "What makes you think I would be?"

"Well, you have a number of fundraisers and other charitable drives attributed to your name," she said, her words the perfectly round type of someone who'd grown up in the Atlantic northeast.

"Ah, yes, from my time in the Hamptons," she said. "I live full-time in Five Island Cove now. I'm not the PTA President, or on the homeowner's board of directors." Sometimes, Alice missed her old life. She'd get a flash of what her days used to hold, and sometimes it seemed more exciting than working on a laptop in a pitch-black room so her fifteen-year-old could sleep late.

"Of course not," Miss Summers said with a light, airy laugh that was entirely fake. Alice knew; she'd spent over a decade with false laughs and casual waves of the arm that were meant to mean *nothing's important here* when there was always something crucial behind the scenes when one had to lie to keep the conversation going.

"I'm not sure how I can help you."

"You know quite a few people in the cove, I'm assuming."

"Yes," Alice said cautiously. Not as many as Robin or even Eloise, as the Chief probably did literally know everyone.

"Then you know who needs help. My organization is collecting nominations for the residents of Five Island Cove, and we'll be choosing several people to fund in their restoration or repair, replacement of anything lost, or actual cash restitution if things can't be replaced or repaired."

Alice's mouth dropped open, and she couldn't form a thought, let alone a sentence.

"Can I send you an email?" Miss Summers asked. "It'll have all the details in it, along with the nomination form. We want to get started as soon as possible, so if you could look at it and see if there's anyone you would nominate, that would be appreciated."

She paused for a moment, and Alice supposed she

should have a question or two. Her mind was still trying to catch up to "cash restitution."

"You can share the nomination form around the cove," Miss Summers said. "We'll close it when the funds have been used up."

"Okay," Alice said dumbly.

"Great," Miss Summers could breeze through her words like a spring wind coming off the ocean. "I just need that email address."

Twenty minutes later, Alice's computer notified her of a new email, and she practically lunged for the mouse to navigate to it.

Foolishness filled her, because she hadn't gotten Miss Summers' first name, nor the name of the charitable organization, and with every passing minute, she'd felt more and more conned.

The email came from a Sasha Summers, Account Manager at White Sands Worldwide. There was a website, and a physical address in Halifax. Alice still wasn't sure, and she clicked on the website, hoping to see a picture of Sasha.

She imagined her to have long, straight blonde hair, perfectly smooth skin with the exact right amount of blush. She'd be wearing a dark blue blouse, because dark blue always looked amazing on people with fair features.

The website loaded quickly, and it had a security feature in the address. It was populated with recent posts, and it flaunted a professional, clean, crisp design. Every single thing Alice looked at screamed professional and legit, and she started to relax.

She clicked around on different tabs, but the About page didn't have pictures. It did have a bio for Sasha, and she'd been at White Sands Worldwide for twenty years, hailed from "a small island in the Atlantic harbors," and had previously worked at a non-profit organization in Massachusetts.

She worked to find and carry out projects that needed a "white sand touch," and Alice's fears about the organization faded completely.

After closing the website, she read the email in its entirety. There was little more information than what she'd gotten on the phone, and Alice wished her mind had been working properly when she'd had Sasha in person.

She replied to the email, asking where the funding came from, and if any of it needed to be repaid. White Sands Worldwide wasn't a non-profit organization that Alice had seen on the website, and that meant they made money somehow.

She clicked the form to see what it entailed to nominate someone to get the "white sand touch," and it was easily the simplest form Alice had ever seen. That raised a red flag, and she left it open to go back to her email.

Sasha had responded already. *All grants are privately funded, and we've had someone who's a native of Five Island Cove just pledge six figures to help residents there. She wants them to have a magical Christmas. Smiley face.*

"Smiley face." Alice scoffed and sat back from her computer. She folded her arms as she considered what to do.

Her mind flowed in and out like ocean waves, and she could see Robin's face as she began crying over Duke's boat. She could see the broken windows in the house she'd just sold, as well as the trees that had caused the damage.

She saw Matt's face as he showed AJ the pictures of the golf course his family owned. "Over seventy-five percent of it is still underwater," he'd said.

Kelli had gone down to the beach bungalow, and the water line was up to the ceiling. She didn't own it, but the man who did said he couldn't afford to fix the damage. She and Parker were basically homeless.

Eloise had offered her a room here at the inn, but that meant a room she couldn't earn money with. Her mother had a broken leg, and her house had water damage too.

Alice could honestly nominate the entire population of people in Five Island Cove.

She exhaled and sat back up to the computer. "Six figures," she muttered. "How much does a new beach bungalow and a fishing boat cost?"

As she filled out the form for Duke Grover, then Matthew Hymas, then William Bridge and all of his damaged ferries, Alice suspected there would be a price to pay later for free money now.

She couldn't stop herself, though, because she couldn't stand to see her dear friends in so much turmoil.

Kristen, Kelli, Robin's mother, and Alice even nominated herself in conjunction with her new buyers to get the house back to the condition it was in when they'd committed to buying it.

Charlie came out of the bathroom and said he was going to go find the Chief to see what he could do to help out, and Alice barely grunted at him.

She was too busy filling out the form. When she finally finished, Alice sat back, her heart actually thumping in an elevated way, as if she'd just done something exhilarating.

"Please let this work," she whispered, and she closed her laptop. Her kids were off helping around the island, and Alice should be too.

CHAPTER FOURTEEN

Kristen picked through the soggy clothing in what had been her closet. She wore rubber gloves, but a tremor of disgust still squirreled through her.

"There's nothing here worth saving," she said to herself. Rueben and Jean had been helping her salvage anything Kristen identified, but they'd gone inland to volunteer there.

The ferry system had opened up earlier that morning, and Kristen had been texting with her girls. They were all okay, thankfully, and Kristen paused to look up to the ceiling as if she could see all the way to heaven.

Unfortunately, the roof did have a hole big enough for her to see the sky through it, and she stilled completely.

She didn't want to be here. She'd been sleeping at Reuben's for the past two nights, and she didn't want to be there for a third. She got along great with Rueben and Jean, that wasn't the problem.

The problem was this tiny cottage on this slab of rock didn't feel like home anymore. Joel was gone, and while he'd become a different man in her mind than the one she'd believed him to be in person, she still saw him everywhere she looked out here at the lighthouse.

Perhaps it was time for her to find a new spot of Earth to call hers.

The water had swept her car up and over the rocks and down the hill, though Rueben had taken it, along with his, to the garage at the entrance to the parking lot. He'd found both of them and gotten them back to their proper places.

The sun had been shining all day, but it was a weak, winter sun that brought light but not much heat. The interior would still be wet. The RideShare system was completely overrun, as a lot of people were in the same situation as she was—their cars were in some state of disrepair.

Her phone rang, and she knew who it would be —Robin.

Out of all the girls, she'd noticed that Kristen had not given a status update on her house and belongings. She'd only checked in to let everyone know she was alive and well, that Rueben and Jean were doing great, and that the hurricane that had been named a couple of days ago had turned and would not be hitting Five Island Cove.

Most hurricanes didn't form this far north anyway, especially in the winter, and Kristen wasn't surprised by that. What she was surprised by was her unemotional attachment to this place she'd called home for so many years.

She gazed around, looking at the path she'd trod so many times. She knew the way by the feel of the rocks beneath her feet, and she loved standing at the edge of the cliffs and looking out over the water.

To her knowledge, there wasn't anything out in the ocean between this side of Diamond Island and Europe, thousands and thousands of miles away. That amount of water boggled her mind, and she didn't try to hold it there the way she had at other times of her life.

She'd accepted her place inside the vastness of this universe, and she'd made a good life for herself here. She could do it again.

A house was just a house. Cars were just cars. They didn't hold any sway over her, and she could fill a new place with fresh photos, new memories, and loud laughter.

The phone stopped ringing, and Kristen regretted getting so deep inside her head that she'd missed Robin's call. The woman genuinely cared about her as fiercely as a daughter loved their mother, and Kristen lifted her phone to call her back.

Her phone rang again, and Robin's name sat there again. Kristen swiped on the call and said, "Hello, dear."

"There you are," Robin said, half-frustrated and half-relieved. "How are things going over there?"

Kristen looked around the bedroom and turned toward the exit. "Just fine," she said. "Rueben and Jean are off volunteering, and I'm going through the house."

"You haven't said anything about your house."

"It's got some holes in it," she said. "I've decided to leave it all behind. I'm going to be looking for somewhere else to live."

"My goodness," Robin said, her shock palpable even through the line. "Where are you going to go?"

"I don't know," Kristen said, realizing how that sounded. "I'm not leaving the cove, Robin."

"Oh, thank heaven," Robin said with a sigh. "You scared me there for a minute, Kristen." She laughed lightly, and Kristen could hear the anxiety in her tone.

"Duke's boat is lost, isn't it?" Kristen asked.

"Yes," Robin said. "No one has a boat right now. It's okay." She took a big breath. "We're going to be okay."

"Yes," Kristen said, reaching the door and exiting the cottage where she'd lived for the past several years. "Things do tend to work out in the end."

"Sometimes that road is long and riddled with potholes, though," Robin said. "I don't know, Kristen. It feels like every time Duke and I are making some good headway on our bills and debts, something happens to derail us completely."

"I know, dear."

"I'm not going to complain about this," Robin said. "Sorry, Kristen."

"You don't need to apologize to me."

"Will you please come to the inn? It's dry here, and everyone's gone now. There's a room on the bottom floor for you, and I need you here."

"I'm going to come right now," Kristen said, deciding on the spot. "You can help me look for a new place here on Diamond."

"Yes," Robin said. "That sounds great."

Kristen tilted her head toward the uprise of rocks that hid the rest of the island from view. The wind blew, but the wind always came to play at the lighthouse, and Kristen was accustomed to it. In fact, if the wind didn't bluster and blow around the tall, white lighthouse, Kristen would think there was a problem.

"Why do you need me there, dear?" she asked.

"Duke couldn't come, obviously," Robin said. "Though I think he is going to come tomorrow. Our house is slightly wet, and he's working on it with a neighbor today. Anyway." She cleared her throat. "Promise you won't say anything to the others?"

"Always," Kristen said.

"AJ is pregnant, and just so happily-in-love with Matt. It's great. It is. It's just so...different than my life. Alice has Will she's texting with every five seconds. Eloise and Aaron are busy around the island, and they have each other. Kelli is...someone else, Kristen. You won't even recognize her. I just...I feel like I don't fit."

Ridiculous, Kristen wanted to say. Robin was the glue that held them all together. She fit, because she created the container they all existed in.

"Of course you fit," Kristen said. "I'm sure it feels like you don't, though. Can we back up to AJ is pregnant?"

Robin told her the story of how they'd been told, and she related an up-and-down version of AJ that Kristen recognized from her teens. "So she's off her meds, and wow, you can tell."

"That's not good," Kristen said. "She's going to need a lot of help over the next few months."

"She's moving here," Robin said. "So she'll be around. She's moving in with Matt."

"Oh, so she'll be on Diamond too."

"With me, you, and Alice," Robin said, and that seemed to perk her up. "Please let me know when you get on the ferry. I worry about you."

"I know you do. Are they doing RideShare over there?"

"No," Robin said. "If you text me when you get on the ferry, I'll come down and get you."

"Robin—"

"Don't say no. There's no RideShare. I'm going to be your RideShare."

Kristen knew better than to argue with the woman when she spoke in that voice. "Okay," she said.

"Great." Robin giggled. "I'll get a few things done for this new bride, and I'll be at the station when you come in."

The call ended, and Kristen gave herself a few moments to stand still on the sidewalk down from her house. She looked right, and the lighthouse loomed before her.

She'd had a great life here. A really amazing life.

It was simply time to move on, and Kristen turned left, where the full possibilities of Diamond Island waited for her.

"No, that's the bottom piece," Alice said the following morning.

The moment Kristen had stepped inside The Cliffside Inn, she'd instantly felt at home. The way Alice had rushed at her and held her tightly had helped, as had the vibrant and noisy dinner they'd shared last night.

It reminded her of the parties at Alice's over the summer, and Kristen loved the atmosphere of friendship and acceptance she felt with her Seafaring Girls.

This morning, they'd eaten cold cereal and fruit, and then Eloise had brought out the fake Christmas tree. She and Aaron and the girls had removed all the pieces, and now they were working on getting the different segments to come together properly.

"She's right," Billie said, and Kristen did like having the children around. She and Joel had had two children, but it had been a very long time since she'd had little children or even teenagers in her life.

They switched out the wrong piece for the right one, and Alice started opening boxes of decorations. Kristen joined in then, such a family-oriented atmosphere hanging around them all. Eloise had somehow put holiday music through the speakers at the inn, and Kristen hung a couple of ornaments in the traditional red and green colors, and then retreated to the steps, where she'd set her coffee.

She sipped and watched Alice's twins speak to each other as they passed on their way to and from the tree. Robin laughed with AJ about something, and Kristen smiled at the two of them. They both probably felt like they didn't belong here, but they'd both be wrong.

AJ seemed so happy, and she definitely possessed a pregnancy glow, though Matt wasn't around this morning. His parents owned a golf course, and they had a lot of work to do there.

"Why didn't someone come wake me up?" Kelli asked as she came down the steps. "I'm missing the tree decorating."

"You were so tired," AJ said, turning from Robin. "You've been through a lot lately, and we wanted you to get the rest you needed."

Kelli accepted her hug, and she settled next to Kristen.

She wore a pair of black sweat pants and a bulky sweat shirt with colored butterflies all over it. "It's looking good."

"There's plenty of ornaments," Kristen said, nodding toward the boxes. "Go hang one."

"I really just need some of that coffee," Kelli said, and she still looked tired.

"It's good," Kristen said. "Aaron made it, and he's a master. I'll come with you. You caffeinate up, because I've heard you have an amazing story about the night of the tsunami."

She grinned at Kelli, glad when the other woman let a small smile touch her mouth. "It's not that amazing," Kelli said as she stepped through the fray of people decorating the Christmas tree in the foyer at The Cliffside Inn.

The colored lights would be a welcome addition to all the polished wood and fresh-faced walls. Kristen thought Eloise had done a superb job of fixing up the inn, and making it feel modern yet quaint at the same time.

"Alice mentioned breaking and entering?" Kristen said, following Kelli.

Kelli laughed, and that definitely wasn't a denial. "Aaron needed gas," she said. "I had to go into the convenience store and get the gas can."

"Of course," Kristen said as Kelli went into the kitchen. Kelli did seem different; she was more confident and more articulate. Eight months ago, when she'd come for Joel's funeral, her own shadow had startled her, and

Kristen was just so glad to see her acting more like the person she'd been suppressing for so long.

"Is Julian coming?" Kristen asked, and Kelli's movement in putting the coffee pot back on the burner stuttered.

Oh, there was something going on there, and Kristen lifted her coffee mug. "Never mind."

"He's not coming," Kelli said, sighing. She stirred sugar and coconut-flavored cream into her coffee. "I haven't told anyone yet. I suppose I should."

"If you'd like," Kristen said, hoping she sounded nonchalant. "I'm fine with whatever you want to share."

Kelli's eyes met hers, and Kristen gave her a smile.

"I love you, Kristen," Kelli said, suddenly pulling her into a hug. "You've been so good to me over the years, and you've always seen this gold inside of me I didn't know I had."

Kristen hugged her back, holding her tight as she tried to tame her emotions. She'd just given her one of the best compliments of her life, and Kristen loved her dearly too.

Kelli stepped back and lifted her coffee to her lips.

"How's your mother?" Kristen asked. "Is she a safe topic?"

A ghost of a smile crossed her face again, and Kelli nodded. "Yes, my mother is a safe topic."

"Is she still dating Devon?"

"Yes," Kelli said. "They seem very happy together.

They're coming—I think. That was the plan, at least. They're coming to the dinner on our last night here."

"It seems everyone has invited someone to that," Kristen said. She hadn't, but she painted over the fact that she didn't really have anyone to invite to it with another quick smile. With any luck, no one would notice how melancholy she felt that day, and she'd be able to shake the feeling by lunchtime.

CHAPTER FIFTEEN

Kelli slid one grilled cheese sandwich onto a plate, and then removed a second from the griddle too. "There's six more sandwiches," she said, and several people turned toward her. They all seemed in good spirits, and Kelli smiled at them.

She and Robin had been making sandwiches and heating soup in stages, as many as the griddle in Eloise's huge, gorgeous kitchen at the inn would hold.

They'd fed the kids first, and Kelli inhaled the scent of warm butter as Robin placed six more fully assembled sandwiches on the griddle. They'd been buttering and slicing for several minutes now, and Kelli started pushing plates toward Laurel and Paul, Alice and Kristen, Eloise and Aaron.

AJ and Matt had disappeared somewhere, and Kelli wouldn't be surprised if they'd gone behind closed doors for a lunchtime pick-me-up. It wouldn't be the first time AJ had skipped a meal in favor of sleeping with a boy.

Kelli honestly didn't know how she had the stamina.

"We miss you at lunch," Robin said, taking the spatula from Kelli.

She turned her attention from Eloise and Aaron, who seemed so happy together, to Robin. "I know," she said. "I wish I could come." She swallowed back the jealousy that Robin, Eloise, Alice, and Kristen got together every Wednesday.

If AJ returned to the cove full-time—and it sounded like she would—she'd probably join them. That would only leave Kelli out of everyone, and she already struggled to believe she belonged to this group of women.

That's not true, she told herself sternly. She did belong in this group, and everyone here loved her as much as she loved them. The mind had a special way of bringing doubt into one's life, and Kelli hated that she even thought for a second that her friends didn't want her there.

Robin nudged a sandwich up and then back down, her patience endless. Since her daughters had become teenagers, Robin had perfected the awkward silence where she waited for someone to fill it.

"You can come next week," she said. "You'll still be on the holiday break, right?"

"Right," Kelli said with a smile. She turned toward the stove to stir the soup, which Robin had poured out of a couple of boxes. She did love roasted red pepper and tomato soup, especially with croutons and sour cream, and she ladled herself a bowl, put in the toppings, and turned back to the counter.

Alice and Kristen stood there, and Kelli blinked at them.

"I have to tell everyone something," Kristen said.

Robin jerked her attention up from the browning sandwiches. "Tell-All?"

"No," Alice said, and she rolled her eyes at Robin. "You and the Tell-All."

"I like it," Robin said. "Surely everyone has something to tell."

"AJ's not even here," she said.

"She already said her news anyway," Robin said, glancing at Kelli.

Kelli took a deep breath, because she was done being the timid woman who let life happen to her. She'd driven a van around in the dark, delivering people to safety in the hours leading up to a tsunami.

She could tell her friends about Julian.

"I have something," she said. "I think we should do a Tell-All."

"Traitor," Alice said with a smile.

"Think of something, Alice," Robin said as she giggled. "These sandwiches are almost done." She flipped them one by one, and Kelli took her soup bowl over to the counter where everyone had gathered to eat.

"We're doing a Tell-All," Kelli said to the two couples.

Laurel Baker looked up, clear surprise in her eyes. "What is that?"

"It's where you have to tell everything," Eloise said. "You don't have to—"

"If you stay, you have to Tell All," Alice said, taking the barstool she'd been on a few minutes ago. "I'll understand if you want to leave." She wore a hint of displeasure in her eyes, but it was clear she didn't really dislike the Tell-All. She'd called them plenty of times in her life, that was for sure.

Laurel looked at her boyfriend, Paul, and he got up a moment later. "I think I'm out."

"I'm one hundred percent out," Aaron said, grinning at he leaned over and pressed a kiss to Eloise's forehead. "I'll go find the kids, and we'll head back down to the grocery store."

"Okay," she said, and she smiled as the two men left the kitchen through the door that led straight onto the back patio.

Kelli took Aaron's spot next to Eloise, who asked, "What am I going to say? Everyone knows everything."

"Think fast," Kelli said, glancing over to where Robin still nudged the sandwiches around as if that might help them cook faster. No one wanted a soggy sandwich or one that wasn't browned enough. At least Kelli didn't.

Kristen returned to the counter with a bowl of soup, and only a second later, Robin called that the sandwiches were done.

She turned off the griddle and brought over a sandwich for Kelli and herself, and sat in front of the bowl of soup Kristen had brought over.

"Okay, Kristen wants to go first," she said.

Kristen gave Robin a glare, though she had said she had something to say.

"First, let's clue poor Laurel in to what this is," Eloise said, smiling at the woman.

Kelli glanced at her too, and she almost wished she wasn't there. Kelli didn't know Laurel Baker all that well, though she worked with Aaron and she'd helped track down all the information on Kelli's supposed half-brother a few months ago.

Laurel had mousy brown hair that she tucked behind her ear. It was thin, like Kelli's, and her brown eyes saw everything though they possessed kindness too.

"It can be anything," Alice said.

"It's usually not, though," Eloise said. "It's usually something that's scary to us. Or that we're worried about. Or just a really big piece of news."

"I'll say mine, and she'll understand." Kristen reached over and patted Laurel's hand. "My cottage is a soggy, wet mess. The roof has holes in it, and there's nothing I want there. I've decided to leave the lighthouse and find a small house or condo on Diamond Island."

Kelli stared at Kristen, disbelieving what she'd just heard. Her mouth dropped open, and she kept stirring her soup with one hand as if it had a mind of its own.

"Kristen..." Alice said. "Really?"

"Yes," Kristen said with a nod around to everyone. "It's time. Rueben and Jean are happy at the lighthouse, and I can walk away from it now."

Kelli didn't think she'd ever hear Kristen say those words, because she'd lived in the lighthouse for decades, then in that cottage behind it. Her whole life had been wrapped up in the lighthouse, and it was her past, present, and future.

"That's huge," Eloise said. "How are you feeling about it?"

"Good," Kristen said. "My father always said it would take an act of God to get us off that land, and I guess he was right." She grinned then and picked up her half-eaten sandwich.

"Well, Rueben's still there," Robin said. "Your family is still on that land."

"Very true." Kristen took a bite of her sandwich and shrugged, clearly saying, *That's my news. Who's next?*

Kelli hadn't taken a bite of her lunch yet, and she figured she might as well get the words out of her stomach so she could enjoy her food.

"So it's news a lot like—" Alice started to say.

"Julian and I are getting divorced," Kelli interrupted. "He moved back to Newark a few weeks ago. Last month. I don't know." She looked down into the swirling, pale redness of her soup. "He couldn't run the business from here, but that's not the only reason he went back."

No one said anything, and Kelli could've probably stopped there. Instead, she said, "He begged me to come with him, but nothing's changed." She looked up and right into the eyes of her best friends. She wasn't anywhere near close to crying, and that alone was a testament to how much she'd changed.

"He still wants me and Tiffany, and she's living in our —his townhome in New Jersey. I asked him to file for divorce, since I don't live in Jersey anymore, and he said he would." She nodded and pressed her teeth together.

"Kelli," Alice said. "You shouldn't let him file for divorce."

"Why not?"

"As the defendant, you automatically bear the burden of being labeled the guilty one, whether you are or not."

Kelli's chest squeezed, and she realized she should've gone to Alice first. "If I file, I have to pay the fee," she said, because she might as well admit to everything while she was at it. "And I have to appear in court. I don't live there."

What she was really saying was that it wasn't free to fly to Newark and back. She didn't have anyone to watch Parker, and she had a job five days a week.

As she gazed around at the other women in the room, she realized she had plenty of people to watch Parker.

"Has he filed yet?"

"That's not how the Tell-All works," Robin said.

Alice shot her a look that said, *Are you kidding me*

right now? "We said something after Kristen revealed. This is important."

"Fine," Robin said. "This just doesn't feel like a Tell-All, that's all I'm saying."

"No, he hasn't filed," Kelli said. "At least not that I know of."

"I'll help you with it," Alice said. "I really don't think you should let him file."

"Okay," Kelli said, finally lifting her soup spoon to her lips. The soup was still hot, tangy, and delicious. "Mm."

"Duke's boat is a total loss," Robin said. "We have nothing as far as that goes." She took a crispy bite of her sandwich, obviously done talking.

"Feels short," Alice said dryly.

"Nothing else to say," Robin said around a mouthful of cheese and bread.

"I don't have much," Eloise said. "Other than I'm worried I'll never get my mother up to the inn now."

Kelli smiled at her as warmly as she could. Dawn Hall was a very routined person, and her experiences shaped her opinions and habits about certain things. It had taken Kelli and Aaron an extraordinary amount of talking and convincing to get her to go to the clinic for her leg, because of an experience from decades ago.

Getting in an accident on the way up to the inn would definitely leave a scar on her memories.

"She's here now," Alice said. "She'll be okay."

Eloise nodded, and everyone looked at Alice. Kelli

would be surprised if they forced Laurel to say anything, but knowing Robin, the cop would have to come up with something.

"I became a cop on a dare," Laurel said, looking around at everyone with wide, round eyes. She almost looked like she'd been fed to the lions, but she wasn't going to go down without a fight. "Then I liked it so much, I've moved up and become a detective."

"That's great," Alice said with a genuine smile. "You and Paul seem—"

"You don't have to say anything about Paul," Robin said. "Alice, she said something."

"I'm just saying," Alice said. "You police me to death, Robin. You really don't have to be in control of *everything*."

Kelli burst out laughing, and she was the only one for a few seconds. Eloise finally joined in, and then Kristen and even Laurel. Finally, Robin's stoic exterior broke, and she dropped her eyes back to her plate. She didn't speak though, and Alice only smiled.

"Sorry," Kelli said. "Sometimes listening to you two snipe at each other is really funny."

"It really is," Eloise said, still giggling. "Though I do agree with Alice. She wasn't doing anything wrong, Robin."

"I know," Robin said, keeping her gaze down. "I apologize, Alice."

"Me too," Alice said, and Kelli had learned from her

long ago that she could be right about something and not have to say it. She'd seen Alice do that so many times in their math class growing up. Alice had been terribly smart with numbers, and she'd sit quietly while Roger Bushman went off about something or other that was completely wrong.

"I'm up," Alice said. "I had a woman call me yesterday. She's from a company called White Sands Worldwide, and they're a charitable organization with a native of Five Island Cove who wants to donate money to the people here who've been impacted by the tsunami. I submitted all of us."

She gazed around at everyone, her chin raising an inch or so, almost daring someone to say she shouldn't have.

"I gave them Robin and Duke's name and said they lost his fishing boat. I told them about Kelli's house, and Matt's golf course. I submitted Will's name, because he needs help with the ferry system, and my name with my buyers, as my house on Rocky Ridge has some damage. I put in your mom's name, Robin, because her house is a wreck, and yours Kristen, because I assumed you'd need something at the lighthouse, what with it being right on the east coast cliffs and all."

She cleared her throat and looked at Eloise and Laurel. "She said they just want to make some Christmas wishes come true. They might not even pick any of us."

Silence draped over the kitchen, only to be broken by

Robin's sob and the scraping of her barstool as she got up and engulfed Alice in a tight hug.

Tears came to Kelli's eyes, and she said, "We could use a Christmas miracle."

"We sure could," Eloise said, reaching for Kelli's hand. She squeezed, and they smiled at each other.

Everyone got up then, surrounded Alice, and started firing off questions to find out more details about this charitable organization and how soon they'd find out who would get their Christmas miracle.

CHAPTER SIXTEEN

Robin heard her phone buzzing on the nightstand next to her bed, but her brain couldn't seem to force her body to do anything about it. It fuzzed and blurred, and she rolled over, a groan coming from her mouth.

She wasn't sure how much time passed before someone touched her shoulder, and Mandie said, "Mom, Dad's freaking out and wants you to call him."

That woke Robin, and she sat straight up, nearly knocking into Mandie, who'd bent over her. "Freaking out? About what? What did he say?"

Mandie fell back a couple of steps, her eyes widening. Robin couldn't believe she'd slept late enough to have the sun shining through the slatted blinds, illuminating her daughter's face. "I don't know. He called, and he sounded frustrated that you wouldn't answer your phone. I told him you were up late with your friends, and he said to wake you up." She looked disgruntled, like Robin and Duke had interrupted something important she'd been doing.

Probably kissing Charlie, Robin thought, surprised her mind had room for such a thing. Duke never freaked out. He hardly ever got frustrated with her at all, and she reached for her phone.

"Thanks," Robin said. "What are you and Jamie doing?"

"Laurel's showing us how to do self-defense," she said. "I probably missed the elbow throw." She grinned, and before Robin could process that, and look at her phone, and think about what could possibly have Duke in a tizzy, her daughter was gone.

Duke had called a couple of times, and she had multiple texts from him.

Robin, I need to talk to you.

I just got a phone call from someone, and they said we've been selected for a grant to replace my fishing boat.

Robin, can you pick up?

I'm calling Mandie.

Her heart beat faster and faster as the words from his second text settled into her mind. They'd been selected. Their Christmas miracle was going to come true.

A sob started low in her belly, but she swallowed against it. She'd cried too much in the past several days, and she was done with that. She didn't know how else to deal with the endless pit of worry in her stomach, and it had accompanied her since her husband's birthday, when he'd come home and said *The Lady Hawk* had been damaged.

With the tsunami, he'd said she was gone.

The worry inside Robin didn't cease as she tapped to return his calls. She'd know within one word whether this was good news or bad, though a corner of her mind wondered how getting a replacement fishing boat for free could be bad.

"Robin," Duke said, his voice full of excitement, and her constant companion of anxiety and worry eased a little bit. They didn't completely go away, and Robin wasn't sure they ever did. They seemed to wait in the wings, ready to pounce at any sentence anyone said, or anything Robin ever read.

"Sorry," she said. "I didn't go to bed until late, and I've been so stressed."

"One less thing to be stressed about," he said, laughing. "I just got a call from a man named Gene Yardley, and he said we were nominated for a grant from this place called White Sands Worldwide, and they're helping people to recover from the tsunami. And they chose us!"

He laughed in his deep voice, the one that always brought a smile to Robin's face. His laugh always made her want to laugh too, and she joined in with him the way she often had. The pesky tears came again, but they didn't slip down her face.

"What else did they say?" she asked.

"He said they'd be sending me an email with all the details, and then someone would literally be on the island this afternoon to meet with me."

"Wow," Robin said, her head starting to spin. She glanced at the clock, in complete shock that she'd slept until nine-fifteen. She was the type who got up at five-thirty every morning to get things done before her family woke up.

"I'm headed to the ferry right now," he said. "So I'll be there in about an hour. We'll do that gift exchange you told me about, and go to lunch, and then could you come back to Diamond with me this afternoon? I want you there with me to meet with him."

"Of course," Robin said, standing up. She'd completely forgotten about the gift exchange, not to mention lunch. Duke had originally planned to spend the whole day at the inn with his family, spend the night, and they'd all go home in a couple of days—on Wednesday, which was Christmas Eve.

Eloise's first guests were set to arrive that afternoon, and Robin couldn't believe the few days they'd planned to spend at the inn for the holidays were flying by so quickly.

Ruined, she thought, a level of bitterness in mind and body that she didn't understand. She saw her friends a lot now, and she looked forward to Wednesdays with a fervor she embraced.

There was supposed to be something special about Christmas, though, and Robin hadn't felt it yet. They'd spent yesterday putting the inn back together after pulling it apart to make room for whoever showed up at the door. Those that didn't do that had gone down the cliffs to help the stores, businesses and private citizens who needed it.

"Great," Duke said. "I'll see you soon. I'm so excited. I hope that email comes really fast."

"Me too," she said. "Call me if you get it before you get here."

"I will." The wind blew across the microphone on his phone, and Robin knew she needed to let him go.

"I love you," she said.

"This is going to be exactly what we need," he said. "I love you, too, Robin."

The call ended, and Robin quickly got in the shower, got dressed, and got on her computer. She had a wedding in six days, and there were at least a hundred details that needed to be done before then.

She answered the emails from the coordinator at the venue, all of them modifications due to the storm. Her bride would have to deal with it, because decorations, backdrops, and docks had been damaged.

After downloading the pictures Judy had sent, she sent them along to her bride, who confirmed that whatever they could do would be just fine. *We're just so glad we have somewhere beautiful to be married. Thank you, Robin.*

Robin smiled at the gratitude coming through in the text, and she moved on to the next thing. Gina had called from the florist shop, and Robin returned her call. Her worry needled through her as Gina started talking, and it took a moment for Robin to realize what she was saying.

"So nothing's changing?" Robin finally asked.

"No," Gina said. "We're on schedule, and we'll be at Victoria's Wharf at eleven-thirty on Sunday."

"Amazing," Robin said. "Thank you so much, Gina. I'm meeting with Callie after the New Year, and I'll need to come sit down with you then. She's texted me again that she wants flowers literally everywhere. Her budget just for flowers is eight thousand dollars."

Gina whistled, and Robin heard her physically flipping a page. She still used a paper planner for everything, and Robin enjoyed the quirks of her personality. "Let's set something up right now," she said. "For an order like that, I won't want to miss anything."

"Okay." Robin clicked over to her online calendar. She color-coded every bride, and she could easily see Callie Lyman's appointments, as they were lime green. "I'm meeting with her on the third. The wedding is on May fifth, so we'll have four months."

"I could at two o'clock on the fourth," Gina said. "Or... not until the seventh, but that would be an eight a.m. appointment, and I know you like those mornings."

Robin did. She liked getting up early and getting a lot done by lunchtime. Then she'd stop working on weddings and focus on home and family. She only wanted to work part-time, but the weddings could take over her whole life if she let them.

"Let's do the seventh," she said. A two o'clock meeting meant she wouldn't be home when the girls got out of school, and though Mandie had said she'd keep an eye on Jamie and the mean girls, Robin wanted to be there when Jamie walked in the door.

She moved on to the food for her upcoming wedding, then the digital invitation proofs, which had come in last night. She forwarded all of that to her bride, texted her to say she had, and closed her laptop.

Her stomach roared at her about eating, and Robin felt like she was missing out on something happening at the inn. If there was anything Robin hated more than the constant worry running through her veins, it was missing out on something her friends or family were doing.

Downstairs, she found AJ and Matt sitting with Eloise and Aaron at one of the tables that had been repositioned in its proper spot in the dining room. They had empty bowls and plates in front of them, an indication that there had been food at some point.

"There you are," AJ said, rising to her feet. She wasn't showing at all, but Robin couldn't help sweeping her eyes down the length of AJ's body to check. "I was about to sic Alice on you." She grinned at Robin, who smiled back.

"I'm tired," she said. "I didn't sleep hardly at all on Saturday night."

"I don't think any of us did."

"I also didn't sneak away at lunchtime yesterday to

nap." Robin raised her eyebrows at AJ as they went into the kitchen, and AJ laughed.

"It was a great nap," she said. She moved over to the sink and put the dishes down inside it. "There's oatmeal and cold cereal. Matt wanted to make blueberry pancakes, but Eloise said those are for tomorrow."

"I won't be late tomorrow morning then," Robin said, reaching for a bowl. She and dairy didn't get along very well, so she opted for a scoop of oatmeal without any of the honey and sugar sitting there.

A shriek filled the air, and Robin spun toward the back door to see Kelli standing there. She held up her phone, her face bearing a load of excitement that had Robin's pulse thumping.

"I just got a call from Marian Usher. She said I've been selected for a grant to get me into a new house here in the cove."

"You're kidding," AJ said, already moving toward her. The two of them embraced and laughed together. The pair ended up jumping up and down like giddy teenagers, and Robin finally thawed from where the news had frozen her to the floor.

She hugged Kelli too, and said, "Duke got a call too. They're going to replace his boat."

"This is so amazing," Kelli said, gushing now over everything Marian had said. She finally exhaled, her chest rising and falling so fast. "She said someone will meet me on Diamond Island at some point this afternoon." She looked back and forth between Robin and AJ. "Do you think it's okay that I go?'

"Of course," AJ said.

"I'm going with Duke," Robin said. "This is *huge*, Kelli. We'll do the gift exchange and go." A rush of trepidation moved through her at the thought of seeing what state her house was in. Duke had sent pictures, but seeing things in person made them more real in a way pictures simply couldn't do.

Aaron came into the kitchen, and Robin turned toward him. He looked like he had something to say, and she took a couple of steps toward him. "What is it?" she asked.

"Eloise is talking to someone about a grant for her mother's house."

Robin froze again, sure she'd heard him wrong.

Aaron hooked his thumb over his shoulder. "And Matt took a call and left for a minute, then came back with a huge smile on his face, saying he had to run out front to call his parents and to let AJ know."

AJ came to Robin's side, and her hand slipped into Robin's.

"I guess he talked to someone too, and they're going to fund the restoration of the golf course." Aaron tilted his head, his eyes burning with curiosity and a smile nowhere in sight. "What's going on? Who's sending all this money to do all of this?"

CHAPTER SEVENTEEN

AJ wasn't sure if the reason her stomach kept cramping was because of the morning sickness, the excitement flowing through the inn, or Aaron's refusal to see the bright side of everyone getting their Christmas miracle.

He wore a perpetual frown as Eloise explained what her caller had told her. "Then Forrest said that they'd get my mother's medical records and make sure she didn't have a massive medical bill either." She wore excitement in her dark eyes, making them shine like black gold. "So with the water restoration and any sewing machine replacement—I explained that she was a seamstress by trade and needed those machines—she'll be back to new in no time."

She seemed so happy, and AJ reached over and squeezed her hand. Aaron did not.

"They're sending someone to do an evaluation on the golf course," Matt said. "Today. *Today.* I just can't believe it. They don't waste any time." He looked around at the group, and a rush of gratitude for the accepting nature of her friends filled AJ.

They'd assimilated him into their group without question, with a smile and open arms, simply because he was important to AJ. She was important to them.

Robin had already told everyone what she knew about Duke's conversation with yet a different person from White Sands Worldwide. AJ didn't care how many people they employed or how many came to Diamond Island.

She wanted everyone to get what they needed to move their lives back toward normal.

They all sat around a couple of tables they'd pushed together in the dining room, and once Matt stopped talking, silence fell over them.

Then Kristen's phone rang on the table in front of her. Every eye flew toward it, and she leaned in. "I don't know the number."

"Answer it," Alice said. "I submitted your name too." She gripped her phone like it alone would keep her sane. She'd put in her name, along with her buyers, and she hadn't gotten a call yet.

Kristen swiped and tapped to put the phone on speaker. "Hello?"

"Yes, hello," a round, crisp female voice said. "This is

Tonya Sharpino from White Sands Worldwide. Am I speaking with Kristen Shields?"

A roar from the group rose up, and AJ started laughing. Out of all of them, only Aaron looked like he didn't like what was happening. Everyone else looked as if someone had shown up with stunning pellets and they'd all been hit multiple times.

Kristen raised her hand, and that got people to quiet down. "Yes," she said. "This is Kristen Shields."

Tonya laughed, but it was still clearly professional. "I can see you're with friends."

"Yes," Kristen said, pure sunshine pouring from her expression now. AJ's heart expanded ten sizes; perhaps Kristen wouldn't have to leave her generational land on the edge of the cliffs, next to the lighthouse she loved so much.

"I'm happy to say that you were nominated for some help from our charitable foundation, and we've selected you to receive some funds to help you get back on your feet following the tsunami."

Kristen pressed one hand to her chest, though she had to be expecting Tonya to say exactly what she had.

Robin giggled and squeezed Eloise's hand on one side and Laurel's on the other. AJ let her eyes linger on the second woman, who'd somehow integrated herself into their small group fairly easily.

AJ wondered how she did that. AJ had never been able to integrate herself into any groups without consistent, persistent effort, and sometimes she still felt like an outsider in a lot of ways.

Alice sat back, pure disbelief on her face. Her eyes started to fire a lot the way Aaron's were, and when they looked at each other, AJ could tell they were having a silent conversation she didn't understand. Some of her enthusiasm faded, though, because she couldn't see why they should be concerned about this.

Alice herself had told them about White Sands Worldwide. She'd submitted all of their names. Why had she done that if she was worried about something?

Tonya finished telling Kristen about how they'd send someone to Diamond Island that afternoon—same as everyone else—and that they'd go to Kristen's home to assess the damage. "Things will move from there," Tonya said. "You have somewhere safe to stay in the meantime? We can put you in a hotel."

"I have somewhere to stay," Kristen said, and before her call ended, Alice's phone rang.

She jumped to her feet, looking at her phone as if it had transformed into a poisonous snake and might strike her right at the jugular at any moment.

"Oh, my word," she breathed just before she strode out of the room. As she took the steps up into the lobby, she lifted her phone to her ear.

AJ met Kelli's eyes, and they got up together. She wanted to know who was on the phone with Alice, and she'd eavesdrop if she had to.

Alice paced in the foyer, her eyes unhappy and her eyebrows drawn down. "Yes, I understand," she said, glancing at Kelli and AJ. "What I'm asking is where the money is coming from."

She shook her head and spun on her heel again, her shoulder-length brown hair swinging with the movement. Everything about Alice had stayed neat and trim, despite the past several months of turmoil in her life.

AJ hugged herself as Alice said, "I want to know who the benefactor is. I want to know the terms of this 'donation' before I agree to anything." She paused near the check-in podium and kept her back to Kelli and AJ.

A seething sensation started in AJ's stomach, and she moved one hand there to press against the nerves. She did feel somewhat sick again, and she wasn't even sure why.

"She's worried," Kelli said. "Do you know why?"

"No," AJ murmured, most of her joy diffusing now that Alice—one of the smartest women AJ knew—wasn't hopping around with a giant grin on her face. Perhaps Aaron's concern was valid.

She turned back to the dining room and walked away from Alice just as she started to say, "No, that's not okay. I need..."

AJ would get caught up with everything she suspected or was worried about once she got off the phone. "Matt," she said, touching his shoulder.

He turned away from the group and looked up at her, his smile wide and beautiful. "Hey." He stood and took her into his arms. "Can you believe this? It really is going to be okay."

Enveloped in this new energy, AJ wasn't sure why she'd been tense only ten seconds ago. She gripped the feeling and stepped back slightly. "What did...who called you from White Sands?"

"A woman named Sasha," he said.

That name rang a bell, and AJ tilted her head. "I think that's the same woman Alice talked to a day or two ago. The one who told her about their charity." AJ found herself needing a lot more information.

She was a sports reporter, and she knew how to dig to get information. "I'm going to get my laptop," she said. "Then I want to know every word that woman said to you on the phone." She realized that several others were looking at her too. She gazed around at Eloise, Robin, Laurel, Kristen, and the others. She wanted all of their stories too. Every name.

"I want to talk to everyone too," she said. "I just need to get my computer. Then I want all the details."

"Finally," Aaron said almost under his breath.

AJ nodded and started back toward the foyer.

"What is she looking for?" Robin asked. "They're a charitable organization. They help people."

Other voices spoke, but AJ had long legs, and she'd ate up the distance back to Kelli already. She expected to see her best friend hugging herself, eyes wide, as she continued to listen to Alice.

Instead, Kelli stood with one hip cocked, a frown on her delicate features as Alice said, "Well, I'll meet you there, but I want full details. I want to see a contract. I want to know what I'm signing away, and to whom, before a single dime is spent on me."

She turned and faced AJ and Kelli. "That goes for everyone," she added. "I'm not going to let anyone take advantage of my friends."

AJ felt her passion and determination, and it dove through her too. The last thing she wanted was to see anyone in this inn get hurt in any way. She hurried past the podium while Alice continued to listen to whoever had called her. She darted into the room she and Matt had been assigned and grabbed her computer.

Back in the lobby, she caught the backs of Kelli and Alice as they returned to the dining room, and AJ hurried to follow them. Her head throbbed, and she felt somewhat unsteady on her feet, but she pressed forward.

"Okay," she said, setting the laptop on the table. "One at a time. I want names, what they told you, all of it."

AJ sat down and opened a new notes document. She'd started a countless number of these, and her fingers knew exactly what to do.

"I talked to Tonya Sharpino," Kristen said.

"Forrest Bell called me," Eloise said.

"Marian Usher," Kelli said.

"Sasha Summers," Matt said, and his eyes were wide

now too. AJ wished she could erase the worry in them. She didn't want to cause that.

"I spoke to her originally," Alice said quietly. "Just now, I got a call from Carol Grady."

"How many people work there?" Laurel asked. "Seems like a big group."

AJ watched her and Aaron exchange a glance while her fingers flew through typing the names. She'd spent so much of her career on a keyboard that she didn't have to look at her hands to type.

"Robin?" Eloise prompted.

"I didn't talk to them," Robin said. "I don't know who it was. Duke said, but I didn't think it was important." She still looked slightly perturbed that they were having this conversation at all.

"Hello!" a man called, and Robin sucked in a breath, jumped to her feet, and ran toward her husband. She shrieked as she launched herself at him, and he laughed as he caught her around the waist and picked her right up.

AJ actually envied the petite woman. AJ would never launch her six-foot-tall frame at a man, no matter how little she weighed. But Robin was eight inches shorter than her, and she fit right against Duke's upper half with her legs around his waist.

He put her down a moment later, and they both came back into the dining area. "They want to know who you talked to this morning," she said.

"A guy named Gene Yardley," Duke said. "I just got a

text from him too. Diamond Island downtown park pavilion, four o'clock."

As if summoned by the time and place announcement, Matt's phone chimed. AJ glanced at it as he did, and she watched as he swiped it open.

He looked up, his eyes even rounder now. "I just got the same text." He held up his phone as if people wouldn't believe him.

AJ stared at it, quickly typing in the exact wording. She wasn't sure why this was bothering her. Perhaps because it bothered Alice.

"Can we table this for now?" Eloise asked.

"Yes," Robin said, glaring openly at Alice and then AJ. "It's time for the gift exchange. Then we're having a holiday luncheon."

"This could be something," AJ said.

"No, it's not," Robin argued. "It's a charitable organization helping people after a natural disaster. There are a thousand companies, churches, and groups like this."

"We did organize as a church and go to Bell Island when they had their beach cleave off into the ocean," Kristen mused. "No strings attached."

"I'm sure everything is fine," Eloise said, but AJ watched Aaron gape at her. "Robin's right. Alice wouldn't have submitted any of our names if she hadn't done her research first anyway." She turned her gaze to Alice, as did everyone else.

"They seemed legitimate," Alice conceded, her voice

much softer than the one she'd used when speaking on the phone only a few minutes ago. "I think we should ask a lot of questions and read the fine print before any of us sign anything." She surveyed the group, and most people nodded their assent.

That made sense to AJ, and she typed in one more note before closing the lid on her laptop. "Gift exchange," she said. "Everyone get your kids, and let's move over to the couches. It'll be more comfortable, and I put the treats over there."

She led the way, because the gift exchange had been her idea. AJ had always wanted a family tradition of a pre-Christmas gift exchange with her loved ones. For a few years after she'd finally finished college, she'd tried with her brother and sister. But neither Amelia nor Ryan had been too keen on the idea. They'd done what she'd wanted, because AJ knew how to get what she wanted.

In the end, she'd decided it was too much work to try to make sure the three of them stayed close simply by purchasing a couple of gifts each year. As time went on, she knew that wasn't how relationships were built anyway. They needed constant care, continual nourishment, and unfeigned love to be able to succeed.

She thought of her sister out on Pearl Island with their father. Amy was the youngest, and she claimed to simply understand their father in a way AJ did not. She'd been at home with him for two years after AJ left for college, and she'd stayed on the island furthest south to raise her family.

AJ wondered if Amy was happy. Surely she was. She'd been married to a man named Donovan for ten years now, and they had two little girls AJ had flown home to see when they were both newborns.

Her guilt was as sharp as ever as she waited for everyone to settle down and for all the kids to make their way into the lobby area. Once they were all seated, with their gifts on their laps or nearby, AJ picked up the bowl she'd prepared.

"Okay," she said. "I'm going to draw a name, and whoever was assigned that person will present their gift." She smiled around at her friends, old and new, taking a moment to enjoy them for who they were.

Alice, for her unwavering strength and refusal to compromise on what she thought was right.

Robin, for her mothering spirit and the the way she could unite all of them so easily.

Eloise, for her good heart and kindness to AJ, even if they were cut from opposite sides of a cloth.

Kelli. AJ's dear Kelli, who'd never judged her, criticized her, or done anything but support her. Kelli smiled at her, and AJ nearly burst into tears.

"Thank you for indulging me with this," AJ said, her voice tight. "I think we should make it a tradition. It certainly seems like we're all going to be living here from now on, and we could take turns hosting each year."

She looked around, her hope bright as she took in the men and women present with them. She noticed that Alice and Kelli had settled beside one another, the only two women there without a boyfriend or significant other. AJ knew keenly how that felt, and her heart expanded for her friends.

"I'm sure I could do it," Alice said. "I love a good holiday party." She grinned too, and somehow, that broke the tension that had accompanied them to the gift exchange.

Robin agreed, and Eloise said the inn would always be available, though that surely couldn't be true. She'd want the inn to be filled with paying guests, not her friends.

"Family traditions are important," Laurel said from right next to AJ, and AJ felt a kinship with her she hadn't expected to feel.

"Okay." AJ drew in a deep breath. Her fingers fumbled over the little slips of paper she'd made. She finally grabbed one and pulled it out. "Robin." She put the basket down, because she wouldn't need it again unless the chain moved to someone who'd already given away their gift.

Robin grinned and stood up. "I had Grace." She walked over to the girl who sat on her father's lap, and it was as if the whole world smiled as Robin handed her a box wrapped in bright purple paper.

"I didn't know I was going to get a gift." Grace looked up at Robin with eyes full of wonder.

"What do you say?" Aaron asked.

"Thank you," Grace said, finally reaching to take the gift. "I just open it now?" She looked around, some measure of fear in her eyes.

"Yep," Eloise said. "And then you give your gift to your person." She glanced at AJ. "Right?"

AJ nodded, unable to speak. She loved the magic and love that Christmas brought with it, and she was glad she'd volunteered to put together their meals and activities.

Really, once she'd sent an outline of the few days they'd be at the inn together, everyone had stepped up and volunteered for things. Kelli would run the family tradition luncheon in a few minutes, and Alice and Kristen had partnered up for the big finale dinner the day before Christmas Eve.

Grace opened her gift, and her smile was as wide as the Atlantic Ocean when she pulled out a pair of pink jelly shoes. "I've always wanted a pair of these." She gazed at them as if they were Dorothy's ruby red slippers. "Thank you, Robin."

She slid from Aaron's lap and went to hug Robin, who embraced her with a warm smile and her eyes pressed closed.

AJ reached for Matt's hand, because she knew in that moment, she was going to be okay. She might not know what she was doing as a mother most of the time, but she could learn. She wanted a little girl like Grace to spoil and love, and she couldn't wait for her baby to be born.

The fear and trepidation about being a mother and if she had the internal fortitude to stick with it when her mother hadn't disappeared. It wasn't there anymore, and AJ hoped the doubts and darkness would stay away forever.

CHAPTER EIGHTEEN

Laurel clung tightly to Paul's hand, noting that he didn't seem to mind. He even adjusted their hands a couple of times during the gift exchange. She hadn't anticipated being here for this, but they'd been working so hard around Sanctuary Island, and as it was her and her partner's assigned island, it felt like the right place to be.

The Chief had planned to take this week off already, and he'd been coordinating everything from The Cliffside Inn. Laurel, Paul, Connor, and three other cops that had been on Sanctuary when the tsunami warning had come in had been working around the island to get things put back together, and Laurel half-wished she'd gone down to the beaches again this morning.

She and Paul had lingered to help with breakfast, and she hadn't known how to slip away from this gift exchange. She'd tried, but Eloise had said she was welcome to stay.

Laurel hadn't felt welcome in very many places throughout her life, so she'd stayed. She and Paul didn't have gifts for anyone, and no one would have anything for them. She found she didn't care as she watched Alice present Kristen with a hot water pot.

"It's wonderful," Alice said. "You put in the water, and it's hot in about a minute. I know you love your flavored hot chocolates in the winter." She bent down and hugged Kristen, then turned and picked up a basket that had been hiding beneath her chair. "In fact."

She gave the basket to Kristen, who pulled out different pouches of at least a dozen different types and flavors of hot chocolate. The older woman swiped at her eyes, and Laurel marveled at the relationship between all of them.

She'd never done Seafaring Girls, but she wished now that she had. She wouldn't have been in the same group as everyone else, of course, as she was probably a decade younger than Eloise and her friends.

She glanced at Eloise, who sat on the couch with the Chief and his girls. She fit there, and Laurel was once again so grateful she hadn't ruined anything between them last fall.

Eloise met her eyes, and Laurel smiled quickly before ducking her head. The exchange went on, with Kristen giving a customized planner to Robin. "It has all the dates of our birthdays, anniversaries, luncheons, and get-togethers already in it," she said as she sat back down.

Robin gazed at the oversized planner as if she'd died and gone to heaven. She opened the front cover and gasped. "Kristen." She looked up, her eyes wide but so happy. "Where did you get this?"

Kristen smiled and said, "Show everyone."

Robin held up the book so everyone could see it, gently moving it around the circle of couches and chairs where people sat. "It's us as Seafaring Girls."

"That's the day we did our final test on that yacht," Kristen said fondly, her face a picture of joy. "I found the negatives in a filing cabinet at Rueben's, in the lighthouse. I printed a whole bunch of them." She nodded to the planner. "They're inside."

Robin leafed through the booklet, stalling only a few seconds later. She grinned and tipped the book up again. "Look, El. You and Aaron are in the planner." She showed them, and even Laurel could see the big, red heart that had been painted around a date in April.

"I need to get in that thing," AJ said, and every eye flew to her. "What?" she asked. "I said Matt and I were talking about marriage."

"Talking is different than being engaged," Alice said, her gaze sliding to Matt. He shifted a bit, but he didn't say anything.

"Let's keep this thing moving," Duke said, patting his wife's knee. "We still have lunch to get through, and the lines at the ferry station are long."

"Right," Robin said, though she was definitely communicating something to AJ from way across the room.

An hour later, Laurel helped put together the last of the luncheon by taking the spinach and artichoke dip out to the patio.

Eloise had bought and installed heaters into the lattice work of the pergola that covered the patio. She'd told them about her plans to put flowers in it during the summer months and continue to use the space as much as possible in the winter with the inclusion of the heaters.

Two long tables had been set up between the pillars of the pergola, and all the food had been put there. A couple more tables spread underneath the roof, and teens, kids, and adults milled about.

The other cops had come back from their work for lunch, and Laurel put down the dip and migrated toward them. She felt at home at Paul's side, especially when he swept his fingers along her waist in a light touch.

She glanced up at him, and he inclined his head toward her. "My sister is planning to meet us at my house this afternoon. We could go together to yours after, if you'd like me there."

Laurel's heart skipped a beat. "I would love that, Paul. Thank you."

He smiled, pressed a kiss to her forehead, and they

both turned toward Kelli as she said, "Okay, everyone. Settle down. It's time for our family recipe holiday luncheon."

Laurel loved being here. These women reminded her of what it was like to spend time and holidays with family, and also how much she missed doing exactly that. Her parents lived in Nantucket now, and Laurel worked a lot, as Five Island Cove seemed to be a place tourists came for the holidays. She didn't think she'd minded, but now, surrounded by the air and attitude of family, she knew she did.

Kelli started explaining the food, saying that Alice had brought her mother's deviled eggs, which apparently she made for Christmas dinner every year.

Alice smiled and nodded, and Kelli went on to say she'd made her grandmother's cranberry and walnut cookies. "She served them every Sunday afternoon in December," Kelli said, a small smile on her face. "I remember loving them as a little girl, and I decided I'm going to make them every year too."

She looked at Robin. "Robin is the queen of the kitchen, and she made the candied ham and cheesy sliced potato casserole. Her mother's been serving ham for Christmas for decades, so that makes it special for our luncheon too. El?"

"After my dad left," Eloise said, stepping next to Kelli. "My mom and I just made as many dips as we could for Christmas Eve. Queso dips, chili cheese dip, dill dip for veggies, and this spinach and artichoke dip." She gazed at the pan Laurel had carried out, and Laurel could feel the safety and spirit of Eloise's and her mother's special times together.

Eloise looked up at her mother, who already sat at a table because of her broken leg. Billie, the Chief's oldest daughter, sat next to her, and they looked at one another too, something familial moving through them.

Laurel could practically taste it in the air, and there was nowhere she'd rather be than right here. If she couldn't have her family with her, she wanted to be with these people. With Eloise, Alice, Kelli, Robin, Kristen, and AJ.

She wondered if that was even possible. She couldn't infiltrate their group; she knew better than that. But they had accepted her, and she hoped she'd be able to find a place where she fit among them.

"Anyway," Eloise said. "It was my favorite, and that's why I made it for us today."

AJ didn't cook, but she adored pumpkin pie, so she'd bought one of those to share. "There's ice cream in the kitchen," she said. "We always had pumpkin pie and ice cream on Christmas night." Her smile said how happy her memory made her. "In fact, the day my mother left, my dad served pumpkin pie and ice cream for dinner."

That turned the atmosphere down slightly, but AJ kept on smiling. "It has good memories and bad, I suppose, but it's a family tradition, so I thought that's what I'd do."

Kristen put her hand on AJ's arm, her smile all-knowing. "I brought my potato rolls," she said, looking out over everyone. "I make them for all kinds of holidays, but always Christmas."

"Let's eat!" Kelli said, and the teenagers swarmed. Laurel stood back, watching them and simply basking in the energy they all brought together. Separate, they were great people. But together, she felt like they were unstoppable.

She wanted to be unstoppable too, so when AJ said, "Come eat, Laurel. Paul. Come on," Laurel went. It was nice to feel like she was wanted and welcome somewhere, and that was exactly how AJ had just made her feel.

"There's a spot here," Alice said when Laurel turned from the buffet, her plate overflowing with food.

"Thank you," Laurel said, setting her plate down and giving Alice a smile. "Thanks for letting us cops crash your party."

"Oh, please," Alice said with a light laugh. "You can come to anything you want. In fact, some of us go to lunch every Wednesday." She put a tiny bite of bread in her mouth. "Of course, Robin sometimes makes us spill all of our secrets, so you might not want to come."

"I *make* you?" Robin demanded from a few spots down the table, and Laurel simply laughed.

"There's Tell-Alls, and New Truths, and first rights of refusals, and *all* kinds of other things," AJ said as Paul took a seat across from Laurel. "Honestly, you should probably ask Aaron to work every Wednesday."

"You don't even come to the lunches," Alice said.

"I will," AJ said. "Once I move here."

"When is that happening?" Alice asked.

AJ glanced over to the buffet, where Matt stood talking to Duke. "Oh, I don't know," she said airily, and Laurel caught the look of skepticism on Alice's face before she wiped it away.

She wasn't sure what that was about, but she didn't know AJ all that well. She knew her name, and that she didn't live in Five Island Cove. She knew AJ had played sports and done well, that she'd made a name for herself inside sports journalism, and that she was pregnant with her boyfriend's baby.

Laurel had once thought there would be nothing more magical than carrying her boyfriend's baby. She'd been there, though, and she wasn't sure she'd ever be ready to go there again.

Her eyes locked on Paul's, and he watched her with one eyebrow slightly higher than the other. "I'm sorry," she said, looking left to one of Alice's twins. "I missed something."

"I'll say," Alice said. "Your handsome boyfriend over there asked if you wanted to go to dinner tonight after you assessed the damage on your houses, and you just...stared."

An embarrassed flush rose through Laurel, and she defaulted to what she always said. "Sorry. I was just thinking about something." She looked up at Paul, catching the quick grin on Alice's face that said she'd been teasing Laurel.

"I'd love to go to dinner if we can find somewhere on Diamond that's open."

"You're not going to stay here tonight?" Eloise asked, leaning past a couple of people to look toward Laurel. She sounded like she really wanted Laurel to stay another night.

Laurel looked down at the shirt she wore. It wasn't hers, and she honestly didn't know who'd donated it to her. "Depends on what my house looks like," she said. "I'm up on Browning Road, so I might be okay."

"We've got to get back to work at some point," Paul said, catching Laurel's eye. "We don't even know what the station looks like."

"The station is almost cleaned up," the Chief said, his voice carrying easily though he didn't lean forward like Eloise had. "I've got Mitch and Gina on it."

"Oh, well, Gina," Paul said with a grin. "I'm surprised we all don't have detailed to-do lists, organized by block, per island."

"Give her until tonight," the Chief said, laughing afterward. Laurel, Paul, and a couple of other cops down by him joined in.

On Laurel's other side, AJ and Kelli started talking in low voices about White Sands Worldwide, and Laurel kept one ear on that conversation. The cop inside her wouldn't just let it go, because she'd seen the look on the Chief's face.

He hadn't let it go either, and she wouldn't be one bit surprised if he'd already texted someone who had more free time and more privacy than he currently had to dig up anything he or she could find on the charitable organization that sounded too good to be true.

Laurel had some personal experience with things like that. Sometimes things that sounded too good to be true started out okay, and then quickly delved into the world of nightmares.

So she listened, but she buttered her roll like she wasn't, even when Kristen leaned across the table and joined the conversation.

CHAPTER NINETEEN

Kristen hated the distrust running through her bloodstream. She'd never considered herself a jaded or distrustful person. Her default wasn't that someone was lying to her. When Joel had come home late at night and said he'd been up at the lighthouse going over their quarterly reports, she'd believed him.

She hadn't even *thought* he'd lie to her.

Since his death and all the secrets that had come to light, though, Kristen found herself questioning everyone and everything. She hated the doubt circling through her, especially when it was herself she couldn't believe.

She'd spoken to Tonya on the phone with everyone listening in. Everyone had heard the phone call, even AJ. She hadn't detected anything nefarious or alarming about the woman's voice, her delivery of the news or finer details —which, as she listened to AJ and Kelli chat, hadn't really been very fine at all—or her request to meet on Diamond Island that afternoon.

She'd gotten a text just like everyone else. Her phone had simply been on silent, and she hadn't alerted the group to it the way Matthew Hymas had. She sat next to the man, who watched AJ and Kelli too. He didn't say anything, and it wasn't until Kelli asked, "Do you think we shouldn't go?" that Kristen decided to join the conversation.

"I think we absolutely should go," she said. "The only way to get more information is to show up to get the information."

"I feel like I need a handbook of questions to ask," AJ said, and Kristen felt that deeply. She'd have loved a manual of what to ask when her husband came home late, or left early, or didn't want her to go with him when he had to go out to the claw to check the lantern.

Sometimes he went in rough waters, and Kristen worried about him the whole time. Sometimes he'd gone during calm seas, and he'd spend a few days there stocking their emergency supplies, topping off fuel, and fixing the shelter.

The claw was just a patch of sand out in the water shaped like a rooster's foot, and there was a lantern there to guide boats into the right waters to reach the docks on Diamond Island. There was a rudimentary shelter, but it was waterproof and had a bed and plenty of food and emergency supplies.

He could've met any number of women out there and Kristen would've never known. She'd never asked. She'd never suspected anything.

Familiar foolishness ran through her, and she pressed against it mentally. She was tired of feeling like she was the one who'd done something wrong by not suspecting that her otherwise devoted husband was cheating on her.

You didn't do anything wrong, she told herself for probably the hundredth time since Joel had died.

"So we'll go," Kelli said, her voice strong enough to pull Kristen out of her damaging thoughts. "Let's make a list of questions before we go, and let's commit to asking anything we can."

"I should've brought out my laptop," AJ mused, and Matt reached across the table and covered her hand with his.

"Tell me why you're suspicious."

"Did you see Aaron Sherman?" she asked. "He wasn't jumping up and down for joy, and I don't know. It triggered something inside me. Sometimes there's more to a story."

"And sometimes there's not," Matt said, and Kristen nodded before she could tell herself to do it. He glanced at her, and she met his eyes. She didn't know him personally very well, but she knew his parents. They were lifelong residents of Five Island Cove, and his mother was one who'd brought food to the funeral luncheon.

She gave him a warm smile, which he returned. He

looked back at AJ. "Right, babe? You sometimes think you have a story, but when you look further into it, you don't."

"Yes," AJ admitted. "Sometimes."

"The point is," Alice said, joining their conversation from the other side of Laurel. Kristen watched the woman for a few seconds, and anyone who underestimated her would be sorry. Kristen could simply sense the quiet strength inside her. Her dark eyes carried it too, though she didn't speak up much and could easily be forgotten.

"We don't know which is it," Alice finished. "It could be something, but it might not be. We owe it to ourselves to ask all the right questions before signing anything."

"What did your caller say when you questioned them?" AJ asked. "Did they say who the benefactor was?"

"She would not say," Alice said. "Carol—the woman who called me—said she actually couldn't disclose that information to anyone. There's something strange about that. If you're literally going to help a group of strangers on a tiny group of islands where you don't live, why can't they know who you are?"

"Maybe we do know who they are," Kristen said, bringing every eye to her. She didn't normally thrive in the spotlight, but she could handle the heat of it just fine. She looked around at everyone. "Just because White Sands is in Canada doesn't mean the benefactor is."

"The woman I spoke to the first times said they grew up here." Alice reached for her glass of sweet tea. "That they wanted to help residents here, because they were once one."

"There you go," Kristen said. "Perhaps they still are, and she just *implied* they didn't live here anymore."

Alice met her eye, and Kristen looked steadily back at her. Alice had a good head on her shoulders, and Kristen usually listened to her. She wasn't sure if she just wanted everyone to have the happily-ever-after they sorely needed this Christmas or if she just couldn't stand the thought of another obstacle to overcome.

Another secret to bring to light.

Another painful decision to make. *Not painful,* Kristen thought. *Impossible.*

"Well, I'm going to go to the pavilion at four," Kristen said, groaning as she got to her feet. "I'm going to see what they say."

"Who do you think will be there?" AJ asked, and Kristen collected her mostly empty plate and walked away. AJ loved to speculate more than anyone else Kristen had ever met, and she supposed that had helped the woman in her line of work.

Right now, all it did was bring a sense of uneasiness to Kristen's stomach she could do without. She put her plate in the large trash can on the edge of the patio, the air much cooler out here, as the heaters didn't extend their arms of warmth quite this far.

Kristen ran her hands up her sweatered arms and gazed out over the empty pool to the ocean north of the island. It was a crystal clear day—cold, but clear. She could easily see the southern edge of Rocky Ridge, and she started walking toward it.

She went past the pool and all the way to the edge of the lawn here at The Cliffside Inn. Eloise had done a good job of getting everything cleaned up and ripped out, and she'd detailed her plans for the spring landscaping at one of their recent lunches.

A sense of satisfaction ran through Kristen now, because there was nothing she loved more than seeing her girls and her children achieve their dreams. Eloise had loved the inn growing up, and to see her back here, thriving, in love, with a wedding and a family on the horizon almost brought Kristen to tears.

"I swear I can see my house from here," Alice said as she stepped next to Kristen.

Kristen smiled and folded her arms as another chill scurried across her shoulders. "I think it's that one with the light glinting off the big windows out front." There was a light winking into the daylight from the sun's reflection, but it wasn't Alice's.

They giggled quietly together, and Kristen did love Alice so dearly. "Why are you worried about this opportunity for everyone to get their lives back together?" she asked.

"I don't know," Alice said with a sigh. "Only that I am."

Kristen disliked it when Alice said she didn't know

something. She usually at least had an inkling of an idea, but she just didn't want to say it out loud. "Robin and Duke need that boat. It's the only way they make any money."

"I know," Alice said quietly.

"Do you?" Kristen asked. "All the way, Alice? They're living in her mother's house for nearly free, and they barely still make ends meet." She kept her gaze on Rocky Ridge, miles and miles away, half wishing she could walk all the way there.

"I didn't know that," Alice murmured.

"I know you're not rolling in money anymore," Kristen said. "I just wasn't sure if you knew Robin never has."

"She's such an amazing woman," Alice said.

"And yet you snipe at her every chance you get."

Alice sighed, but she didn't deny it. "I love Robin with my whole soul. She knows that. I thought everyone else did too."

"We do," Kristen said. "I know your bickering is in good fun. I just...she is carrying a huge load right now, and getting a new fishing boat is literally a saving grace for the two of them."

Alice let several seconds of silence go by. "Think of how terrible I'll feel if I'm responsible for getting them involved in a charitable organization that isn't so charitable," she finally said. "I think one reason I'm worried is because it will be my fault if this turns out to be a bad thing."

Kristen nodded, glad the truth had finally been spoken. "We're all adults here."

"Yes, but Robin and Duke are ready to sign anything that's put in front of them," Alice said, turning to face Kristen. "That's not smart or responsible, and I don't want them to find themselves in a worse situation, because *I* submitted their names on that stupid form."

"You sound like Robin now," Kristen said with a smile. "Always carrying the weight of everyone, when she should just worry about herself."

Alice shook her head, her smile barely there. "I spent a lot of years thinking only of myself," she said. "I try not to do that anymore."

"Please," Kristen said. "The moment you had those babies, you've worked only for them."

Alice folded her own arms. "I could use some advice about them, actually."

"You should talk to Robin," Kristen said, reaching to put her arm around Alice's shoulders.

Alice smiled and leaned her head against Kristen's shoulders. "I should. She might know what to do with a daughter who wants to go out with a boy who's no good for her."

Kristen simply stood with her, glad some of Alice's anxiety had disappeared. She was sure they were both thinking about what would happen at four o'clock in the downtown park on Diamond Island, and Kristen wondered if it was too early to leave for the ferry station.

Behind her, she heard people start to talk and move, and she and Alice turned back to the group. Robin put a stack of plates in the trash, tugged down the sleeves on her hooded sweatshirt and started toward Alice and Kristen.

"I'm going to go get my purse," Kristen said. "You two have a good chat." She stopped to give Robin a hug.

"You're leaving?"

"I'm going to get my purse so we can go to the ferry." She smiled. "Alice wants to ask you something."

Robin wore a dark edge in her eyes as she looked past Kristen to Alice. Kristen patted her on the shoulder. "She needs your advice. Do try to remember that they all look to you for help."

Robin's eyes rounded, and her gaze flew back to Kristen's, but she was already stepping around Robin. She knew Alice and Robin had been arguing more than usual lately, but deep down, they were the very best of friends. They understood each other on a level most people didn't, because they were so very much alike.

"Help them sort through things," she whispered to herself as she went inside. She met Dawn Hall in the entryway, struggling to get her left crutch past the edge of the wall. "Let me help you." She hurried forward and dislodged the rubber end from where it had stuck. "There you go."

Dawn stumbled slightly, but her smile came quickly. "Thank you, Kristen."

"How are you?" Kristen asked, putting her hand on

Dawn's lower back. "How's the leg? What can I help you with?"

"I'm going to be just fine," Dawn said, hobbling ever so slowly down the hall to her bedroom at the back of the inn. "Thankfully, I can run a foot pedal with both legs, and Eloise is so close now."

"That is a blessing," Kristen said. "Are you excited for the wedding?"

CHAPTER TWENTY

Alice hugged Robin the moment she arrived, her guilt slicing through her chest in a painful wave. "I'm so sorry for arguing with you," she said. "And for saying you make us say things we don't want to say."

Robin simply gripped her, and Alice let the silence and emotion between them stitch up the wounds between them. She finally cleared her throat and stepped back. "Kristen said you needed my help with something?"

Alice took a moment to press her hand to her mouth, trying to quiet the unrest in the back of her throat. Whenever she had a problem, Robin had helped her. Whenever she'd had to admit very hard things, Robin had encouraged her and said she could weather whatever storm came from the decisions Alice made.

No one had helped her more over the summer, as

Alice went through her divorce and moved her children back to Five Island Cove, than Robin.

"Ginny has a boy who's asked her to a dance," Alice said. "Charlie insists he's not a nice guy, and that he sleeps around with a lot of girls, and he's targeting Ginny."

Robin said nothing, though she surely had formed an opinion the moment Alice had started speaking.

"I don't know what to do. Ginny sometimes feels like I take Charlie's side, and that's what she's accused me of here. Charlie feels the same way from time to time, and I feel stuck." Alice rolled her neck left and right, trying to work the stress and exhaustion from her muscles. "What would you do?"

"I have no idea," Robin said, her voice muted and quiet. "Jamie has a mean girl trying to befriend her, and Mandie said this girl has gone through a lot of girls, using them up and spitting them out."

"Sounds similar, except one's a girl and one's a boy."

"Who's the boy?"

"Cameron Heights." Alice hadn't said another word to Ginny about him since yesterday morning, but she'd need to before her daughter went back to school after the New Year.

"Hmm." Robin hummed in such a way that led Alice to believe she knew the boy or his family. "I'm going to go with Charlie on this one, Alice. Mandie told me that he went to the movies with her group once, and he tried to kiss every girl—her included—before the night ended."

Alice sighed, her mind racing now. How could she gently lead Ginny to the idea that she couldn't go out with this boy?

"Sometimes they have to make their own mistakes," Robin said.

"Not this kind," Alice said, her thoughts going down dark roads where she had to take her daughter to the hospital and make a police report of a sexual assault. She'd protect Ginny from that at any cost. It was worth her daughter being angry at her for the rest of her life, if that was what it took.

"How are you feeling about Charlie and Mandie?" Alice asked. They regularly spoke about their children dating one another, just so they could be on the same page when it came to the relationship.

"Good," Robin said, finally tearing her gaze from the horizon to look at Alice. She looked tired, with plenty of lines around her eyes. Alice wanted to wrap her in a hug and tell her she'd fix everything. She couldn't though. Not this time.

"Charlie is a good boy," Robin said. "He's respectful to me and Duke, and he respects Mandie."

"Doesn't mean he won't sleep with her."

Robin shrugged. "You know, I used to be so worried about that. Mandie's a pretty girl, with lots of curves. She's had boys coming by the house for a few years now. Charlie's by far the best of them." She smiled at Alice. "You've done a great job with him."

"Thank you," Alice murmured, her eyebrows drawing down. "You're not worried about them having sex?"

Robin shrugged again, and Alice thought she was in really bad shape. "I don't think it's the worst thing that could happen, Alice. I really don't."

"You're kidding." Alice gaped at her, her eyes widening as they tried to take in more of Robin's face in an attempt to understand. "Robin. What is wrong with you?"

"I think..." Robin met Alice's eyes, pure fear in hers. "I think sometimes there are bigger problems than two teenagers who mutually agree to an intimate relationship."

"This is about Duke's boat."

Robin looked away, but Alice saw the darkness in her eyes anyway. "We need a fishing boat."

Alice nodded, because she couldn't argue. People needed a place to live too. Matt's family needed their golf course to be open to pay their bills. Dawn needed her sewing machines. Out of everyone, Alice's situation was very low on the scale, and she recommitted herself to helping her friends in any way she could.

"I just need to ask a few questions this afternoon," Alice said carefully. "I don't want you and Duke to get into an even tougher situation."

"I appreciate that, Alice," Robin said. "I do. I just...we need that boat, and I'm going to do everything I can to get it." She turned around and patted Alice's shoulder. "No matter what you ask and what the answers are, I'm going to do anything and everything in my power to replace my husband's fishing boat."

She walked away, and Alice felt like the earth between them was splitting with every step she took, creating a chasm that she'd never be able to bridge.

A couple of hours later, Alice disembarked from the ferry along with everyone else. They'd had to wait through two other ferries, and they'd be very lucky to make it to the pavilion by four o'clock. Alice had decided to leave her twins at the inn, and they'd kept Parker, Mandie, and Jamie with them.

Aaron had brought his girls with him, as they hadn't been back to Diamond Island since the tsunami, and they all wanted to see the state of their home. After the meeting in the park, Eloise would go with them to the house, and the group would split up.

Alice wasn't sure why, but she didn't want Laurel and Paul to go. She didn't want the other cops to return to their homes. She wanted everyone to come back to the inn that evening, though they had no dinner planned the way they'd done when they'd all stayed at her house on Rocky Ridge.

She liked being with good people, and she liked talking to her friends. She didn't want to go by the house she was supposed to be moving into next week, and she didn't want to see the state of the things she and the twins had moved over the past few weekends.

Still, her feet moved her, and she got in the first Ride-Share she could, cramming inside next to Kelli and Kristen in the back seat of a sedan. Aaron, Eloise, and the girls had taken the car in front of them, and Laurel, Paul, and all the cops got the extended RideShare in the form of a minivan behind them.

Alice could admit her nerves, but she didn't. Not out loud. She also didn't show them on the outside, ever. She'd learned to box them up very early in her life, and she was still very good at it.

"I think I'm going to go out to Rocky Ridge for Christmas," she said to Kelli. "Are you going to see your mother?"

"Yes," Kelli said. "That was the plan, and her house wasn't too badly damaged." She smiled at Alice and reached over to squeeze her hand. "I know you're just trying to do what's right."

"I don't want to hurt you," Alice said, looking away. "I'll just keep my questions to myself. Everyone's going to make their own decisions anyway."

I'm going to do anything and everything in my power to replace my husband's fishing boat.

Alice would've done the same for Frank, once upon a time. Robin loved Duke very much, and it was actually a nice reminder for Alice to see it.

Before she knew it, the driver of the car pulled up to the park with the words, "Diamond Downtown."

"Thank you," Kristen said, already paying for the ride. Alice wished she wouldn't. She wasn't sure how much money Kristen had, but she didn't need to pay for everyone's ride.

Alice got out of the car and held the door for Kelli. After closing the door, she faced the park. Eloise and Aaron were already there, of course. Matt, AJ, Duke, and Robin got out of another car just down the street, and they started across the wet grass toward the pavilion.

Everywhere Alice looked, she saw evidence of water and debris. The people on this island had been busy cleaning up, the same way they had been on Sanctuary. She wasn't sure what her new house looked like, but in that moment, it didn't matter. She'd clean it up and get it habitable, just like everyone else.

She wasn't going to quit. She wasn't going to let a little saltwater ruin her life or change her plans. She held her head high as she walked down the sidewalk toward the pavilion where it seemed no one else was.

It certainly wasn't warm enough to bring children to a park to play, and everyone else had so much work to do they weren't out enjoying the winter sunshine.

"Alice," someone behind her said.

She turned at the sound of her name in an unfamiliar, male voice. Kelli, who walked in front of her, stopped walking too, coming to Alice's side.

A man had just gotten out of a car, and he'd turned back to pay the driver. He was tall, with a head full of sandy blond hair and a dark blue jacket straining across his broad shoulders and narrowing at his waist.

He turned back to her, and Alice knew who he was instantly. Her heartbeat stopped completely, and heat filled her face. "Will," she said.

"Ohhh," Kelli whispered. "He's looking at you like he wants to kiss you right now."

Alice didn't even look at her as she stepped back the way she'd come.

"Alice," Will said again, grinning. He jogged the last few steps to her and wrapped her in a hug as he laughed.

Alice had no idea what to do with such happiness and joy. She couldn't remember the last time a man had even smiled in her direction, not to mention laughing as they greeted her.

She felt stiff in his arms, and he stepped back quickly. "Sorry. Are you not a hugger?" He looked at her with those dark, navy, dazzling eyes she definitely remembered. "Seems like I remember you being a hugger."

"Hugging is fine," Alice said, reaching up to tuck her hair behind her ear, suddenly feeling very out of place. She could only hear the comments from Charlie and Ginny about his daughter, and she wondered if she should break things off between the two of them before anything even started.

The way her blood pulsed through her veins, though,

and Alice didn't want to do that. She lifted her head and looked him right in the eyes. "It's so good to see you." She hugged him again, this time joining in with him as he laughed. "Sorry, that was a weird greeting. I just—I'm surprised to see you here."

She pulled away and looked down to his casual tennis shoes and back to his face. He wore a pair of jeans with his jacket zipped up so she couldn't see his shirt. He was so... not Frank, and Alice really liked that.

At the same time, her heart sank all the way to the cold cement at her feet. If Will was here, his nomination had been selected too.

"I got a phone call from someone at this place where they're helping people impacted by the tsunami," he said easily. "White Sands Worldwide? I'm supposed to get more details here." He looked past her to the pavilion while Alice's throat dried right up.

Why hadn't he texted her that he'd gotten a phone call? *He's really busy*, she told herself. He was responsible for all the water transportation in the cove, which was significant.

"They say they can help get the ferry system all the way operational with a little bit of money and some extra manpower to help get things cleaned up quick." He grinned at her and reached out as if he'd tuck her hair. He did just that, sending fire cascading down the side of her neck and into her ribcage. "What are you doing here?"

CHAPTER TWENTY-ONE

Eloise looked over her shoulder to where Alice and Will had stopped on the sidewalk. She really wished she could transform into a fly in that moment and buzz around to hear what they were talking about. Her own heart pounded, and she forced herself to turn around.

No one waited for them in the pavilion though, and Robin's anxiety had started to wear on Eloise's patience. The girls wouldn't last long here, and Eloise pulled out her phone to check the time.

Two minutes until the clock ticked to four. White Sands Worldwide seemed like the type of organization that would be prompt, and Eloise swallowed back her own nerves.

"Billie," Aaron said. "Why don't you and Grace take my card and go get a soda?"

"Really?" Billie asked, and Aaron smiled at his daughter. He took his wallet out of his back pocket and withdrew the card. He handed it to his eldest and said, "Do not leave Grace behind. Stay together."

"Do you want something?" Billie asked, tucking the card into the back pocket of her jeans. She pulled down the ends of her hat to cover her ears.

"Yes," Aaron said with a smile. "You know what I like."

"El?" Billie asked, and she loved hearing her nickname in the girl's voice.

"I want strawberry basil lemonade," she said. "If you're going to Station Ninety-Nine."

"Got it," Billie said, and she reached for Grace's hand. The two girls walked away, and Eloise couldn't help the fondness for them that filled her.

"It's just us," Alice said as she stepped next to Eloise. "Did you notice that?"

"What?" Eloise asked.

Alice wore a look of fear and anger at the same time. "Sasha Summers called me and said she had a form people could fill out for the grants. I didn't tell anyone else about it, but she said she was going to call other people."

She glanced around, her expression turning darker and darker. "She obviously didn't. We're the only ones here. The seven people *I* submitted. That's it. We've all been chosen. We're the *only ones* who've been chosen."

Eloise looked around, and sure enough, there wasn't anyone there besides the people Alice had nominated for the disaster relief. "I'm not sure that's a bad thing," she said. "Maybe she just figured she'd gotten enough nominations, and she didn't call anyone else to let them know about the project."

"I need to call her," Alice said, already swiping on her phone, though she hadn't saved the number.

An ache spread through Eloise's body, causing a sharp pain in her lower abdomen. She instinctively curled into herself, and Aaron noticed. His eyebrows went up, and Eloise just gave an almost imperceptible shake of her head.

She loved him so much, and when her brother had shown up at the inn a few months ago, breathing threats and knowing every little iota of business she and each of her friends were involved in, Eloise had turned inward.

She'd narrowed down what was the most important things to her, and she'd landed on her relationship with Aaron, his girls, her mother, and her friends. She would sacrifice anything for them, and she'd given Garrett what he wanted—all the property he and their father had amassed through their illegal card games at the inn. All the money.

Eloise sometimes thought about what her life—and the lives of those she loved—would be like with the money. She would've been able to help Robin and Duke with their fishing boat, and they wouldn't be standing under this pavilion in the freezing cold, waiting for an unknown savior.

She could've helped Alice so she could keep the vacation home she and her children had been living in. Alice claimed not to care about the house, but Eloise didn't see how that was possible. Alice had always liked nice things —expensive things—and she'd never apologized for it.

Eloise glanced at her now, and she could simply feel the unrest that existed in Alice, though she hid it masterfully.

She looked around at everyone there, and they all held such a special place in her heart. She wanted only what was best for all of them, as well as her mother, whom she'd left at the inn with all the kids. Worry darted through her, but she reasoned that her mother had a phone, and there were plenty of people to help should she or the children need it.

Eloise had gotten to know her neighbors up on Cliffside Drive over the last six months, and they were all very nice people.

Robin and Duke wore the most worry in their faces, as well as the most hope. As their contribution to the activities, they'd taken the movie night for that evening, back at the inn. AJ had suggested they could bring popcorn or brownies, and she knew Robin would have something delicious to present.

Eloise was making blueberry pancakes and candied bacon for tomorrow's breakfast, and she was glad Paul had volunteered to help. He'd been a good friend to Aaron for many years, and Eloise could see why they got along so well.

Alice had said she and Kristen would take care of the last, final dinner tomorrow evening, and then everyone would leave on Wednesday morning to make room for Eloise's first guests at The Cliffside Inn.

Her stomach flipped, as it had been doing every time she thought about having real, paying guests at the inn again. There would be no gentlemen's club this time, and no dastardly card games. Just good food, a family atmosphere, and the peace Eloise had always felt at the inn.

She'd been living in the small suite behind the inn, but come April, things would have to change. The apartment wasn't big enough for a family of four, and Aaron needed to live on Diamond Island.

Eloise hadn't made a final decision yet, but she suspected that she'd hire a manager to live in that suite. She'd thought about offering it to the chef. No matter what, she needed someone who could be on-site for any issues. It really all depended on whether or not she could keep The Cliffside Inn full and thriving.

"They're late," someone said, and Eloise glanced down at her phone again. Sure enough, it was after four, and she twisted to look behind her again. Another vehicle hadn't arrived, and she'd have known by now anyway, as cars made noise.

Another minute ticked by, and then another, and the tension riding in the air increased with each breath.

"How long do we wait?" Alice asked, and Robin threw

her a dirty look. Surprisingly, Kristen did too, and Eloise simply watched everyone. She was very comfortable on the outside, and she often picked up cues from other people by keeping her eyes open and her mouth closed.

"El," Aaron said very quietly. "I have a bad feeling about this."

"Should we go?" she whispered. "The girls aren't back yet." Some of her apprehension belonged to what they might find at his house. There didn't seem to be a rhyme or reason to how some buildings had been damaged while others hadn't, and all she'd been able to do was pray.

He'd asked his parents to take Prince, his dog, and Aaron wanted to stop by there too. First, to check on his parents, and second, to get the dog he loved. Eloise wasn't sure if they'd make it back to Sanctuary tonight, and she told herself it was okay. The ferries started early, and she could get back and get breakfast going in plenty of time.

Alice said something quietly to Will, and they started talking in low voices. Alice trilled out a laugh, and Eloise stared at her in surprise. She hadn't seen Alice flirt with a man in a very long time, and she started to giggle too.

She turned into Aaron's chest to stifle the sound, and he asked, "Do you hear that?"

Eloise pulled away, and she cocked her head to the side, trying to hear what he did. "Sounds like a helicopter."

Kelli and Kristen moved toward the edge of the concrete and stepped onto the soggy grass. They looked up into the sky, and Kristen said, "It's a helicopter, and it's coming this way."

Everyone bustled out from under the roof of the pavilion and looked up into the sky, even Eloise. She'd seen helicopters before, of course, but for some reason, none of them could look away from this one.

"Are they going to land that thing right here?" AJ asked.

"Is that legal?"

"Can they do that?"

There were too many people there for Eloise to identify all the voices as people continued to chatter and ask questions that no one answered.

The chopping sound of the blades came closer and closer, growing louder and louder as the helicopter itself grew larger with each passing moment.

Eloise found it remarkable that such a vehicle could fly at all, and she watched the hulking black machine in the bright blue sky with a bit of wonder amidst all the uncertainty streaming through her.

She ducked behind Aaron, and everyone stepped back inside the pavilion as the helicopter made ready to land right there in the park.

Aaron's phone rang, and he pulled it from his pocket. "Yes," he said, practically yelling. He said a couple of other things, but she couldn't hear him over the deafening noise of the helicopter.

He hung up and turned his back on the park and the

vehicle that had just touched down. "Eloise," he yelled. "We need to go."

"Go?" she yelled back. "They just got here."

"We don't want to be here."

She didn't understand, and he said something else she couldn't hear. She shook her head, and Aaron's frustration showed all over his handsome face. He tapped furiously on his phone and held it up for her to see.

I just talked to Ben, and he said the benefactor is Diane Proctor.

Eloise read the sentence over and over, her confusion doubling. "Diane Proctor?" she asked, but no one could hear her. She knew that name, but it wouldn't come forward and remind her of how.

Aaron's mouth moved, and he typed on his phone again. He held it up, but the blades had started to slow, and the group had begun to inch forward again. She stepped past Aaron without looking at his phone, which he hadn't held up again anyway.

Three people had already stepped out of the helicopter and were currently hurrying toward the pavilion with their hands up to cover their bent heads. They all wore extremely professional clothing in dark blue or black, and Eloise hadn't seen such pressed slack or such suffocating skirt suits in a while.

She'd been wearing jeans and ratty T-shirts for months, and she worked with a variety of handymen, tradesmen, and others who dressed the same way she did to get their jobs done.

Robin stepped forward first, of course, and she shook the hand of the lead blonde woman, both of them smiling like jackals.

Aaron put his hand on Eloise's waist, but they couldn't leave now. "Eloise," he said anyway, a hefty dose of warning in his voice.

The helicopter finally powered all the way down, and another woman disembarking from the helicopter drew her attention. She carried prestige and power in her step and the stance of her shoulders, and it was clear to Eloise that she'd be the one funding all of the projects in Five Island Cove.

A few people were still exchanging pleasantries with the other three people who'd arrived first, but it didn't take long for everyone to turn their attention to the tall, blonde woman wearing a pair of gray slacks, a pair of black heels, and a long, duster jacket that clearly cost thousands of dollars.

She was Alice times ten, with probably millions more dollars than Alice had enjoyed in her prime. She wore her wealth in the set of her smile and the way her eyes didn't crinkle with the movement. Her arms swung naturally at her sides, as if she'd made many walks like this before and knew exactly how to do it.

Her hair fell below her shoulders in straight, shiny strands, and Eloise half-expected a stylist and makeup artist to emerge from the helicopter too, because this woman was exquisite.

Eloise took a step toward her, because she also seemed somewhat familiar.

"El," Aaron said again.

She ignored him, because AJ had just let out a shriek filled with horror and despair. She stepped past Matt though he said, "AJ? What's wrong? Is it the baby?"

She stopped just past the group that had gathered, and Eloise saw her fingers curl into fists. She had a power stance too, and hers was much more aggressive than the other woman's.

Everything made sense when she asked, "Mother?"

CHAPTER TWENTY-TWO

AJ couldn't believe her eyes. This could not be happening. This person she hadn't heard from or seen in thirty-five years could not be standing in front of her.

Her heartbeat sprinted through her body, and her heart itself thrashed against the cage her ribs made around it. What was she supposed to say? How was she supposed to feel?

How dare her mother come here, dressed like she owned the world, with a grand entrance in a helicopter she wouldn't dare get out of until the blades had stopped?

AJ wasn't sure if she should find the nearest object she could and hurl it at her mother's perfect face, or rush toward her and wrap her arms around her. The feelings shot through her at the speed of light, and her thoughts were so tangled she couldn't make sense of anything.

"Mother?" someone repeated, but AJ honestly couldn't decipher vocal tones at this point. Someone touched her, and she jerked away from it.

"Hello, AvaJane," her mother said, not denying that she was, in fact, Diane Proctor.

"Thank you so much for coming," another woman said, her voice as fake as plastic. She wore a false smile too, and AJ's stomach heaved.

"I'm going to be sick," she said with a moan, and she turned around. Thankfully, Matt was there, and he took her into his arms to support her.

"Come sit down," he said, but AJ didn't want to sit down. She wanted to know why her mother was there.

"I'm Marian Usher," the other woman continued, and AJ could still feel Diane's eyes on her. "Not all of our account managers could come, but I'm going to be talking with Kelli and Will."

"I'm Forrest Bell," a man said. "I need Eloise and Duke with me."

"Right here," Robin chirped, and AJ couldn't believe her.

She turned back to watch Robin step to the man's side. Duke went with her, but no one else had moved at all. AJ's numbness started to wear off, though it had only started a few moments ago.

"I'm Carol Grady," the last woman said. "I have Alice and Kristen with me."

"Who's she?" Alice asked, her voice tight and professional.

"I'm Sasha Summers."

"Why did AJ call you mother?" Alice asked.

"Because I'm her mother."

"We're leaving," Aaron said before Alice could ask anything else, and AJ watched as he and Eloise looked at one another. They had an entire conversation without saying anything, and Eloise finally nodded, acceptance spreading through her expression.

Eloise held AJ's gaze for a moment, then another.

"Why are you leaving?" Forrest asked, obviously confused.

"We're not taking any money from AJ's mother," Eloise said. She surveyed the whole group. "None of you should. Do you know who she is? Do you realize what she's done?"

"Eloise," AJ said, not sure why she didn't want her to say anything badly about her mother. Perhaps AJ wanted to outline and detail all the horrible things she'd dealt with over the years. The pure inadequacy she'd suffered. The hours of time and thousands of dollars she'd spent in therapy. The hundreds of men she'd slept with as a way to try to forget that she'd been abandoned by the one person who wasn't supposed to ever leave her.

"Will you be the one funding the projects?" Alice asked, her eyes never leaving Diane.

AJ didn't want cower in her boyfriend's arms, and she

straightened to face her mother. She had so many things and people she needed to face, and she had to be strong even when she didn't feel like she could be.

Without her medication, every day and every hour was harder than normal.

Be strong for the baby, she told herself. *Be strong for yourself.*

Her mother had the audacity to come here, and surely she'd known AJ would be there. She'd known her false identity would be revealed.

"What do you want?" she asked.

Diane's eyes went right back to her, and AJ held the gaze steadily. She could still remember the last time she'd seen her mother, and she'd seemed so big back then. So powerful and so wonderful. She'd kissed AJ goodbye in the morning before school, and she'd been gone in the afternoon.

She'd left a note for the family, which her father had burned a few years later on his birthday, claiming it was his gift to himself to finally move past the woman who'd ruined his life and his children's lives. He'd taken to drinking a lot more after that, and AJ hadn't thought he'd really moved past much of anything.

AJ had fended for herself through much of high school, as Ryan was older than her and gone by the time she was a sophomore. She'd watched out for Amy as much as she could, and she'd spent time with the boys that made her forget her situation and helped her feel good about herself. She'd left the cove the moment she could.

"I want to help the people in Five Island Cove." Diane adjusted the designer purse she carried on her forearm.

"You only told me about the nomination form," Alice said. "You knew who I was, and you knew I'd nominate all my friends."

Diane turned to Alice and gave her a winning smile. "Yes, dear. You did great."

AJ couldn't stand the idea of her mother making Alice feel small, and she watched Alice shrink right in front of her.

"Get back on the helicopter and go," AJ said, stepping forward again. She'd protected Amelia from Joel. She'd stepped out of line in college and in her job, too. She had to in order to get the interviews she wanted, or stand up to coaches who'd pushed the team too hard.

She was tired of being pushed around.

"All of you," she added. "We're not interested in my mother's money. By the way, her name is Diane Proctor, not Sasha Summers." She scoffed at the ridiculous name.

In her mind's eye, she watched their Christmas miracles disappear into a white horizon. Matt's golf course would simply find another way to get cleaned up and reopened. Kelli could find another way to get a new place to live.

"AvaJane," her mother said in a placating voice that grated against AJ's nerves. "Don't be like this. These people need help, and they're not going to turn it away because you don't like me."

"I don't *like* you?" AJ said, her voice full of incredulity. She started to laugh, aware of how manic it sounded. "My name is not AvaJane, Diane. It's AJ. You'd know that if you hadn't abandoned me and my two siblings when we were children." She turned back to Diane's co-workers. "Did she tell you this story? That she walked out on us one day, and she has literally never once looked back?"

She glared at her mother, feeling wild and out of control. "Seems like she went off and found herself someone else to use. A rich man, I suppose. She is a horrible, terrible person, and no, I don't like her. But that's not even a strong enough word."

She folded her arms. "I hate her."

"AvaJane," her mother started.

"It's *AJ*," AJ barked. "I don't have to stand here and listen to a single thing you say." She turned and started to march away, expecting everyone to follow her. Only one set of footsteps did, and she wasn't surprised when Matt caught up to her.

"I came to see if we could patch things up," Diane called after her, and AJ spun back to her.

"Patch things up?" she said, practically running back toward her mother. "Patch things up?" She came within feet of her mom, who now wore a slightly scared expression. "You patch things up with a friend you miscommunicated with about lunch. Or a boyfriend you didn't text back the way you should have."

Her chest heaved, but her mind suddenly cleared. "You *left* me, Diane. You abandoned me and walked away from your whole life, because you didn't want your children, husband, or life anymore. Who does that?"

She shook her head and let her gaze slide down her mother's tight, trim body. She'd probably had plenty of surgery to look the way she did, because AJ knew Botox when she saw it. Her mother's face barely moved, for crying out loud.

"You're an awful person. The worst type there is. Paying to drain a golf course isn't going to change that."

"I was hoping we could talk," Diane said.

"You're delusional," AJ shot back.

"There's no chance of forgiveness?"

"How does one erase the past thirty-five years and call it okay?" AJ shook her head. "You're delusional *and* stupid."

She didn't have anything else to say, which surprised her. She'd thought a lot about what she might say or do if she ever came in contact with her mother again, but now that she was faced with the very woman that had caused her the most damage in her life, she had nothing to say.

She scanned her mother again, all the way down to her expensive heels, turned, and walked away.

Hours later, she'd cried more than she had in the few days after she'd learned she was pregnant. Matt had speculated that her mother had found out somehow, and that was why she wanted to make amends now.

AJ didn't much care why. She wasn't going to sit down to lunch with her mother and "patch things up."

As she curled into the couch and looked out Matt's front window, a fresh wave of emotion rolled through her. She didn't want to face the past. She wanted to leave it lying where it was, so she could step forward into a new future as a wife to a wonderful man and mother to a baby she'd always dreamt of having.

At the same time, terror's tight grip on her heart kept whispering that she'd never be a good mother, because she'd had a mother who couldn't stick around long enough to teach her how to love a child.

Tears streamed down her face again, because no one had followed her and Matt. She'd left them all standing at the pavilion, and even when the RideShare car had come to take them to Matt's parents' house, they'd all still been there, talking to the four people who'd come to rescue them.

AJ drifted in and out of consciousness as she dozed. Matt had gone to the golf course with his father, leaving AJ alone in his house. It hadn't suffered too much damage. The water line came up three feet on the house, but the front door sat up seven steps, and none of the salty ocean water had entered his home.

Therefore, everything was dry and habitable, and AJ wiped her face as she experienced a wave of gratitude for that.

She'd been going back and forth in her decisions for the past couple of hours, and once again, she thought she needed to get out to Pearl Island.

Now, a voice boomed in her mind, and AJ stood up. Her face felt like someone had packed mud on it and let it dry, and as she moved, her skin cracked.

She didn't take time to pack. The ferry system was operating on reduced hours, and if she wanted to be on Pearl that evening, she needed to go now. Luckily, a Ride-Share car sat right around the corner, and she made it on the last ferry from Diamond to Pearl.

During the ride, she texted Matt. *I had to go see my sister. I'm fine, and I'll let you know when I'll be back.*

It wouldn't be that night, and AJ realized she'd left the house without a change of clothing, a toothbrush, or a plan of any kind.

Her nerves buzzed, and she felt sick to her stomach again. She'd normally stand when she rode the ferry, enjoying the crisp sea breeze in her face. Today, though, she sat indoors, the weather and darkness too much for AJ to endure.

She had to wait for a ride on Pearl, and she had to look up her sister's address to give it to the driver.

Soon enough, she stood on the front porch of her sister's house, her fist raised to knock. She'd started her trip to the cove with a scenario so much like this one, and AJ dug down deep to find the well of courage she needed to rap on the door.

Knock, knock, knock, knock.

"Just a second!" someone yelled from inside, and AJ's chest vibrated as she took a breath.

A few seconds later—or maybe a minute, AJ wasn't sure of time anymore—the door opened. A girl no older than seven or eight stood there, and AJ saw the Proctor genes plainly in her face.

She had no idea what to say to her niece, as her emotions hung on a thread already.

"Who is it?" Amy called, and AJ broke into a sob.

The little girl scampered away, closing the door in AJ's face.

She told herself to get it together. She couldn't break down and act like a lunatic on someone's front porch.

"...did she say?" Amy asked as she opened the door again. "She might need help." She met AJ's eyes, and Amy stilled. "Oh." She looked down to AJ's feet and back to her face.

"I do need help," AJ said, glad her voice had worked. "Mom's in the cove, and I didn't know where else to go."

Amy's eyes widened, and she stepped out onto the porch. "Mom's back in the cove? Where?" She actually seemed eager to go see her.

"Somewhere on Diamond," AJ said as a gust of wind

kicked up. Combined with the winter darkness, it made it far too cold to stand around on the porch talking.

"Did you see her? What did she say?"

"She showed up to save me and my friends from all the damage the tsunami did."

Amy gasped and covered her mouth. "You're kidding."

"I wish." AJ shivered, and she held her purse tight against her chest.

"Come in," Amy said, stepping back. "Darcy, go heat some water for coffee."

"No coffee," AJ said. "It gives me heartburn."

Amy cocked her head, her expression troubled. "You love coffee."

"I know," AJ said. "I do. It's just...the baby doesn't like it." She put one hand on her stomach, and Amy's eyes bulged out of her head.

"You're pregnant?"

AJ nodded, more tears threatening to flow down her face. She stepped inside the house, noticing how perfectly warm and quaint it was. "What are we going to do about Mom?"

"Come tell me everything," Amy said. "Mary, we need hot chocolate."

"Can I have some?" another little girl asked. "The kind with the marshmallows?"

"Yes," Amy said, though AJ got the distinct impression she would've normally said no. She glanced at Alice as they walked through the living room and into the kitchen.

"Donovan's down at the restaurant, but I can call him to come home."

"You do what you want," AJ said.

"Girls, you remember your Aunt AJ, don't you?" Amy nodded to the older girl who'd answered the door. "Darcy will get you a mug. Mary, ask her what kind of hot chocolate she wants."

Amy was so good at giving information without seeming like she was, and AJ loved her powerfully in that moment. As her girls did what she asked, AJ stepped over to her and grabbed her in a hug.

"I miss you," she said, letting her tears flow. "I'm so sorry I've disappeared too."

Amy held her tight, the two of them seemingly unwilling to be the first to let go.

"I'm a mess," AJ continued. "I'm not married and pregnant with Matt Hymas's baby. His golf course is mostly underwater, and our mother pretended to be someone else so she could come here and 'rescue me.'"

AJ hadn't even realized she felt that way until she vocalized it. She'd often felt like she needed to be rescued, but she certainly didn't want that help to come in the form of the person who'd held her underwater for so long.

She stepped away from Amy, noting the fear in her younger sister's eyes. AJ collapsed at the kitchen table and let her niece put a mug in front of her. "Thank you, Darcy." She hugged the little girl and let Mary show her the flavors of hot chocolate they had.

With hot water in her mug, and the marshmallow mint powder getting stirred in, Amy said, "Start at the beginning with Mom." She glanced down to AJ's stomach. "We'll get to Matt Hymas." She grinned and lifted her mug to her lips.

AJ felt a flicker of joy when she thought of Matt, but he was quickly dampened with images of her mother in those fancy clothes, her hair stunningly perfect, and her almost disdainful voice making the reason why she and AJ didn't have a relationship *AJ's* fault.

"I used to think I wanted Mom to come back," AJ said. "Standing in front of her, though, and...I don't know." She sighed. "Do you think there are times when we just can't forgive each other?"

Amy finished swallowing and set her mug on the table. "Honestly, AJ?"

"Yes," AJ whispered. "Honestly, Amy. Tell me honestly."

"Yes," she said. "Sometimes our own self-preservation has to come before forgiving someone who hurt us so badly that we'd be damaged again by doing so." She reached over and put her hand over AJ's. It was so comforting, and AJ disliked herself for not coming to visit more often.

AJ nodded and smiled at her sister. "I'm sorry I'm such a mess."

"I know who you are, AJ," Amy said, withdrawing her hand. "You do the best you can, and I've always known and appreciated that." She stood. "Now, I do have a pizza noodle casserole in the oven, and you haven't even started the story about Mom yet."

AJ almost didn't want to tell it. At the same time, there was no safer place than her sister—someone else her mother had left behind and had likely never thought about again. That thought alone was enough to get her to open her mouth and start the story about the phone call Alice had gotten just yesterday.

CHAPTER TWENTY-THREE

Robin stood in her office and looked at the neat piles on her desk. Their house sat on a slope, she'd learned, because only the back of their property had suffered any damage at all.

The back yard still had water in it, and while their neighbors had started to pump the standing water out of their yards, Duke and Robin hadn't done anything yet. There wasn't anywhere for the water to go anyway.

They didn't have beachfront property, and all they'd do is pump the water from their yard into someone else's, or onto the street. It wasn't hurting anything at the moment anyway.

The back patio had remnant stains of standing water, but it was gone now. Duke had set up the fans and blown out the moisture in the kitchen and dining room, and only the vinyl near the sliding glass door had peeled up at all.

Her husband would fix it, and just as soon as they replaced the carpet in the living room, they'd be back to living normally.

Robin's chest pinched, because if Duke didn't get up in the morning and drive the girls to school, then head to the docks and *The Lady Hawk*, that would not be life as normal.

She had no idea what he'd do if he didn't fish, and she lifted her hand to her mouth to chew on her thumbnail. She normally wasn't a nail-biter, but life had thrown a few curveballs this year.

Robin turned to the Christmas tree she'd set up in front of the bay window in her office. They'd planned to spend the holidays at home, after their brief time at The Cliffside Inn, and Robin had been wrapping presents and putting them under the tree all month.

The cheery red, green, white, and blue packages didn't have to think about the right course of action. In a few days' time, the paper would curl into ribbons of smoke as Duke fed it to their fireplace on the wall opposite from where Robin stood.

Darkness had started to fall, and Robin and Duke had opted to come back to the house here on Diamond rather than returning to the inn. Mandie and Jamie said they'd be fine, and Eloise's mother was there. Alice was going back tonight too, and Robin had asked her to check on the girls.

Robin sighed as she moved over to the desk and sat down. She couldn't recall ever being this mentally tired.

When she'd been pregnant with Jamie, she'd hardly been able to sleep for the last month before she'd come. She'd been so tired then too, but in a different way.

"I hate not knowing what to do." Robin Grover knew what to do in almost all situations. Her personal convictions usually illuminated a clear path, and all she had to do was employ her bravery to take the first step.

She opened the folder for the wedding in just a few days, and she moved the catering post-it from the left side to the right. She pulled off the one labeled *band* and threw it away. The bride and groom had taken care of that and Robin didn't need to follow-up with it.

She moved a couple more notes, including the ones for the flowers and the e-invites, and surveyed the two that were left.

She needed to get down to the venue and see for herself what she'd be dealing with. Judy, the event coordinator for the beach-side wedding hall, had sent pictures, but Robin suspected things changed on an hourly basis.

While she had the venue booked and confirmed after the tsunami, she didn't move it to the right side of the folder. The last post-in never got moved from the to-do side to the done one until the morning of the event.

Décor. Robin always had a separate list for décor as well, and she checked it to make sure she had everything waiting in the bins near the entrance of the office.

She got up to go through them again, because it would

give her hands and mind something to do, when Duke appeared in the doorway.

"What are you thinking?" he asked, leaning against the doorway and folding his arms.

Robin drank in his dark features that had always called to her female side. He'd started to get some silver among the brown and black, and she liked that a whole lot too.

"I don't know," she said. "It's Diane Proctor." Those words didn't mean the same thing to him as they did Robin, and she wasn't sure how to explain.

Aaron and Eloise had left the pavilion without listening to the pitch. After AJ and Matt had gone, Eloise had said everyone should do what they thought best, but that she didn't want any part of Diane Proctor's money, and that she believed taking it would put a wedge between her and AJ she didn't want.

Robin didn't want that either. She simply hadn't been able to walk away. Alice and Kristen had stayed as well. Laurel and Paul had left, as they didn't have a nomination in play anyway. Robin suspected they'd come as a support to Aaron and to offer a second opinion after the pitch.

Will Bridge had stayed, never more than a few feet from Alice. Kelli had stuck close to Alice as well, and Robin had never felt more isolated from her friends. She was used to being the center; the one who brought them all together; the one who they asked for advice.

"I feel like maybe I'm not thinking clearly because I

want the boat so badly," she said. "I feel like Eloise is right. If we accept the help, there will always be this invisible wedge between me and everyone else."

Duke nodded, his jaw set. His eyes were dark and harbored some anger, but also acceptance. "I know how important your friends are to you."

"But how important *should* they be?" she asked, desperate for him to tell her what to do. The decision here was hers; they both knew it. He wanted to accept the money and get a new boat. Robin wanted that too.

She simply thought there was a price to receive it, and she wasn't sure if she could pay it.

"No matter how I look at it, we end up in debt," she said. "One is monetary and our own. We go get a loan for a new boat. We pay it off. The other is a debt all the same—to Diane Proctor. One I have no doubt she'll call on us to repay at some point in the future when it suits her needs."

Robin had listened to the pitch, and everything sounded far too good to be real and true.

A new fishing boat, free and clear. Paperwork to be signed, of course. Alice had taken hers and said she'd go over all of it and let everyone know what they were really signing.

"Heard from Alice?" Duke asked as if the question had been summoned by Robin's thoughts.

She shook her head and bent to open the box she needed to go through. "I don't want to decide myself."

"What kind of debt could Diane Proctor call in?"

"That's just it," Robin said. "Who knows?" She pulled out a box of mini fish bowls. She'd fill them with sand when she arrived at the venue and put flowers in them for the décor on the altar.

"She's not a nice person, Duke. She left AJ and her siblings without a word. She hasn't called, texted, sent cards, nothing in thirty-five years." Robin couldn't imagine what kind of person could do that, let alone a mother.

The woman she'd seen that afternoon barely looked a week older than AJ herself, and Robin supposed she'd needed something more fulfilling than motherhood in her life.

Robin didn't understand that on a fundamental level. Being Mandie and Jamie's mother was the single most fulfilling thing she did with her day. She'd organized and planned over a hundred weddings. They didn't matter to her nearly as much as making sure her daughters knew they were loved, that they had dinner, that they had someone to talk to after school if they needed it.

"I'll do what you want," Duke said.

"I know that," Robin said. "But you're putting a ton of pressure on me, Duke." She tossed him a disgruntled look, though she didn't want to fight with him. It wasn't his fault; this situation was impossible.

"I know what you want me to do. I know what Eloise and Alice and AJ want me to do. I feel like no matter what I decide, I'm going to have someone upset with me."

She just needed to decide which was the lesser of the

two evils. Duke would forgive her eventually. Would her friends?

Then there was the question of whether her friendships were so important that she'd choose them over her own husband's needs. Her own family's needs. Even over herself.

And added to that was the complication that the money would be coming directly from AJ's mother. Robin felt certain that she'd be climbing straight into bed with the devil if she did that, and not only would she lose AJ, she'd lose her soul too.

She shook her head when Duke remained silent. "I think we need to explore every avenue to replace your boat," she said quietly, her hands stilling after she set the fish bowls on her desk. "Not take the first one that comes along, because it seems easy."

"It seems *too* easy," Duke said.

"Yes," Robin agreed, turning to step into his arms. He uncrossed his arms easily, though he didn't smile. He didn't kiss her neck the way he usually did. He just held her against his chest, and they breathed in and out.

"Can we get a loan?" he asked in a whisper.

"We'll have to see," Robin said. "I think there are probably going to be plenty of banks and credit unions helping people in the cove right now."

Duke did dip his head and sweep his lips along her ear. "So what do you want to do?"

She knew every day he couldn't go out on the water was a day of lost income.

"Am I selfish if I ask for more time?"

"Let's call Margie in the morning," he said. "Am I selfish if I ask you to come to bed with me right now?" He pressed his mouth to her neck. "The girls are gone, and it's never just us."

Robin leaned her head back as an answer, and Duke took what he wanted from the delicate skin there. He pressed into her, and said, "Are we still going back to Sanctuary in the morning?"

"I don't know," Robin whispered. After the meeting in the pavilion had ended, the group had disbanded without hardly a word to one another.

They were supposed to meet at the inn for breakfast—it was Eloise's contribution to their holiday activities. Robin pulled her phone from her pocket as Duke's mouth dropped even lower. "Eloise hasn't texted," she said, pulling in a breath as his lips found her collarbone.

No one had texted.

"Mm," Duke said, his hands sliding up under her shirt.

"I'll find out after," Robin said, lacing her fingers through his hair and adding, "I love you, Duke."

"Love you too, baby," he said, claiming her mouth now. Robin managed to focus on her husband and her relationship with him for a while.

She lay in his arms and listened to the strong beat of his heart, the steady rise and fall of his chest so comforting to her. After a long time, she rolled over and picked up her phone.

No one had texted yet, and Robin hesitated to be the first. Maybe it was time for someone else to play the role of the mother hen, the one who initiated the get-togethers, the Wednesday lunches, the activities.

So she put her phone down and rolled back to Duke's side.

CHAPTER TWENTY-FOUR

Kelli smoothed back her son's hair and smiled at her mother as she put a bowl of chicken noodle soup in front of Parker. "There you go, sweetie," she said, bending over to place a kiss on the boy's head. "You sure you don't want anything, Kel?"

Her mother met her eyes with concern in hers, and Kelli shook her head.

Devon, her mother's boyfriend, sat on the couch in the nearby living room, and Kelli sure did like him. She wondered when they'd get married, but now didn't feel like the time to ask.

"You have nothing?" her mom asked.

Kelli shook her head. "We have a few sets of clothes," she said. "The cottage is soaked from floor to ceiling, and I was renting the furniture anyway."

The sense of helplessness and defeat hung around

Kelli's neck like a noose. She hadn't told her mother about the phone call and offer to get her into another house without any cost to her.

Kelli already knew she wouldn't be taking the offer. She'd heard AJ's voice and seen her face when she'd spoken to her mother, and Kelli would rather forfeit her own life than hurt AJ.

She'd stayed for the meeting, because she hadn't had the courage to leave alone, and everyone else had seemed like they were staying.

"You didn't have much damage," Kelli said, taking a seat at the table while Parker ate.

Her mother bustled around the kitchen. "I lost a few trees in the back yard," she said. "Honestly, I think they took the brunt of the waves. I also upgraded the house for severe storms a couple of years ago." She joined Kelli and Parker at the table, a couple of plates of pie with her, despite Kelli's denial of it already.

"Mr. Highway next door didn't do it when the guy came through town, and his place is in a lot worse shape than mine." She lifted her coffee mug to her lips and took a sip.

Kelli gave her mom a smile and actually picked up a fork. She'd just taken a bite of the blueberry pie her mom bought from another neighbor down the street when her mom said, "You can stay here if you'd like, Kelli. You're always welcome."

"Thanks, Mom," she said. "I think just for tonight.

Tomorrow, I might want to leave Parker so I can figure out somewhere for us to live."

She didn't say so, but she really wanted to find a place in a single day so she and Parker would have somewhere for Christmas Eve.

The boy had turned nine recently, but he still believed in Santa Claus. Kelli thought of the gifts that had washed away with the waves that had come through the cove, and her throat tightened.

She wouldn't have time to replace them anyway, and perhaps she could just put her head down and cry.

No, she told herself. She wasn't going to let life steamroll her. She thought of the woman who'd broken a window and driven a nine-passenger van all over Sanctuary Island. She needed her to make an appearance and find an apartment and a few gifts.

"Of course," her mom said. "I have to work in the morning, but Devon can take him."

Their eyes met, and Kelli hesitated. She liked Devon, and Parker did too. But she'd never left her son with someone like him before.

She found herself nodding, because she was in a unique situation, and that meant she had to do things outside her sphere of normal. "I'll be gone all day, I'm sure," she said. "I have to find a place to live."

Her thoughts went straight to the house on Seabreeze Shore, and she knew she could live there.

For some reason, she'd been thinking of it as a last

resort. The house wasn't ready to be lived in yet, but it had weathered the storm well too.

The house sat up on the cliffs, and there had definitely been water up in the yard. The patio had shown evidence of moss, but the house itself was undamaged and dry.

Perhaps tomorrow, she should focus on finding a few gifts for Parker, and they could have their own Christmas in the house where she'd grown up.

Kelli immediately balked at that idea, and she wasn't sure why. It was time to move forward. Move on. She couldn't keep holding onto a piece of the past without using it. Her hand was simply growing sore, and she wasn't doing anything constructive.

"Let's call my friend Dixie," Kelli's mother said. "She knows everything about the real estate market in the cove." She actually picked up her phone to make the call. She looked at Kelli with her light eyes, and Kelli looked into her mom's gaze. So much of herself was found there, and Kelli smiled.

"Thanks, Mom." She leaned over and hugged her mom. "Call her. I need a rental, though. I can't afford to buy right now."

"Dixie always thinks people should buy," her mom said. "Fair warning."

Kelli was getting better and better about putting her foot down, and she'd just tell Dixie Dutton that she wasn't going to buy. Plain and simple.

"Dixie," her mom said. "It's Paula Watkins. My

daughter lost her rental home in the tsunami. What have you got with two bedrooms, decently furnished, for a good price?"

Dixie obviously started talking, and Kelli's mother gestured for her to get something to write with. "Oh, is that right?"

She pulled the phone from her ear and tapped the speaker button. Dixie's voice came through the line mid-sentence.

"...show her in the morning if she's willing to commute."

Kelli nodded, because she'd literally spent her life commuting from the outer islands to Diamond. She and Parker made the journey each morning, though the ride from Sanctuary was easy at only seventeen or eighteen minutes.

"Yes," Kelli said, finding her voice. "I'm willing to commute, ma'am."

"Kelli," Dixie said, her voice filled with warmth and smiles. "It's good to hear from you."

"I missed most of what you said," she said. "Can you say it again?"

"Sure," Dixie said. "I told your mother I've got a client who called this morning to say they're going back to the mainland tomorrow quite last-minute. His mother apparently fell, and he's going to spend some time with her. A few months at least, he said." Dixie spoke so fast, and Kelli didn't even try to type any notes into her phone.

"He works from home, so he's here sometimes and in Maryland sometimes. His place is nice, and he asked me to sublet the apartment if I could. It's fully furnished, and he'll have a cleaning service go through it tomorrow, so it likely won't be ready until the day after, so just in time for Christmas."

Kelli pressed her eyes closed, feeling the stars line up just for her.

"How much?" Kelli asked, her voice barely making it out of her mouth.

"He's quite reasonable," Dixie said. "I haven't even listed it yet, because well, there's so much going on right now."

"If I can afford it, I'll take it," Kelli said. "You won't need to list it."

"It's nine-fifty, usually," Dixie said. "But like I said, David isn't particularly fussy about it. He owns it, so he's not trying to pay a mortgage or anything. Last time, it took me a few months to even rent it at that price. What can you afford? I'll just tell him that I had to list it for lower to get a renter in quickly."

Kelli had been paying eight hundred for the beach bungalow, and it had a prime location and a short commute. "What island is it on?" she asked. "How far is the commute to Diamond?"

"It's on Bell," Dixie said. "The direct ferry to Diamond takes thirty minutes. The house is a twin home, and the neighbor next-door is quiet as a mouse. It's a five-minute walk to the ferry too, so you don't need a car, and you won't have RideShare fares."

"I can afford eight hundred," Kelli said, opening her eyes and looking at her mother. She wore apprehension in her gaze, but she nodded. "I'm available in the morning to see it."

"Perfect," Dixie said. "Give me a second..." Silence poured through the line, and Kelli's heart started pounding like a drum. "About nine?" Dixie asked. "I can take you by there before I catch the ferry to Pearl for another showing at ten."

"Oh, do you live on Bell?"

"Yes," Dixie said. "It's the best island in the cove." She wore plenty of pride in her voice now. "See you at nine."

"Yes," Kelli said, and she tapped the red phone icon to end the call. She exhaled, a smile slowly spreading across her whole face. "Mom, I can't even believe that just happened." She picked up her fork again and took a much bigger bite of pie. "I'll take Parker with me to look at the house, but then I'll need to go take care of a few things on Sanctuary. Can Devon still take him?"

"I can," Devon said, coming into the kitchen. "We can go mini-golfing."

"It's winter, dear," Kelli's mother said with a smile at her boyfriend as he leaned down and touched his lips to her forehead. "Kelli has hopefully found a place to live, but she and Parker are going to be here tonight."

"Sounds good." He gave Kelli a kind smile, and she

returned it. She hoped that when she found another man to love that he would be a lot like Devon—kind, handsome, and devoted to making sure she was blissfully happy.

Kelli ate a whole piece of pie before she announced she was going to go take a bath and get ready for bed.

In the bathroom, with the door closed and locked, she texted AJ. *Are you okay? Where are you?*

I'm staying with Amy for a bit, AJ said. *You?*

I'm at my mother's. Sheer gratitude came over Kelli that she could go to her mother when she needed her. *Glad you went to see Amy.*

AJ didn't answer, and Kelli suspected she didn't know how to explain her aversion to visiting Bell Island whenever she came to the cove.

Kelli didn't normally push anyone, least of all AJ. This time, she sent another text. *Are you going to see your dad?*

I am, AJ said. *It's time, and I don't know what I have to hide anymore.*

Kelli nodded to herself, sitting right there in her mother's house, on the closed toilet. "I'm not going to take the money from White Sands Worldwide," Kelli said out loud to herself as she typed out the message. She inhaled for a long few seconds as the message spun and sent.

Her phone rang, and AJ's name sat there. "Hey," Kelli said.

"You stayed, though, right?" AJ asked.

Kelli wasn't sure if she was upset or not. "Yes," Kelli admitted. "Eloise and Aaron left as well. Everyone else stayed." She held her breath, wondering how AJ would take that news.

"Everyone has to do what they want," she finally said.

"I'm not taking the money," Kelli said. "I think I've found a new place to live already, and I wouldn't use your mother no matter what. I know what you've been through because of her."

"So does everyone else," AJ said quietly.

Kelli didn't want to disagree with her, so she said nothing. The truth was probably somewhere in the middle of what AJ thought was true. Kelli knew a lot of what AJ had endured as a teen, because they'd ridden the ferry together to school each day. Alice, Eloise, and Robin didn't. They only knew what AJ said to them, and for the last year or so before they'd left the cove for college, AJ had distanced herself from everyone, even Kelli a little bit.

"It's on Bell," Kelli said. "The apartment. I'm meeting the realtor at nine in the morning. If you'd like, I'll go to your dad's with you afterward."

"Would you?" AJ asked. "You're not going to the inn for breakfast?"

"Are we still doing that?" Kelli asked.

"We're not?"

"You're going to go?" Kelli was aware they were both asking questions and not answering any.

"I wasn't planning to go," AJ said. "I...wish I was a forgiving person, Kel, but I'm not. I haven't forgiven my mother for leaving, and I'm not sure I'd be able to look

Robin or Kristen in the face, knowing they chose her over me."

Kelli wanted to say it wasn't so black and white. Of course Robin wouldn't be choosing AJ's mother over AJ, but it was good to know how AJ viewed the situation.

"No one said what they'd do," Kelli said. "It was weird, actually. You left, and Elise chastised all of us, and she and Aaron left too. Paul and Laurel went with them, and then your mom—" She cut off, because maybe AJ didn't want to know. Kelli cleared her throat. "We got the information, and then we all just sort of...left without saying anything to anyone."

AJ didn't say anything, and Kelli cleared her throat again. "I'm glad you're okay."

"I'm glad you are," AJ said. They said their good-byes, and Kelli stared at her phone until it darkened.

Someone needed to ask about breakfast in the morning, but Kelli didn't know what to say. "You should at least tell El you can't come," she said. She started typing, deciding to keep the message short and sweet.

CHAPTER TWENTY-FIVE

Laurel rode in the passenger seat of Paul's police car, her heart starting to pound as he made one last turn onto her lane. She'd seen so much damage already. Power poles down, and trampolines in a tangled mess of metal legs. There had been water way up on the beaches just down from Paul's house, and he had standing water in his front yard.

"This doesn't look bad," Julie, his sister, said from the back seat. "Your house is on a higher street, Laurel."

"Mm." Laurel didn't quite know what to say. Julie was a couple of years younger than Paul, and that made her a couple of years older than Laurel. She did mother Paul a little bit, as their mother had died several years ago. Julie was married with three kids, and honestly, she reminded Laurel a lot of Robin. Robin mixed with Alice, which made her smile, because it felt like Robin and Alice hardly got along.

They were both strong women though, and Laurel liked them each in different ways.

"Screen door is off," Paul said as he pulled up to Laurel's house. She normally loved coming home to her pale yellow rambler, the bright blue shutters and front door such a contrast to the mellower paint on the house.

She'd done all the painting herself, during one of her reinvention periods. She'd learned how to write screenplays once upon a time too, and she'd grown all of her own herbs for a year. Laurel couldn't stand to sit still for very long, and she liked to keep her mind and hands busy with new things.

She'd never been cross-country skiing, and it was definitely on her bucket list. If she couldn't leave the house every single day, she'd probably go mad by dinnertime.

She got out of the cruiser and looked toward the house. The screen door was bent sideways on the hinges, and as Paul came around the car, he said, "I can fix it, Laurel."

"Thank you," she said, reaching for his hand and feeling more centered and like herself as his fingers wrapped around hers. "It doesn't look like the water went too high." That was one good thing about water—it left marks.

It wasn't hard to see where it had gotten to, either, and the line on her house sat just below her front windows. It had definitely crested the bottom of the front door, and Laurel wondered if it had seeped inside.

If so, she'd have wet carpet and linoleum, and the feet of her furniture would likely be soggy too. She took the first step up the sidewalk, noting that her rose bushes looked much worse than they had when she'd gone to work on Saturday morning. They likely wouldn't come back in the spring, and Laurel loved roses so much, she'd go get new ones to plant.

The rose bushes represented a time of new growth for her. They were one of the first plants she'd put in the yard of this new house—the first she'd bought on her own, and the first place she'd lived after she'd finally ended everything with her abusive ex-husband.

She glanced at Paul, as she hadn't quite told him about Owen yet. The first and only time she'd mentioned him, she'd called him a boyfriend. In her mind, that was all Owen had ever been, but she knew the state of Massachusetts would show something different.

Owen had forced her to marry him, and she'd had to pay to file for the divorce, show up in court, and deal with all of it. At least Owen hadn't come to contest anything. She'd assumed he'd found someone else to terrorize, and she'd seriously considered pressing charges against him for something, simply to protect anyone else he might meet in the future.

She'd met with Deputy Chief Charles, and they'd gone over all of Laurel's complaints. Owen hadn't kept her confined to their home. He had forced himself on her sexually, but they were married, and the Deputy Chief had said it would be a very hard case to prove, and even harder to win. In the end, she'd done nothing, and Owen had left the cove. Laurel had started the healing process.

It had been a long four years, and she'd lovingly clipped roses every spring and all summer as a reminder that she could bloom again, year after year, tragedy after tragedy.

She climbed the steps first and keyed in the code to unlock the door. The satisfying whir of the deadbolt and resulting click met her ears, and she turned the knob. "At least I don't have pets," she said, looking over her shoulder to Paul.

She wanted to share more of her life with him. He'd been nothing but kind and patient with her. She'd run to him after Eloise had found her and Aaron in the Chief's car together, but that situation had been explained and handled.

Laurel hadn't been intimate with Paul yet, and he hadn't brought it up either. The very idea still had her stomach in knots, though she enjoyed kissing Paul and cuddling with Paul and being with Paul.

The scent of something salty and stale met her nose, and Laurel turned away. "It's wet," she said. Not only that, but a distinct breeze blew through the house now that the front door stood open, and that meant there was something ajar or broken at the back of the house.

"I guess I have shoes on," she said, taking the first step into the house. Paul followed, with his sister right behind him. She flipped a light switch, and the light came on. The bulb popped in the next moment, and Laurel flinched away from the cracking sound and the resulting darkness while Julie yelped.

They'd left the pavilion an hour ago, and darkness was definitely starting to settle over the island. They'd first gone to Paul's, where his sister had been staying with him for the holidays. Julie and Paul were close, and she'd been putting her husband and kids to work around Paul's house to get it back to a fully functioning dwelling.

They'd gone there first, and sure enough, Julie and her family had been working hard. Paul's house had looked great, and Laurel supposed she could stay with him.

Her sister had texted to say her house had some damage, and she'd be staying with her boyfriend. Laurel wondered if they'd have an extra bed for her too.

She walked behind the couch positioned perpendicular to the front door, her goal the next light switch on the next corner. This time, the bulbs stayed on, flooding the kitchen, dining room, and living room with warm, yellow light.

"The window above the sink is broken," she said, a chill moving down her arms despite the jacket she wore. Paul stepped right behind her, his eyes sweeping everything too.

Laurel wanted nothing more than a hot shower, some

fresh clothes, and a cup of hot broth. She and Paul had been wearing the same clothes for days, and while it worked for him because he was tall, silver, and sexy, she desperately needed some time to freshen up.

"I don't think you're staying here tonight, Laurel," he said quietly.

"I'll text Lyle and tell him to get another bed ready," Julie said. She turned around and retraced her steps. "It's freezing in here. I'm going to go wait in the car." She closed the front door behind her, and neither Paul nor Laurel moved.

"I want to make coffee in my own pot," she said. Laurel wasn't much of a traveler, and she liked being home more than anywhere else. "I want to shower in my own bathroom, with my own soaps and oils."

"I know, sweetie." Paul put his arm around her waist, and Laurel leaned into his strength. "I think it's too late for the ferry back to Sanctuary, though I'm sure Eloise would let you stay there for a while."

Laurel shook her head. The past few days with Eloise Hall had been really good for Laurel, as all of the awkwardness between them had dissipated quickly as they'd banded together to help others. "Eloise said the inn is full starting on Christmas Eve. I can't ask her to give up a room someone has paid for."

"There's room at my place," he said as if he knew Laurel was thinking about calling for a hotel. The problem was, they were full too, as many people around the cove were dealing with the exact same situation Laurel now found herself in.

"There's really not," she said. "Besides, you and Julie have family traditions for Christmas, and I don't know." She finally tore her eyes from the broken window and the flapping curtains to face Paul.

He looked at her with those bright brown eyes, his beard grown out and oh-so-sexy. "I feel like I'm crashing your family Christmas."

"Laurel." He didn't say anything else, but his eyes searched hers for several long moments.

"Paul," she said, deciding she might as well lay everything on the line. "Remember what I told you about my ex-boyfriend?"

"You've not said much, actually."

She nodded, a lump forming in her chest that made it hard to speak now too. "He wasn't my boyfriend. He... brought a preacher to the house and forced me to marry him. Technically, he was my husband."

Paul's eyes widened, and they searched more earnestly. "Laurel, I have no idea what to say."

"I don't have any kids," she said. "I am not whole in a lot of ways, Paul. That's why I can't...I haven't...I want to be with you. But I understand if you'd prefer to be with someone who's ready to move a little faster than I currently can."

"No," he said, shaking his head. "I'm not looking for someone to sleep with. I mean." He ducked his head. "Of course I want to sleep with you. I'm a man, after all, and you're an incredibly beautiful, talented, smart woman." He was whispering by the end of the sentence.

Laurel took his face in both of her hands and lifted his chin so they could look at one another.

"I'm not *just* looking for someone to sleep with," he said. "If I wanted that, Laurel, I'm sure I could find someone."

She was sure he could too, which was why she'd said what she had. "I don't want to slow you down."

"You're not," he said. "Laurel, I know we haven't said many serious things yet, but I like you very much." He smiled and pressed into one of her palms. "I'm enjoying getting to know you, and I want to be with you. Just you."

Laurel smiled up at him, tipped up, and touched her mouth to his. This kiss wasn't anywhere near as passionate as some of their others, but it said much, much more. It was far more intimate, and Laurel enjoyed the way his mouth trembled against hers in such a sweet, vulnerable way.

She didn't get to see Paul like this very often, as he was an alpha-male officer on Chief Sherman's force. He was the Assistant Chief. He'd achieve the rank of Captain soon, if Laurel knew anything about how the Chief worked—and she did.

He pulled away and touched his forehead to hers. "Okay, Laurel?"

"Okay, Paul." She breathed in the musty and musky

scent of him, as they'd both been using perfumes and colognes to cover up their days-old clothing. "I like you a whole lot too, so you know." She pulled away and stuck her hands in her pockets. "Julie's right. We can't stand around in here. I'm going to go get some clothes and I'll meet you back in the car."

Paul nodded. "Are you going to stay with me or find a hotel?"

Laurel tore right down the middle. "I don't want to sleep on an air mattress."

"I have a king-sized bed," Paul said. "Nothing you don't want to do, Laurel. I told you that once, and I meant it."

Laurel's eyes rounded, and she was the one searching his face now. He'd never lied to her, though, and she had no reason to distrust him now either. "Give me five minutes," she said, turning away from him.

She hurried down the hall to her bedroom and pulled a bag from the top of her closet. The bedskirt had definitely been wet, as it showed a salty crustiness that only came from ocean water. The carpet here seemed dry, though, but Laurel knew she'd have to rip it out and replace it.

She didn't have money for any of that, at least not on a house-wide scale. "One step at a time," she muttered to herself, thinking of the last four years of her life. She'd made it through them one step at a time.

She thought of her relationship with Paul. They were

making things work one step at a time. If she stayed in his bed with him that night, that would be a huge step in her mind, and she honestly didn't know if she was ready to take it.

She knew how to pack jeans, sweaters, socks, and shoes. She added several uniform pieces, as she didn't have the next few weeks off of work. She and Connor should be back out on duty tomorrow, in fact. She needed to check the schedule and see what Gina and the Chief had been working on.

Her thoughts went to Chief Sherman and Eloise, and the brave way they'd stood up to their friends. They did what was right, according to what they believed, and Laurel wanted to do the same.

She gathered her personal toiletries, thankful for her own brand of shampoo and conditioner, and started down the hall again. She'd have to call and get someone to come install a new window. She could rip out old carpet and get the subfloor drying herself. Paul could fix the screen door, and she could start to replace the flooring throughout the house.

She could run a load of sheets and towels and anything else necessary through the washing machine, and she could get fans to dry the legs and feet of her couches and chairs.

This tsunami had caused a setback in Laurel's life, but it was not a roadblock she couldn't get around.

She skipped down the steps and practically ran down

the sidewalk toward Paul's cruiser. He waited next to her door, a handsome smile on his face that made her blood run hotter.

"Got everything?" he asked, reaching for her bag.

She handed it to him, and he started toward the trunk. "Yes," she said. "Enough for now, anyway. Paul, I'll...stay with you."

He swung back toward her, surprise etched in every line of his face.

Laurel shook her head as she giggled. "Don't look like that. I've stayed over before."

"In the guest room," he said.

"You held me while I slept."

"Can I do that tonight?" He turned away and lifted the trunk, which had already been opened. "Hold you while you sleep?"

Laurel watched him lift her bag inside his truck and close it. Their eyes met from several feet apart, and she asked, "What will your sister think of us sleeping in the same room?"

"I'll just kindly remind her that I'm forty years old," he said. "And you're a consenting adult, and what we do behind closed doors in my home is entirely up to us."

Laurel grinned at him. "I so want to be there when you say that to her."

He laughed and shook his head. "I thought you liked Julie."

"I do," Laurel said. "I like her a lot. But Paul, come on.

You have to admit she's like your mother, who I do not think would approve of us sharing a bed, even if there's nothing going on but sleeping."

Paul took her into his arms again. "I wish you could've met my mother. I think you'd be surprised. She wasn't as traditional as you might think."

"Then why did Julie tell her husband to set up another bed for me?"

"She probably doesn't want me to get hurt," Paul said. "You're not the only one with a crazy ex in her past."

Laurel looked up at him, shock cascading through her whole body. "You've said nothing."

"Like I said," he said. "We haven't talked about a lot of serious things yet."

"Maybe we should."

"We will," he promised as he reached to open her door for her. She slid into the passenger seat and buckled while Paul went around the vehicle and got behind the wheel. "Jules," he said. "Tell Lyle we don't need another bed. Laurel's going to stay with me."

In the rearview mirror, Laurel watched her facial expression change, and she had a very hard time suppressing her giggle.

"I'm forty years old," Paul said, grinning at Laurel. "It's my house, and what Laurel and I do behind closed and locked doors is none of your business."

Julie opened her mouth and a squeak came out. Paul

started the car as he started to laugh. "There you go, Laurel."

She reached across the console and all the equipment and squeezed Paul's hand. They hadn't reached the end of the block when Julie said, "I just texted Lyle."

"Great," Paul practically bellowed.

"As long as the door is locked, Paul," Julie said next. "You have three nieces and nephews who love to come see you first thing in the morning."

"Oh, it'll be locked," Paul said, grinning at Laurel again. She smiled back, but the moment had lost some of its humor. She watched out the window at the piles of debris alongside the road until it was too dark to see them anymore, her thoughts revolving around her sleeping arrangements that evening.

Her phone chimed, and she released Paul's hand to check it. Kelli had texted the group with, *I have to go see an apartment in the morning at nine, so I won't be able to make the breakfast. I'm sorry, Eloise. I then need to find some quick presents for Parker, as all of ours washed away or got ruined. Anyone up for shopping about eleven?*

No one had responded yet, and the need for Laurel to do so pressed against her heartbeat. She didn't know what to say though, because she'd never planned on attending the breakfast at the inn tomorrow morning. She should be working, and she started tapping to get to the station spreadsheet that would confirm if she was on duty or not.

CHAPTER TWENTY-SIX

Eloise read Kelli's text nearly the moment it came in. She sat at the dinner table with Billie, Grace, and Aaron, the four of them sipping the organic tomato soup she'd warmed and eating crispy, buttery grilled cheese sandwiches.

Eloise hadn't been able to eat much, and she'd said even less. Aaron wasn't particularly chatty that night, and even Grace had stopped talking about her class, the gift exchange, her ice cream, and what she hoped Santa would bring for her in just a couple of days.

"Dad?" Billie asked, looking up from her phone. Aaron and Eloise were so off their games, everyone had a device at the dinner table with them, and Eloise looked away from Kelli's message that said she wouldn't be at the inn for the group breakfast in the morning.

She honestly expected everyone else to drop out too,

and her heart felt like it physically plummeted into her feet.

"There's a holiday party tomorrow," she said. "Kim has these tennis courts at her house, and her dad turns them into an ice skating rink in the winter." She glanced at Eloise. "Could I go? Addie is going to be there, and Kara."

"Who else?"

"Kim's a year older than us." Billie shot a glance at Eloise. "She also has an older brother, and he's invited some friends. I don't know everyone who'll be there."

Aaron looked at Eloise too, and she gave an almost imperceptible shrug of her shoulders. "I thought we were spending the day at the inn tomorrow," he said. "El is hosting the holiday breakfast, and we have the big, concluding dinner in the evening. What time is the party?"

"It's in the afternoon," Billie said as Eloise started shaking her head.

"No?" Aaron asked.

"I don't know about what's happening tomorrow," Eloise said, pure misery in her words. "Kelli just texted to say she can't come in the morning, and...I don't know." She picked up her sandwich and took a bite, but the bread, butter, and cheese didn't taste nearly as good as it usually did.

"I can ride the ferry myself," Billie said. "I'll be back in time for dinner."

"Everyone else will come, though," Aaron said. "Kelli's

in a unique situation, because she needs an entirely new place to live."

Eloise's phone chimed again, and then again, but she didn't have the heart to look at it. If she'd made everyone put their phones in the basket like she normally did so they could enjoy a family dinner together, she wouldn't even know she'd gotten new messages.

"I don't want you riding the ferry alone, Bills," Aaron said while Eloise chewed and swallowed. She'd never experienced a sandwich that tasted so much like sawdust before, and she knew it had everything to do with her mood, and nothing to do with Aaron's cooking.

"I'm old enough to ride the ferry," Billie said. "Lexi does it every single day for school."

"There are monitors on the ferries just for students," Aaron argued back. "School's not in session right now, and there would be no one there to keep an eye on you."

"I don't need anyone to keep an eye on me." Billie looked at Eloise. "Kelli puts Parker on the ferry alone sometimes."

Eloise couldn't argue with that, and she'd learned to simply let Aaron and Billie go back and forth a little bit. She didn't need to be the peacemaker between them, and honestly that felt like an impossible task anyway.

She picked up her phone to see that Alice had texted, but not in the group string. Robin too, also privately just to Eloise.

My children are at the inn, so I'll be there, Alice had said.

If you don't want to have the breakfast, I understand. Perhaps you and I could go out with your mother and the twins.

Duke and I are going to the bank in the morning to explore our options, Robin had said, which caused Eloise's heart to lift and leap in a new way. If Robin didn't take the money from White Sands Worldwide, Eloise couldn't imagine anyone else would.

She'd already made her decision, and her stomach writhed with the way she'd lectured everyone else. That was not something Eloise normally did. She respected the differences in people, and she normally allowed everyone to make their own decisions without giving them her opinion—especially when they hadn't asked for it.

She'd been toying with sending an apology for hours, but once she and Aaron had arrived here, they'd been working to clear away any debris that would threaten the structural integrity of the house, sweep the water out of the garage, and mop up the little bit that had come in through the sliding glass door.

Other than that, Aaron's house hadn't suffered too much damage, and Eloise had thumbed her way through an article in the Cove Chronicles about how the most damage had actually been on Rocky Ridge and Sanctuary Island, due to the rockiness of those islands. They'd had landslides and cliffs cleave off into the ocean due to the impact of the waves. Diamond, Pearl, and Bell had suffered from flooding, but not much else. Boats, of course, were now toothpicks, and Eloise's mind wandered to Robin and Duke once more.

"If it's okay with Eloise," Aaron said, and Eloise looked up from her phone. "If she's having the dinner, we've committed to that, and you'll need to be there. Family comes before friends." He nodded at Eloise, and she looked from him to Billie.

"I already said I'd be back in time for the dinner," Billie said, her bright eyes pleading with Eloise. "And if you're doing the breakfast, I won't miss that either. The party is at two, Eloise."

"It's fine with me," she said, another text vibrating against her fingers. Kristen had sent this one, and it read, *Is everyone canceling, Eloise? Would it be beneficial to have breakfast here at the lighthouse? No one would have to ride a ferry.*

Eloise suspected AJ would, and Kelli definitely would need to ride a ferry. She didn't know how to answer anyone, and she didn't want to have a holiday breakfast that was meant for six with only four.

Three, she thought. *If you're lucky.*

She, Alice, and Kristen would be the only ones there, and Eloise felt things in her life splintering in a way she detested.

Robin didn't normally shy away from hard situations, but she'd been presented with something incredibly difficult, and she'd retreat to her core—Duke—until it was solved. AJ could leave the cove and never return. Eloise had seen her do it before.

Kelli just needed some time to catch her breath, and Eloise decided to answer her first.

I'm glad you found somewhere to potentially live. I hope the apartment is amazing. She sent that message, already thinking of and then typing another one. *Would you come to breakfast if we did it later? We could go shopping together afterward.*

Yes, Kelli sent back. *I just need to find a few things so Christmas isn't completely ruined.*

Eloise navigated to Alice's text next. *Would the twins be willing to bring my mother to the lighthouse for breakfast? Kristen has offered, as most of us are here on Diamond tonight. Thoughts?*

She sent a similar text to Robin about having a later start-time for the breakfast, and her heart pumped extra-hard as that one swirled and then sent.

Aaron got up from the table, and Eloise put her phone down. "Sorry, sweetheart," she said. "I'm sort of managing a crisis."

"I can imagine," he said, dropping a kiss on the top of her head. "We're fine. I'm going to get the tiny one in the bath, and then we can put a movie on."

Eloise nodded, noticing that Billie was not in her spot at the table. Aaron went down the hall with Grace while Eloise waited for her friends to text back.

The twins can bring your mother, sure, Alice said.

Keep me updated. I'm actually at dinner with Will, but I can call you later, if that's easier to coordinate something.

Eloise smiled at the thought of Alice on a date, and she'd seen her proper, sophisticated friend with the scruffy, laid-back ferry owner. *Have fun*, she sent.

Robin hadn't answered, and Eloise quickly sent a message to AJ that said, *I hope you're okay. I'd love it if you'd let me know you're somewhere safe. Aaron and I have room for you here if you need a place. I won't ask you any questions.*

She wanted to invite her to breakfast in the morning, but she had serious doubts AJ would respond to the text as it was, so she left it at that.

Aaron returned to the kitchen and picked up Grace's plate.

"What did I miss with Billie?" Eloise asked, shoving her phone in her back pocket.

"You said she could go to the party," Aaron said. "She ran down the hall to find the perfect outfit for ice skating." The dishes clacked as he put them in the kitchen sink, a sigh extending past the end of the noise. "I worry about her at a party with older boys."

"As you should." Eloise stood up and took her plate mostly full of food into the kitchen. She threw it away and put her plate on top of the others. She slid her hand along Aaron's waist, glad when he lifted his arm over her shoulders. "She's a beautiful girl, and she's articulate, fun, and smart."

"You're not easing my mind," Aaron said dryly.

"Sorry."

"You said once she wouldn't do anything with a boy, but I'm not so sure. She definitely likes boys."

"All seventh-grade girls like boys," Eloise said with a smile. "It's mostly harmless." She turned toward Aaron and tucked herself into his chest.

"Not for boys," Aaron murmured. "They have hormones they don't understand and can't control." He ran his lips along the curve of her ear, and Eloise shivered in his arms. He brought out the fire in her with a simple touch, and she couldn't wait to be his wife.

"Kind of like some men I know," she whispered as he committed fully to kissing her neck.

"Mm," he said with a chuckle. "It's been a while for us."

"It has?" she asked. "It's been two nights, Aaron."

"I like listening to you breathe next to me," he whispered, sliding his lips up the length of her throat. When he got near her mouth, Eloise kissed him fully.

"I like your body," he murmured, his hands wandering down her sides. "I like the way you kiss me, and I like the way you touch me, and I like the way you say my name."

"Wow, Aaron," she said, shivering as his hands slid back up her body and into her hair. "I'm glad I know 'a while' for you is two days, though."

He pulled away as he laughed quietly, and Eloise felt

the loss of his touch and kiss as keenly as anything she'd ever felt.

"Do you think you'll ever tire of me?" Eloise asked, draping her arms around his neck and looking into those dark eyes.

"No," he said as Prince tried to nose his way between the two of them. He pushed the dog away with a smile and the words, "Stop it, Prince. I'm kissing my fiancée, and you'll have to get used to it."

"What if you do?" Eloise asked, feeling very unsure of so very many things. If her friendships, which she'd thought were so strong, could crumble and fall, why couldn't her marriage and relationship with Aaron?

It felt so real and seemed so strong to her, but the doubts still lingered in her mind.

"I'm not going to," Aaron said. "I love every minute we have together. I love talking to you, and when something good happens, you're the first one I want to tell. If something bad happens, you're still the first one I need to tell, because you'll make things okay."

He smiled softly at her and let his eyes drift closed as he leaned his forehead against Eloise's. They breathed in together, and the moment of comfort and safety between them made Eloise fall in love with him all over again.

"Plus, I'd make love to you morning, noon, and night if I could," he whispered.

"I'm tired already," Eloise said with a smile.

He pulled back and grinned at her too, the gesture fading quickly. "You like making love with me, right?"

"Of course," she said. "I just...I'm worried I won't be able to keep up with you. You seem to have an incredible sexual appetite."

"For *you,*" he said. "I have an incredible sexual appetite *for you,* Eloise Hall. I think you're sexy, and smart, and articulate, and now you know why I'm so worried about Billie."

"You should just hope she doesn't ever have a boyfriend who knows how to tell a woman exactly what she needs to hear, kiss her like he's in love with her, and is incredible in bed."

Aaron blinked at her and then laughed again. "I am in love with you, El." He touched his lips to hers in a sweet kiss. "I don't just say things—I mean them." He brought her closer, the strength of his muscled body tight and hard against hers. "I want to take you to bed right now."

"You'll have to wait," she whispered, though she did move her fingers up the side of his face and into his hair.

He pulled in a breath. "See?" he said, his voice all air. "I like the way you touch me." He leaned into her touch and closed his eyes again.

"Eloise?" Billie called, and Eloise jumped away from the girl's father.

"Yes," she said, already walking toward the hall.

"Can you help me with my hair?" Billie appeared in the mouth of the hallway, and she only looked at Eloise.

"Sure," she said. "What are you thinking for the party?" She followed Billie back to her bedroom, where the girl had a vanity covered with makeup and hair supplies. "Is Jake going to be there?"

"Yes," Billie said with guarded eyes. "He told Lexi that he likes me, and she started flirting with him like crazy." She rolled those big, blue eyes now. "Sometimes I don't get her."

"Well, if he likes you already, surely she won't steal him away."

"That's exactly what she's trying to do," Billie said. "She's good at it, too, because she's pretty and blonde and popular."

"You're pretty and blonde and popular," Eloise said.

Billie scoffed. "My hair is practically brown. Some girl in my PE class said it was *dirty* blonde last week." She reached up and touched her hair. It was dirty blonde, but Eloise loved it. She reached for the brush and started stroking it through Billie's hair.

"I've always wanted hair this color," Eloise said. "Lots of women pay a lot of money to get hair this color." She let a few seconds go by. "Billie, you know you're way too young to have a boyfriend, right?"

"I know," Billie said. "It's not really a boyfriend, El." Her eyes met Eloise's in the mirror on the vanity. "It's like, he'll hold my hand at parties, and everyone will know we're together. But that's about it."

"No kissing?"

Billie shrugged. "I don't think I'd mind kissing Jake." She grew nervous, if the way she picked up a couple of elastics and started twining them around her fingers was any indication. "I've never kissed a boy, Eloise. Is it hard?"

"No," Eloise said slowly. "I—" She put the brush down and turned to sit on Billie's bed. The girl twisted in her chair and looked at Eloise, her expression practically begging for more information.

"I should ask your father before I talk to you about this," Eloise said.

"No," Billie said. "Please, don't do that." She got up and closed the door. "He won't be mad. He loves you."

Eloise ran her hand through her hair and took a calming breath. "Billie, I love you."

Billie's eyes widened, and then she jumped out of her chair and hugged Eloise. "I love you, too, Eloise."

Eloise pressed her eyes closed and held the girl tightly. "I want you to know that, because then you'll know that I'm not trying to make your life harder." She eased back and looked into Billie's eyes.

"Bills, boys and girls are different. Sex is a wonderful, beautiful thing between two people who love each other."

Billie nodded, her eyes wide and round. "Like you and my dad."

Eloise swallowed, her thoughts down the hall on Aaron and what they did in his bedroom. "Yes." She cleared her throat. "You know what sex is, right?"

"Yes," Billie said, and she didn't seem embarrassed about that, or talking about this.

Eloise nodded, her own heart pounding. "Sex is normal and natural between two people in a loving, committed relationship. Teenagers usually are incapable of that kind of relationship, so I wouldn't advocate for you to do that with anyone until you're in love with someone who treats you well, respects you, and loves you as much as you love him."

Billie just watched Eloise with those sober, wide eyes.

"Sex isn't dirty," Eloise said. "It's just...your dad and I worry about you, because you're so pretty, and so smart, and teenage boys have hormones they don't understand."

"Okay," Billie said. "But kissing isn't sex, right?"

Eloise smiled and reached out to run her fingers down the side of Billie's face. "No, Bills. Kissing is not sex. Jake is a very good-looking boy. I think if you have the chance to kiss him, you should."

"What?" Billie blinked rapidly, her smile growing on her face. She so rarely smiled that Eloise grinned back at her.

"There's just one problem with kissing a boy at your age," Eloise said, retracting her hand and leaning back as she tried to tame her smile. "You have to be alone to do it, and Bills, it's not a good idea for you to be alone with a boy."

"But is it hard?"

"No," Eloise said. "Kissing is really fun, Bills. It's exciting. You just have to be careful with where he puts his hands and be sure to tell him anything he does that you don't like. If he really likes you, and he respects you, he won't do those things."

She looked down at her hands. "Where do I put *my* hands?"

"Usually around his neck," Eloise said, smiling at her. "Or on his shoulders." She paused for a moment. "Billie."

The girl looked up, so much fear in her gaze Eloise almost started laughing. This terrified almost-fourteen-year-old was who Aaron thought was going to sneak off with boys and do things she shouldn't.

"You'll know what to do when the time comes," Eloise promised. "It's not hard, and boys and girls were made to kiss each other. It's natural. Don't think too hard about it."

Billie nodded, but she still looked like Eloise had stung her with one of Aaron's tasers.

"Okay," Eloise said, and she took a big breath. "What are we doing with your hair? Let's do it, so I can go tell your dad what we talked about."

As she wove Billie's hair into two Dutch braids, she listened to the girl talk about her friends and who she hoped wouldn't come to the ice skating party tomorrow. She talked about Jake, and how maybe she could hold his hand on the rink, and that she was going to try to get Daniel to talk to Lexi, because Lexi liked him *so* much, and if they could become "a thing," then Lexi would leave Jake alone.

Eloise loved listening to Billie and asking questions. She learned all kinds of new terminology, and she couldn't wait to hear how things went at the party. She was also keenly aware of what she didn't hear: her phone chiming.

None of her friends had texted back.

CHAPTER TWENTY-SEVEN

Kristen hadn't heard back from Eloise, and her nerves, stomach, and mind weren't happy about it. She'd felt like this before, and the only way to soothe the ache radiating through her body was to get everyone together and talk.

She'd had to do it when AJ and Robin had both been nominated for Homecoming queen. Something as simple as that had caused a divide between the five girls that had concerned Kristen.

She'd gotten them all together in the living room of the lighthouse and she'd forced them to talk. There had been cookies and the guise of passing off a few things in their Seafaring booklets.

"You can't trick them now," she said to herself, the walls of the guest room in the lighthouse closing in on her.

The living space here was small, and Kristen was grateful her son and his wife had offered it to her in the first place.

They lived on the bottom level, which housed the master suite, living room, and kitchen. This level up from there had two bedrooms, a bathroom, and a larger living area.

She got up and left the guest room, padding over to the couch in the living area. She didn't turn on the television or move over to the built-in counter to heat a pot of water for tea. The electric kettle Alice had given her sat there, and Jean had brought all her favorite herbal teas, and assortment of mugs, hot chocolates, and even instant coffee.

There had been muffins and pastries, all of which Jean had made herself. She'd been delivering them to the people who lived on this stretch of road that bordered the east side of Diamond Island. Everyone over here had some measure of damage, and while Kristen had been at The Cliffside Inn, Jean and Reuben had been hosting others who'd suffered some home damage. They'd managed to get their roofs fixed and their bed set up again, and they'd gone home.

Jean had a big community breakfast planned for tomorrow morning, and they were hosting it in the parking lot here at the lighthouse. Kristen could easily invite her girls, and no one would say a word.

She clutched her phone, which had become a lifeline

for her since Joel's death, trying to make a decision about what to do.

Inhaling, Kristen looked down and started typing. *Emergency meeting at the lighthouse at 10:30. Please let me know if you can make it. Jean is serving breakfast for the community in the parking lot.*

Before she could second-guess herself, she sent the text to her five girls. Instantly, guilt hit her. She'd just usurped power over Eloise's planned group breakfast. She wasn't sure if that would comfort Eloise because she didn't have to make a trip to the inn to get the food, or if it would make her feel insignificant and sidelined.

She tapped quickly to call Eloise, but the line just rang and rang. She didn't leave a message, and immediately called again.

This time, Aaron said, "Kristen, it's Aaron. El's down the hall with Billie, and the bedroom door is closed. Can I have her call you back?"

"Of course," Kristen said, her throat so dry that her voice came out like a croak. "How is she? I'm worried about her."

Aaron took a moment to answer. "She's feeling complicated things, as I'm sure most of you are."

Kristen nodded though Aaron wasn't there to see her. "I'm so glad she has you," she said, her voice barely there.

"Funny," he said, his tone serious and calm. "I was thinking the same thing about you."

A sob gathered in Kristen's throat, and she swallowed hard against it.

"I'll have her call you," Aaron said. "I'm not sure what's going on with her and Billie, but she hopefully won't be too much longer."

"Thank you," Kristen managed to push through her narrow throat. The call ended, and she knew exactly what she was going to do.

Or rather, what she was *not* going to do.

She added another text to the new string that said, *I love you all, and all are welcome at any time. I will not be accepting the offer from White Sands, just so everyone knows, but I will support any decision any of the rest of you make.*

With that sent, the unrest in Kristen's soul quieted. She leaned back against the couch and sighed, wondering how long it would take for someone to answer, and who would be first to say they'd either be there or they wouldn't.

That first text was always the most important, and Kristen knew it would set the tone for the other responses she'd get.

Her phone vibrated against her leg, and she jolted upright to check it.

Alice had said, *I'll be there, and I'm calling Ginny right now to have her bring all the food Eloise bought for us, if that's okay with El. I will help cook it.*

Relief spread through Kristen. Alice was a good first

responder, and if she came, Robin would likely come. And if Robin came, Kelli and Eloise would come. And if Kelli came, AJ would too.

I can make 10:30 work, Kelli said. *I might be late, though. I'll stay in touch.*

AJ didn't answer, and she hadn't messaged on the bigger group thread either, the one with Laurel, Paul, Aaron, Duke, and even the twins.

Long minutes passed, and Kristen finally got up and went back into her bedroom. Finally, Eloise called, and Kristen nearly knocked her phone to the ground in her attempts to pick it up.

"I'm not going to be offended if we move the breakfast to the lighthouse," she said instead of hello. "I've just spoken to Alice, and she's having the twins bring the food and my mother. We'll all be at the lighthouse by nine to begin cooking."

Kristen silently wept, touched by the goodness of Eloise Hall. "Okay," she managed to say.

"Okay," Eloise repeated back to her. "Aaron and the girls are coming too, but he can take them and the teens down to the beach while we have our meeting."

"Okay," Kristen said again.

Eloise took several moments before she asked, "Did Robin respond to you privately?"

"No."

"She told me she and Duke are going to a credit union in the morning. I bet she'll come after that."

"Okay."

"Kristen?"

"Yes?"

"I love you too."

Kristen repeated the sentiment back to Eloise, not minding that her voice revealed how she felt.

No one else called or texted, and Kristen settled back onto her pillow, her heart healing beat by beat.

The following morning, Alice, Charlie, and Ginny arrived first. Charlie had his hand on Dawn Hall's back, and he never moved more than a foot from her. She was a slight, dark-haired woman the teenager could probably pick up and carry just as easily as she hobbled along on her crutches.

In fact, one step inside the navy blue door of the lighthouse, and Charlie turned to Dawn. "There's a lot of stairs, Mrs. Hall. Let me carry you."

Before she could say a word, Charlie had taken her crutches and handed them to Kristen, who stood on the landing of the steps that led down, and he swept Dawn into his arms.

She gave a little shriek, and Charlie asked, "Kristen, we're going down two levels, or one?"

"Two," she said, preceding him down the steps. "We'll

cook down there, and then we can join Jean for the breakfast in a half an hour."

She arrived on the bottom level to find Jean putting four more Belgian waffles on a sheet tray in the oven. She slid it back inside and turned with a smile on her face.

She was a completely different person than the one who'd come to live in the lighthouse this past summer, and Kristen stepped over and embraced her.

"Thanks for letting us crash your breakfast."

"It's just fine," Jean said. "I've got all the sausage done and warming. I'm making waffles until nine-thirty, and Rueben is getting the tables out of the storage right now."

Charlie grunted as he set Dawn on the couch, and Alice and Ginny brought up the rear, the two of them talking in low voices. Neither of them looked very happy, but Alice painted over her frown with a smile as she arrived in the kitchen and put a large package of pancake mix on the counter.

"Good morning, Jean," she said as if she and Jean were the best of friends and hadn't seen each other for a while. They hugged even, and a moment later, Eloise's voice came down the steps.

"Hello?" she called. "We're here."

"Come on down," Kristen called up to her, hurrying that way. "Do you need help carrying anything?"

Eloise's footsteps came slowly down the steps, carefully, the way Eloise did everything. She arrived with nothing in her hands, and she took Kristen into a tight hug.

"Don't stop there," Aaron said from above. "I've got too much milk to slow down."

"Sorry." Eloise flattened herself against the wall and let her fiancé by. He grinned at her and then Kristen, carrying four gallons of milk as he passed.

Billie and Grace arrived last, and they both carried juice and muffins too.

"You didn't have to bring anything," Kristen said, taking the large container of mango pineapple juice from Grace, who looked like she was about to drop it.

"The twins couldn't bring everything." Eloise followed Kristen into the small kitchen and living room, said hello to Jean, and started opening cupboards to find a bowl. "Plus, I didn't want to impose on Jean's event."

"It's fine, Eloise," Jean said. "There's going to be so many waffles." As if Eloise needed proof, Jean opened the double waffle-maker and popped out one waffle, twisted it, and got out the second. She put them both on the sheet tray in the oven, which probably held another two dozen waffles already, and turned back to the second maker on the counter. "I'm going to cut these in half, and I probably have twice as many as I need."

"So we can have two breakfasts," Aaron said, eyeing the crispy, brown waffles.

"You already ate breakfast, Daddy," Grace said, and everyone started laughing, even Aaron.

"No one eats three breakfasts," Eloise said, her smile so pure and so genuine.

"I'll run five miles every day for a week," he said, reaching for her. "No problem."

With all the people, the space felt cramped, but Kristen wouldn't have it any other way. She wanted these people here with her, and she couldn't stop smiling.

Jean finished with her waffles, and everyone helped her carry all the food upstairs and out to the parking lot. Rueben had set up tables and chairs, and he was currently visiting with the people who'd already shown up.

Jean welcomed everyone, and Kristen stayed while the others went back downstairs to start cooking their own breakfast feast.

By ten-thirty, Kristen's stomach cried for the want of food, but also because no one else had showed up to the lighthouse.

Rueben had put a table in the larger living room, and Kristen carried the juice and a plate of blueberry pancakes up to it while Alice and Eloise brought the bacon and milk. "Well," Kristen said. "I guess it might just be us."

"Kelli is coming," Alice said. "She just texted to say she's five minutes out."

"I'm surprised Robin isn't here," Eloise said, shooting a worried look at Alice.

"She's not going to take the money," Alice said. "She just needs another plan before she says so."

"None of us are taking it," Eloise said, looking from Alice to Kristen. "Right?"

"Right," Kristen said. "Kelli won't either."

"So it's just Robin." Eloise sat at the table and ran her hands through her hair.

"El, we're going down to the beach," Billie said as she appeared in the doorway.

"Tell me what ferry you're going to be on tonight," Eloise said without getting up.

Billie gave her a small smile. "The five-forty-two from Diamond," she said.

"Your father will be waiting at the station on Sanctuary," Eloise said.

"Yeah," Billie said. "Probably with his lights on." She rolled her eyes. "See you later, Eloise."

"Bye, sweet girl."

Billie left, and the sounds of Grace squabbling with her as they went up to the exit warmed Kristen's heart.

"She's riding the ferry from here to Sanctuary by herself today," Eloise said. "First time."

"She'll be fine," Alice said. "I used to do that all the time. We all did."

"Yes," Eloise said. "Thirty-five years ago."

Alice accepted her point, and Kristen reached for a slice of bacon. Just then, footsteps sounded on the steps, and Kelli came into the room.

"Good morning," she said, and she wore such light and happiness around her person.

"It looks like it is for you," Alice said.

"Yes." Kelli grinned as she set her purse on the side counter and joined everyone at the table. "I looked at a twinhome today, and it's *gorgeous*. Huge windows, and up on a hill that overlooks the ocean." She sighed. "It has two bedrooms, and it's furnished, and it has the most beautiful little patio in the back." She grinned around at everyone. "I'm getting the contract today, and Parker and I can move in tomorrow." Tears filled her eyes then. "If I can get a few presents today, I might be able to give my son a decent Christmas."

Kristen reached over and took Kelli's hand in hers. "I'm so glad, Kelli."

She nodded and brushed her tears away with her other hand while the others expressed their congratulations as well.

A quick beat of silence filled the room before Alice said, "I had an amazing date with Will Bridge last night." She sighed too, and her happiness permeated the room.

"Do tell," Eloise said, propping her head in her hands.

"Not much to tell," Alice said. "After the meeting, he called for Italian food. We picked it up and ate it at his house, which I should say, rivals my vacation home on Rocky Ridge."

"He's rich," Eloise said, grinning. She looked at everyone else. "Of course he's rich."

"That's not why I like him," Alice said, her voice on the edge of deathly quiet.

"I know," Eloise said, and more was communicated in the silence that Kristen didn't quite understand.

"I'm glad you like him," Kelli said. "You deserve someone to take care of you."

Alice looked at Kelli with some surprise in her eyes. "Thank you, Kelli."

"Let's eat," Eloise said.

"No news for you?" Alice asked.

She shook her head, and Kristen was glad she wouldn't have to share anything either. She hadn't taken any steps to find somewhere else to live, but her situation wasn't quite as pressing as Kelli's.

The conversation lightened, and Jean stopped in to ask, "Did you bring Parker, Kelli?"

Kelli quickly swallowed her bite of pancake. "No," she said. "Sorry, Jean. My mother's boyfriend took him to a movie."

"It's okay." Jean flashed her a smile. "You're still bringing him tomorrow, though, right?"

Kristen looked at the hope on her daughter-in-law's face, and then back to Kelli, who was nodding. "Yes, he'll be here at eleven."

Jean smiled then and continued up the steps. A new silence settled over the group, and Kelli cut another bite of her pancake before she looked up and noticed everyone watching her.

"Jean has a special love for Parker," Kelli said. "I bring him all the time."

Kristen barely held back a new flood of tears. "Thank you, Kelli," she said. "It obviously means a lot to her."

Alice nodded, but Eloise had moved her eyes back to the doorway, and she stood up.

"Robin," she said.

Kristen slowly put her fork down, almost afraid to hope that AJ would be behind her.

"Am I too late?" Robin asked, taking a step into the room. Her eyes were guarded, and Kristen couldn't tell how she was feeling. "Our meeting at the credit union ran long, because they wanted to pull our credit and get the loan pre-approval started before the holidays."

She dropped her bag at her feet, her countenance falling slightly. "I'm exhausted, and there better be bacon left."

"There's tons," Alice said, scooting her chair over to make room for Robin. "Tell us what happened at the credit union."

Robin sat down and pulled two pancakes onto her plate before reaching for a few slices of bacon. "We're going to get a loan for the new boat. The interest rates are at zero because of the tsunami, and Margie said we'll get approved easily." She took a bite of bacon. "It's not free, but honestly, I don't think the money from Diane is either."

No one spoke for a few seconds, and finally Eloise said, "Truer words have never been spoken."

"Let's call AJ," Kelli said, pulling her phone from her back pocket. "Like we used to when she lived in New York."

"She won't answer," Alice said.

"If she wanted to be here, she'd be here," Eloise added.

"I'll put her on video," Kelli said as if the others hadn't spoken.

"She might answer if it's Kelli," Robin said. "Be sure she knows we're all here too. I don't want her to be even more upset."

"She's not upset," Kelli said. "At least not at us. She's working through a lot of feelings and emotions right now, and most of her anger is aimed at her mother or herself."

"Just tell her we love her, and we'd love to share our news with her," Kristen said, glancing at Eloise. "I'll have to come up with something, I guess."

Eloise smiled and reached for Kristen's hand. "I will too, if that's what it takes to get AJ on the line."

Kelli's phone rang and rang, and they all waited to see if AJ would answer the video call...or not.

CHAPTER TWENTY-EIGHT

AJ accepted the scrambled eggs her dad had whipped up and put on a plate for her. "Thanks, Dad." She met his eye, and they seemed to say so much more. "Sorry to just show up out of nowhere."

"You're always welcome to show up here out of nowhere," he said, and AJ was glad she'd found him sober this morning. Amy had told her last night that their father barely drank anymore, but AJ hadn't believed her until they'd stood on the front porch and he'd opened the door without bloodshot eyes.

He'd already been dressed too, though it had barely been nine o'clock, and he'd hugged Darcy and Mary. He'd told them to go down to the beach and see if they'd gotten any lobsters overnight, and then he'd offered to make breakfast.

Amy bustled around the house like she'd been there

many times before, because of course, she had. AJ had gazed around at the pictures on the walls, which showed her, Ryan, and Amy at various stages of their lives.

The furniture was new—or at least stuff AJ hadn't seen before. The flooring had been removed and new items brought in. When she'd asked if he'd done that since the tsunami, he'd said no, he did it last year when the carpet had needed to be replaced.

The appliances were clean; the fridge only had bottled water, a half-gallon of milk, and a pitcher of juice inside.

He'd told her about the way he'd stripped the cabinets and re-stained them, and he'd taken her into the back yard, which was a terraced set of wide steps that led down to the beach. Each one bore something her father detailed for her, and AJ had been marveling at everything for over an hour.

Including the steaming breakfast in front of her right now. He'd added cream to the eggs, and plenty of salt and pepper, and while AJ sometimes had a poor reaction to her first meal of the day, she ate the eggs eagerly and asked for more.

Amy paused in her story about Donovan and his attempt to get doughnuts this morning. Apparently, the line had been two blocks long, and Amy had been musing about making her own for Christmas Eve morning.

She hadn't asked AJ if she'd still be with them tomorrow morning, and AJ herself didn't know if she would be or not. She'd originally planned to spend it with

Matt, just the two of them waking up in his bed whenever they felt like it. They'd make something for breakfast, and sip coffee together, and AJ hoped he'd make love to her at some point as well.

She'd told Amy all about Matt, and when they'd reconnected, their long-distance relationship, and the future she hoped to have with him. It had been easy, too, because Amy genuinely didn't judge AJ.

Somehow, getting herself to tell her father about Matt and the unborn child inside her was much harder, and AJ felt the clock ticking.

"What are you doing for Christmas?" her dad asked as he got up to reheat the pan still on the stove.

AJ exchanged a glance with Amy. "I don't know, Dad. What are you doing?"

"Oh, I get up and tend to the shrubs," he said. "Amy said I could come watch the girls open their gifts. She'll feed us." He looked over his shoulder on his way to the fridge. "Are you staying with her?"

"I did last night," AJ hedged. "I've been staying with my boyfriend." She cleared her throat. "Do you remember Matthew Hymas?"

Dad straightened, the carton of eggs in his hand. His eyes were lighter than AJ's, and the source of her more fair coloring. "He was one you went with in high school, right?"

"Right," AJ said, though she'd never gone steady with Matt, or even out on a proper date. AJ didn't date anyone; she'd never had a steady boyfriend until after college.

"I'm seeing him," AJ said. "He lives on Diamond Island, and he's running the golf course. The Hymas's own the golf course."

"Oh, Yancey's son."

"Yes," AJ said with a smile as Dad turned his back on the table and started cracking eggs into a bowl. AJ looked at Amy again, and her sister inclined her head, as if to say, *Get on with it.*

"Matt and I...are probably going to get married," AJ said. "Before the baby comes next year."

Dad spun around, his face arranged into an unreadable expression. "What?"

"I'm pregnant," AJ said with a smile. She refused to be unhappy about the life inside her. She already loved her baby, and she really wanted her father to love it too. "The baby is Matt's, and he's asked me to marry him."

Dad closed the distance between them and AJ stood to hug him. "Congratulations, Ava."

AJ's eyes burned with tears. "Thanks, Dad."

"Why *probably* marry him?" Dad asked.

"He asked her," Amy said. "She hasn't said yes yet." She spoke in a teasing tone, because she wasn't sure why AJ hadn't jumped at the chance to become Mrs. Matthew Hymas. In her words from last night, Amy had said, "You've been in love with him forever."

"Why not?" Dad asked.

"He asked just before the tsunami hit," AJ said. "It's been a little chaotic since then."

Dad nodded and turned back to the stove. The cold eggs hissed as they touched the hot pan, and the scent of scrambled eggs filled the kitchen for the second time that morning.

"Could Matt and I come watch the girls open their presents?" AJ asked, meeting her sister's eyes.

"Of course," Amy said. "He can stay with you tonight if he'd like."

AJ nodded, but she didn't immediately reach to text Matt. "Dad," she said. "When's the last time you saw or talked to Mom?"

Dad spun around again, this time his face a horrible combination of surprise and resignation at the same time. "A long time."

"How long?" Amy asked.

Dad looked from her and back to AJ. "At least twenty years. Maybe a little longer. Why?" He turned and removed the pan from the burner.

"She's in the cove," AJ said, deciding to go right for the jugular. "She works for a charitable organization called White Sands Worldwide, and she's offered all this money to me and my friends to help with the damage from the tsunami."

Dad brought the pan of eggs to the table and clunked it down in front of AJ. "She's here right now?"

"I saw her yesterday," AJ said. "First time in thirty-five years for me."

Dad sat heavily at the table. "I'm so sorry, sweetie." He hung his head. "What happened?"

AJ reached to scoop herself some eggs and said, "Amy, I can't tell it again."

Amy opened her mouth and told the story. AJ interjected every so often to get a specific detail right, and soon enough, the story was out.

"I don't know what my friends will do," AJ said, thinking of the texts she'd received last night and even this morning. She hadn't found the strength to respond, and she knew that a non-response said plenty.

"I thought I could drink your mother away," Dad said. "I thought I could find someone else to dull the pain." He kept his eyes down, and AJ's memories of the amount he'd drank, and then all the women he'd brought home while she was still living in the house streamed through her mind.

"None of that worked," he said. "What's worked is me taking control of my life, working through my thoughts and feelings, and replacing the negativity with positivity." He looked at AJ now, his eyes blazing and strong. "Amy's started to do some of that, and I know you have too."

"I've been trying," AJ said. "I have a very long way to go."

"Then go the distance," Dad said. "I thought I'd need

to confront Diane at some point, but I haven't needed that. Maybe you do."

AJ looked at Amy, who sat at the table with her arms folded. She wore a dark look in her eyes, and AJ wondered if they did need to sit down with their mother and hash everything out. Perhaps there was a dam there that needed to be broken before complete healing could happen.

AJ nodded and started eating her second serving of eggs. When she finished, she thanked her father and added, "Dad, I'm really sorry I disappeared. I didn't know any other way, and I had to go. I had to do something to preserve the little sanity I had, and I'm afraid that hurt you."

She swiped at her wet eyes. "That wasn't my intent."

"I know that, sweetie." He drew her into a hug, and it was so nice to be held by a parent. AJ hadn't had that in quite a long time, and she clung to her father as forgiveness cleansed her from the inside out. "We've all made mistakes," Dad said. "I apologize for being a drunk and leaving you to raise Amy and take care of yourself. I shouldn't have brought home all those women. I never taught you to respect yourself or the the value of intimacy."

"Dad," Amy said. "You did the best you could."

He stepped back from AJ, his eyes broadcasting pure pain. "I know I did, but it wasn't good enough. I know that too. I wish I could change the past, but I can't. All I can do is build the future."

"Grandpa!" Darcy burst through the back door. "Two lobsters!"

"Wow," Dad said, his expression changing in the blink of an eye. "Looks like we're going to be eating like kings on Christmas Eve Eve."

Mary giggled. "Christmas Eve Eve." AJ picked up her plate and started to turn toward the sink when her phone rang. A number sat there that she didn't have programmed into her phone, and she hesitated. She often had calls out to leads and agents, and not all of them were in her phone.

She ignored the call, exchanged a glance with Amy, and went to put her plate in the dishwasher. She'd barely finished that when her phone chimed. She collected it from the table to see Matt's name at the top.

Your mother just called me to get your number. I gave it to her, AJ. I'm not sure if that was a mistake or not, and if so, I apologize.

As she re-read his text and all the dots connected in her head, another message from Matt came in. *Can you call me when you get a minute? I hope your visit with your father is going well. I love you, and I love your heart, and I love your strength.*

She smiled and pressed her phone to her bosom. She loved him too, and while she may not have been in love with him forever, she certainly was now.

While she held her phone against her chest, it rang again, and the screen showed the same number from a few minutes ago. She turned it toward Amy, who was watching their father interact with the girls as they talked about the seafood feast they'd make that night.

"It's Mom," she said, barely loud enough for her sister to hear a few feet away. Somehow, her father heard too, and Dad turned toward them, his eyes wide.

"I'm going to answer it," AJ said. "Do you want to talk to her too?"

"Put it on speaker," Amy said, and AJ swiped on the call so it wouldn't go to voicemail.

"Hello?" She left the kitchen and went to sit on the front porch. Amy followed her, and sure enough, AJ recognized the smooth, crisp voice of her mother as she said, "Hello, AvaJane."

"You're on speaker with me and Amy," AJ said, tapping to put the call on the speaker so her sister could hear too. She sat on the top step on the front porch and put the phone on her knee.

"What do you want, Diane?"

"I was hoping to take you to lunch before I go back to Halifax," Diane said. "Hello, Amelia."

"Hello, Mother," Amy said, and she gave her more respect than AJ had simply by not using her first name. "We just ate breakfast with Dad. I'm not sure we're ready for lunch."

AJ was surprised at the level of passive-aggressive bite in her sister's tone.

"I understand," Diane said.

"Right," AJ said with a scoff. "I'm sure you're so well-versed with how a young daughter feels when her mother disappears while she's at school."

"That's *such* a good point," Amy said. "Did your mother abandon you when you were eight years old, Mother?"

Diane didn't answer, and AJ knew the answer would be no. Their maternal grandmother had been a big help in the first few years after Diane had left, and her death had really pushed Dad into booze and bimbos.

AJ met Amy's eyes, and Amy rolled hers. "I think..." AJ started. "I'd be willing to go to lunch if you're going to apologize and attempt to explain."

"I don't care what her explanations are," Amy snapped, and it was nice to see her lose her cool a little bit. AJ didn't want to feel like the irrational, unhinged sister all the time.

"I don't either," AJ said. "To me, there's no possible excuse for what she's done. I still feel like I need to hear it. I need to know why she felt like she needed to leave."

Amy's gaze glittered dangerously, but she nodded. "I might not be able to attend."

"I can go alone," AJ said, feeling the strength inside her that Matt had spoken of. She'd had wells of strength in the past. They'd allowed her to go back out onto the field when she was injured. They allowed her to let any boy into her bed. They allowed her to carry a baby at age forty-five.

"Is The Saltwater Surf okay?" Diane asked. "Say, an hour?"

"I'm out on Pearl," AJ said. "I don't know if the ferries are running at full capacity yet."

"They're not," Diane said. "We'll be partnering with Mister Bridge to get them back up and running as normal by the New Year." She sounded so proud about it too, and AJ and Amy rolled their eyes at the same time.

For some reason, AJ wasn't angry today. She was simply more resigned, and she did want to unstop the things holding her back so she could take a step forward.

"Let's say ninety minutes," she said, barely holding back her laughter as Amy started to giggle.

"That will be fine," Diane said in a cool, nearly aloof voice. "See you then, AvaJane."

"Diane?" she asked. "I'm not coming if you can't use the name I'd like you to."

Diane Proctor in her current state probably wasn't used to anyone speaking to her like that. Several seconds passed before she said, "Very well, AJ. See you soon. Good to hear your voice, Amelia."

"I'm sure," Amy said sarcastically. AJ jabbed at the phone icon to hang up, because her laughter was going to burst from her. The phone had barely beeped when she and Amy dissolved into giggles.

"Up and running by the New Year," Amy said in a mocking tone. They laughed even harder, and several dark corners that had been lurking in AJ's soul got swept cleaned by simply laughing with her sister.

AJ ARRIVED AT THE SALTWATER SURF BEFORE THE ninety-minute deadline. She sat in the RideShare and watched the clock tick past eleven and watched the meter cross the fifteen-dollar mark.

"Okay," she finally said. "Thanks for waiting. I'm ready now." She touched her smart watch to the sensor in the back, paid her fare, and got out of the car.

The Saltwater Surf was an upscale, slightly unknown seafood bar off the northern coast of Diamond Island. It sat on private property, within a posh, five-star resort.

AJ made her way inside, having met many athletes and clients inside the wealthiest of hotels, clubs, and restaurants. She held her head high as she glanced around, her purse balanced perfectly on her forearm the way all the rich and famous women did.

Her mother rose from a chair several feet from her, and AJ's footsteps slowed. Perhaps this was a bad idea. Perhaps she should've listened to her sister.

Time had strange way of separating into individual threads as it slowed. AJ breathed in, and she could see her mother standing in the doorway, her dirty blonde hair up in a ponytail. She'd waved goodbye to Amy and AvaJane that morning, an apron over her clothes and a smile on her face.

As she breathed out, they walked to the ferry station the way they did a thousand other times. They went to school. They came home, and Ava had argued with Amy about whether or not she could come with her to soccer practice that afternoon.

Another breath in showed her that afternoon in the park. Amy had come with her, because their mother wasn't home, and Dad hadn't come in off the boat yet. The breath out had the years flying by in fast motion, each one filled with empty afternoons, and AvaJane transforming into AJ, the star soccer player.

Then AJ, the girl who slept with everyone. Then AJ, the woman who couldn't make the Olympic team, who grew resentful of her coaches, who dropped out of college only to go back later to get that degree.

She took a step toward her mother, realizing that she'd done a lot of stupid things after her mother had left. She'd also done a lot of amazing things too. "Hello," she said, and all the individual strands of her life merged back into one.

"AJ," Diane said. "Thank you for coming."

AJ made a show of looking at her phone. The breakfast at the lighthouse had started thirty-five minutes ago, and she wanted to be there instead of here with the all the power of the sun. "I need to be back on the ferry by noon," she said.

Diane frowned and adjusted her own purse. "I don't

see how that's enough time," she said. "The Saltwater Surf doesn't serve a fast lunch."

"Let's just see how it goes then," AJ said. "I might be able to buy myself a little more time." She had no idea how long her friends would be at the lighthouse, and a voice in the back of her mind whispered that if she texted just a few words, they'd show up in this insufferable restaurant and rescue her, no questions asked.

"Very well." Diane turned and led the way toward the restaurant's entrance. "You'll be happy to know that only William Bridge accepted our offer."

AJ's eyebrows shot up. "Is that right?" She drew level to her mother, and when she turned to the right to look at her, it was almost like looking in a mirror. The shiny hair without a strand out of place. The perfectly make-upped eyes. The slim figure. *She must be so tired*, was all AJ could think.

She was, and she could admit that one of the biggest reasons she'd transitioned to freelance work was so she didn't have to check each of the five thousand pieces of her life to make sure they all laid flat, behaved, and came together to present the perfect version of herself.

No one was perfect, and she was tired of trying to look like she was.

"Not even Robin?" AJ asked as her mother held up two fingers for the hostess.

She leaned toward the other woman and said, "Under Sasha Summers."

The woman's eyes widened, and she signaled for someone to come over. "Yes, Miss Summers. Your private booth is prepared."

"Why do you use a fake name?" AJ asked.

Diane fixed her with a hard gaze, and AJ had certainly seen her mother angry before. Once, she and her brother had wandered down the street to an elderly woman's house, where they'd eaten strawberry pies and played with her little dog. Diane had been livid, because she hadn't been able to find them.

When they'd finally gone home, Diane had looked at them with this level of danger in her gaze. It had quickly softened into concern and worry, and then tears, and AJ couldn't fathom then that her mother would leave her and her siblings behind only four years later.

She said nothing as a sharp-dressed man led them past all the tables and booths in the regular part of the restaurant. Down a hall they went, and he indicated a doorway to the right. Diane said, "Thank you, Sean," as she stepped inside, but AJ hesitated.

It almost felt like she was committing herself to the dark deep if she went through that arched doorway and into the private booth. She did it anyway, because she'd been in some pretty dark places in her life, and she'd always managed to claw her way back to the light.

The room held a single booth that could easily seat six, and AJ slid onto the side opposite of Diane.

"You can brighten the room with the window and

skylight," Sean said in a smooth tone. "Your waiter is Rich, ma'am, as requested."

"Thank you," Diane said again, and Sean left. AJ didn't have time to ask her how often she'd been here before Rich stepped into the space.

"Good morning, Sasha," he said easily, a smile on his full lips. His eyes darted to AJ and back to her mother. "Do you require a wine menu?"

"We're not drinking this morning," Diane said, deciding for AJ, not that she'd have had alcohol. "Could you bring juice and water?"

"Of course," Rich said, bowing.

"I'll have a mango lemonade," AJ said as he stepped back. He looked at her again, almost like he hadn't been expecting her to speak.

"Yes, ma'am," he said quickly and left.

"What is going on?" AJ asked. "How often do you come here?" If her mother had been coming to the cove all this time, AJ wasn't sure what she would do.

"I don't come here," Diane said. "I own this restaurant, and I requested certain people to see how they do."

AJ didn't believe a single word she said, but she didn't know how far to push her mom either. "Mm hm," she said. "He knew you usually drank wine. Do you drink it with him?" She glanced toward the doorway. "Is there a secret room to sleep with him when you're drunk?"

"AvaJane," her mother said sharply. "Stop it."

"You don't get to tell me what to do," AJ said. "This

was a mistake. Amy was right." She slid to the end of the booth. "Sorry, Diane. Sasha. Whoever you are. I shouldn't have agreed to this." She stood and took a moment to reach back for her purse.

"I go by Sasha Summers," her mother said. "Because then I don't have to think about what I did when I was Diane Proctor."

AJ turned toward her and found the most vulnerable, pathetic look on Diane's face.

"I couldn't do it," Diane said. "Have that name hurled at me every day, reminding me of where I should be."

AJ's heart pounded very loudly in her ears, and she couldn't get her feet to move. She couldn't get her mouth to form another question either, though several ran through her mind.

She sat back down, right on the edge of the long bench seat, and stared at Diane. Long moments passed, and Rich returned with a tray of juice, water, and AJ's mango lemonade. He put no less than eight glasses on the table and lifted the tray again. "Coffee or tea, ma'am?"

"No," Diane said in a quiet voice. "Will you please bring us the continental breakfast basket?"

"The twelve piece or the fifteen?" He shot a glance at AJ.

"Fifteen," Diane said. "I'd also like the seasalt sampler, with the bacon."

"Yes, ma'am," he said.

AJ had eaten at The Saltwater Surf before, and she'd

never heard of those things. They hadn't even been given menus.

Diane looked at her again. "I know what you want to know."

"Why did you leave?" AJ asked.

Diane didn't sigh, and she didn't make a single move to fix her hair. She blinked at AJ, but not rapidly. "I left, because I am weak, and I am a coward. I left, because I wasn't strong enough to stay and fight for the things I wanted."

Confusion ran through AJ. "I don't understand."

"I left, because I'd cheated on your father, and I was pregnant with someone else's baby." A small smile crossed her face, almost like she didn't know she'd made the gesture. "He promised me everything, AvaJane, and I believed him."

Silence hung over them until AJ said, "So you left us for him and this other baby."

"At first," she said. She stared straight at AJ. "I lost the baby, and I lost him. I'd already lost your dad and you kids, and I was too weak to return, apologize, and try to start again."

AJ had not expected her mother to admit to any faults, weaknesses, or misdeeds that would paint her in a bad light.

"Did Dad know?"

"Yes."

"Where have you been all this time?"

"Halifax."

"You obviously have a lot of money."

"I found someone else with deep pockets and a heart of gold. He doesn't know I'm here, and he doesn't know I have three children."

"You *don't* have three children," AJ said, something roaring up inside her. She felt fire in her eyes, and she hoped her mother could too.

"You're right, of course," Diane said.

AJ didn't know where to look, but she didn't want to look at her mom anymore. She wasn't sure this was fixing anything, for either one of them.

"I'm sorry," Diane said. "I know it's not enough, and I know you have no reason to forgive me. I do hope you'll try to accept my apology and my weaknesses. I'm going to tell my husband about you, Ryan, and Amelia when I return home, and I'd like to start seeing all three of you again."

AJ's shock knew no end, and she could only stare at her mom.

Her phone rang, a special blingy type of chime that said whoever was calling wanted her to engage in a video call. Her mind couldn't wrap around the sound, and she held very still.

Rich arrived with a basket as long as AJ's arm and placed it on the table. Muffins and bagels of all varieties had been nestled among the wicker, and a tray of jams, butters, and marmalades went beside it.

"The seasalt sampler is three minutes out," he said.

No one spoke to him, and he left the booth.

AJ's phone rang again, and this time, her mind knew what to do about it. "It's Kelli," she said. "I have to answer."

She tapped on the video icon and gave the device a moment to connect. "Hey, Kel."

"You're on with all of us," Kelli said, her voice happy. AJ looked at her phone to find Kelli holding it out from a table where Robin, Alice, Eloise, and Kristen sat. They'd all crammed together to be in the frame, and AJ's heart took courage.

"Where are you?" Kelli asked. "It's kind of dark there. We can barely see you."

"I'm at The Saltwater Surf," AJ said, and in the next moment, light flooded the booth. She looked over to her mother, who had opened the blinds on the window and the skylight with the press of a button. "I'm with my mom."

Kelli sucked in a breath, and someone said, "Oh, my goodness."

"Do I need to take you off speaker?" Kelli asked, pure worry in her eyes.

"No," AJ said slowly.

"We want you here," Robin said. "At the very least, you have to come to dinner at the inn tonight. Everyone is going to be there, and it's our last event before Christmas."

AJ hadn't forgotten about the dinner, and she said as much.

"None of us are going to take the money," Eloise said. "Even Robin."

"I got a loan at the credit union," Robin said. "I could never do that to you, AJ."

"We love you, AJ," Alice said, and AJ smiled at all of them. They'd called her like this when she lived in New York too, and as they continued to talk, she realized that they had become her family.

She'd missed out on having a mother, but had she? She'd had Kristen Shields. She'd had her sports teams, and her Seafaring Girls friends, and out of everyone, they had not abandoned her. Even when she'd abandoned them.

Tears pricked her eyes, as they'd been doing a lot lately.

Finally, she held up her hand and said, "Guys. Guys. How long will you be at the lighthouse?"

"How fast can you get here?" Kristen asked.

"The ferry from Sanctuary is eighteen minutes," Eloise said. "I bet we can see her in half an hour if we meet her at the station."

"Jean has a car," Kristen said. "I'll see if we can borrow it."

They kept talking, making plans to be at the station to get her in just thirty minutes. AJ let one tear slide down her face, and she said, "Kelli, I'll text you when I'm getting on the ferry."

"Okay," Kelli said. "Remember, the dinner is for everyone." With that, the call ended, and AJ stared at her phone for a second.

Then she lifted her eyes to her mother's and said, "It's our final night together before we go back to our own houses and lives. It's kind of a big deal, and everyone is invited. I'm going to be there with Matt, and...would you like to come?"

CHAPTER TWENTY-NINE

Alice couldn't believe what new level of stress she'd managed to find. Preparing dinner for dozens of people used to be something that thrilled her. Dressing up and painting her face weren't chores. Impressing others was something Alice could do in her sleep.

Tonight, though, she'd already worn one dress backward, only to have her daughter point it out to her right when the water for the pasta boiled over. She'd tossed the tongs to Ginny and raced out of the kitchen to fix her dress. In the end, she'd changed completely, because she couldn't be confident in a dress she hadn't even known how to wear when Will showed up.

He'd arrived five minutes ago, and their eyes had met across the dining room as she'd set a basket of rolls on the buffet table. The lobby and dining area buzzed with merriment, and Alice loved the energy at parties. At least that hadn't changed.

"Is there anything I can do to help?"

She turned at the soft yet powerful voice to find Will only a few feet from her. He held a glass of club soda in his hand, and with that beard and that long hair, he was easily the sexiest man Alice had laid eyes on in quite some time.

"Yes," she said with a smile. "We need that serving platter with the four spots from the hot bar out front. These sauces are ready."

She and Kristen had put together a pasta bar for their last night together. They'd chosen three different shapes of pasta, and prepared four different sauces. Alice could boil noodles, and that was about the extent of her culinary knowledge. Kristen had made a meat sauce, a slow-cooked marinara, a bacon carbonara, and an Alfredo. All four pots bubbled on the stove, and she gave Alice a look as Will nodded and turned to leave the kitchen.

Alice sighed and wiped one hand across her forehead.

"He's handsome," Kristen said.

"I'm so nervous around him," Alice said. "It makes no sense. I knew him as a kid."

"Maybe that's why," Kristen said. "Did you know him like AJ knew Matt?"

"Heavens, no," Alice said, though she'd be lying if she hadn't already thought about sleeping with Will. She'd been so lonely for so long, even when she'd been married to Frank—that was her reasoning at least. "I used to sneak over to his cabin while we were at camp together. We kissed a little, and that's it."

Charlie entered the kitchen, and Alice spun away from the doorway she'd been watching. "Mom, one of Dawn's cats got up on the table and spilled the bread." He plunked the basket next to her.

Alice blinked, not quite sure what to do.

"There's another bag of rolls right there," Kristen said. "Start slicing, you two."

"Right." Alice reached for a knife and handed it to Charlie. She thought she might slice off one of her fingers if she tried to cut the rolls. Her brain had taken a vacation, and it was currently playing second to her hormones.

She hated that, and she didn't know how to get back in control of herself. She had sudden new respect for her son, and she smiled at him as he began slicing the rolls.

"What?" he asked, giving her a wary look.

"Ginny said she wasn't going to go out with Cameron," Alice said. "I thought you'd like to know."

His eyes rounded, and he smiled. "That's great, Mom. Really great."

"Don't say anything to her," Alice said. "The last thing I need is her knowing I'm sharing her secrets."

"Whose secrets?" Will asked, setting the four-well serving dish on the stainless steel workstation next to Charlie. He beamed at the teenager, but Charlie didn't even look at him.

Alice said, "Say hello to Will, Charlie."

"Hello, Will," Charlie said in a monotone. He looked up, the knife still moving. "How are you, sir?"

"Good," Will said with that big smile still in place.

"When is your daughter coming home from Hawaii?" he asked.

Will's face fell, and he cut a look at Alice. Alarms started to ring, and she nearly hipped her son out of the way and told him to go make himself useful somewhere else. She stopped herself just in time, and she hated the grinding in Will's throat.

"Sorry," Charlie said, also glancing at Alice. "Never mind. I'll finish these out there." He tossed the knife in the basket and took the whole thing toward the door.

"I apologize," Alice said. "I don't think he meant to bring up anything sensitive." She knew Charlie didn't like Tori, Will's daughter, and his question had maybe carried a little sarcastic bite. Alice had barely noticed, though, so perhaps Will hadn't either.

"Tori has decided to stay in Hawaii with Sandi," Will said. "I got off the phone with her an hour ago, and I'm afraid I haven't quite processed it."

"Can she do that?" Alice asked, her lawyer instincts perking right up. "Don't you have full custody?"

"Yes," he said. "Tori's a handful, to say the least. She's headstrong like her mother, and a dreamer like me, and that's kind of a dangerous combination."

"She still can't break a custody agreement," Alice said.

"I won't fight her on it." Will looked like he wanted to

shrug, but he didn't. He gazed evenly as Alice. "I'm...I just want her to be happy."

He was a pushover, just like Charlie and Ginny had suspected he was. They'd said Tori got whatever she wanted, and Alice could see it clearly. Still, it might solve one of her problems, because if Tori wasn't around, surely the twins wouldn't have a problem with Alice dating Will.

"What are you thinking?" Will asked.

"She's thinking she better help me get this buffet set up so we can eat," Kristen said. "We're supposed to start in five minutes." She gave Alice a friendly smile and nudged her out of the way. "Grab a ladle, dear, and a pot. It's not hard." She began to ladle the meat sauce into one of the wells.

Alice turned away from Will, still trying to define her thoughts. Thankful for the distraction, she handed Will a ladle and set the pot of marinara in front of him, and together the three of them got everything in the right place and back out onto the hot buffet.

"This is amazing," Eloise said, coming to stand beside Alice as she gazed at the hot bar.

"This is a great investment," Alice said, reaching out to touch the buffet. "Will you do a lot with it?"

"I'm going to steal this pasta bar idea," Eloise said, smiling at Alice.

Alice returned the gesture and gave Eloise a side-hug too. "Thanks for having us all here, El."

"I'm sorry you don't have the big house to host us in

anymore," Eloise said, and Alice was touched by her kindness. No one had acknowledged that Alice might be having a hard time selling the house on Rocky Ridge. Alice was supposed to be stoic and sure of herself all the time. Alice barely had feelings.

None of that was true, and she said, "Thank you, Eloise. I am going to miss that house."

"All right," Kristen said in a loud voice. Alice turned around and stood at her side. "We're ready. Everyone gather over here."

Alice looked around at everyone there, and while they'd started at the lighthouse only eight months ago with just the six of them, their familial group had expanded by quite a bit.

With the kids there, they still had seven extra humans, and when AJ's baby came, that would make eight. She stood next to Matt, and surprisingly, her mother. Alice's smile slipped as she met Sasha Summers' eyes. She wasn't normally so distrusting, but Alice had already seen Kelli get hurt by a family member, and she didn't want AJ to suffer any more at the hand of Diane Proctor.

AJ had filled them all in that afternoon while they relaxed on the top deck of the lighthouse, watching the wind whip the water into white-crested peaks as the waves drove toward shore.

She'd invited her mother, and everyone was allowed to bring who they wanted to the final dinner. Alice had her children and Will with her, and Robin's whole family had come.

Billie had ridden the ferry alone successfully, and she stood next to Eloise, her father, and Grace. She was a gorgeous girl, and Alice's smile hitched back into place when she looked at their little family.

Kelli stood with AJ and Matt, Parker way over by Jamie and Duke on the other side of the room. Rueben and his wife Jean stood with Parker too, and Alice was glad the boy had more people who loved him.

Alice and Kristen stood at the front, and once everyone had settled down, Kristen said, "Welcome to our holiday pasta bar. Alice managed to find pasta in the shape of snowflakes, snowman bowties, and Christmas trees." She smiled at Alice, who knew the next part of the speech.

"Kristen made all of the sauces from scratch," she said. "Charlie cut the rolls, and Ginny made a couple of loaves of garlic bread."

"Santa's elves also came a little early," Kristen said, grinning out at everyone. "They left behind some reindeer cookies, and there's plenty for everyone to have as much as they want."

That was the end of the script, but Alice really wanted to say something else. "Thank you for being here, everyone." Her throat closed slightly, but she was used to powering through emotion. "I'm so glad everyone is spending Christmas in the cove this year, and I hope we can make it some sort of annual tradition."

Kristen put her arm around Alice, and the two women looked at one another. Friendship and sisterhood flowed between them, and Alice loved her Seafaring Girls leader so much.

"All right," Kristen said. "Chief Sherman is going to say grace, and then we'll eat."

A couple of hours later, Alice needed to get out of the heat of the inn. They'd had such an amazing time, with the scent of oregano and tomatoes hanging in the air. She'd eaten far too much chocolate in the form of reindeer cookies, and she'd basked in the candlelight, warmth, and Christmas spirit.

Now, though, she slipped her arms into the sleeves of her coat and stepped out onto the front porch. She quickly zipped up her coat and flipped up the hood. The December night held magic in the sky, and Alice looked up at the stars, wondering if she'd ever believed in wishing on them.

Alice hadn't been a whimsical child, and her father had taught her the stars could show her the way home. She'd loved them for that reason alone, and as her breath steamed in front of her, Alice closed her eyes and felt the peace and stillness of the universe around her.

"Mind if I join you?" Will stepped next to her, and Alice gave him a smile.

"I just needed a few minutes of silence," she said.

"Your friends are great." Will pocketed his hands, which cocked his elbows out slightly.

Alice tucked her arm through the crook of of his arm and said, "Do you want to walk with me?"

"How far are we going?" he asked.

"Not far." She glanced down the road, the moonlight shining on it and making it look like silver. "Just to the rise there and back." She looked at him. "Sound good?"

"I left my hat inside," he said. "If I don't freeze my ears off, I'll be good." He smiled again, drawing Alice's attention to his straight, white teeth, and oh, that mouth. She tore her eyes from his lips and focused on going down the steps without falling. Once her feet were on solid, flat ground, she relaxed a little bit.

"Did things get dried out at your place?" Will asked.

"Enough, yes," Alice said. The new house she'd bought on Diamond Island had suffered some damage. She was covering the cost of the windows in her place, and the sellers of the house she was almost about to own had arranged to have the mold treatments done, bring in the big industrial fans, and get the first level of the house back to normal.

"It helped that the seller is literally Cove Reconstruction."

"That is insanely lucky," Will said. His place hadn't suffered any damage, as he lived on the highest point in the cove.

"How are the ferries coming along?"

"Quickly," he said. "They're sending a fleet of mechanics tomorrow, if you can believe that." He continued to talk about the ways White Sands Worldwide was helping him get the ferry system back to fully operational, and Alice sure did like the sound of his voice.

They arrived at the rise in the road, and Alice didn't want to take another step. If she did, she'd be going down, and she didn't want to climb back up. "It's a beautiful night," she said. "Do you ever ride the ferry at night?"

"Sometimes it's dark when I first go to work in the morning," he said. "Otherwise, no. In fact, it's past my bedtime right now." He chuckled softly, the sound almost echoing around inside Alice's head.

She felt so comfortable with him, like she had nothing to hide. She could be herself and that person didn't have to be perfect.

"So you're a morning person."

"Yes," he said. "What about you?"

"I feel like I'm a morning person and a night owl," she said. "When I was younger, I used to love to ride the ferry at night. Or just be on a boat when the air was the same color as the sea. There's something...exciting about it. I can hear the water; I know it's there, slapping against the side of the boat. But I can't see it." She shivered. "It's like this little thrill."

He turned his head and looked at her, and Alice met

his gaze. "You're an amazing woman, Alice," he murmured.

Her gaze dropped to his mouth, and Alice's mind blanked.

"I want to kiss you," he whispered. "Too soon?"

She turned her whole body toward him and reached out to run her fingers down the side of his face. "Are you going to miss your daughter?"

"Yes," he whispered.

"I can't imagine letting either of my children go live with their father full-time," she said. "I'd miss them so much."

"They're nice kids," Will said, turning to look out over the whole of Sanctuary Island again. "I've liked getting to know them a little bit tonight."

"Thank you." Alice gripped his arm with both of her hands, still pressing her body into his side. "I don't think it's too early for a kiss," she whispered.

Will's smile lit up his profile, and when he turned toward her, the moonlight illuminated the fear in his eyes.

"What is it?" she asked, her own desire firing out of control.

"I haven't kissed a woman in a long time," he admitted.

"You haven't dated?"

"A little bit," he said. "Here and there. Sandi and I split up seven years ago, and nothing's been terribly serious since."

"Is kissing serious business?" Alice teased. "I think we used to do it all the time, and it wasn't too terribly serious."

"Maybe for you," he said, the last word catching in his throat.

Alice's eyes widened as shock and humiliation ran through her. "What does that mean?"

"It means I was serious about us, even way back then. You were the one who thought it was just something fun to do during summer camp."

She searched his face for any hint of a lie, but she couldn't find one. "Will."

"It's okay."

"I'm sorry," she said anyway. "I—I didn't know." It had been exciting to sneak from the girls' half of the summer camp to the boys'. Alice had gotten a thrill just by stealing through the darkness of night, rapping on Will's door, and pulling him outside by the lapels on his collar and kissing him.

"Like I said, it's fine."

"You never asked me out," she said. "Or even to a dance."

"I can't dance," he said. "I didn't take anyone to high school dances." His tone suggested all high school dances were ridiculous, and Alice thought she better keep him away from Charlie.

"You could've taken me to dinner and a movie," she said, still trying to process what he'd said.

"This version of myself can see that," he said. "Thirty

years ago, I could not." He gave her a wry smile, and Alice reached up to put her palm on his cheek, keeping his attention on her.

"I liked you back then, Billy," she said with a smile. "And I like you now, too." She leaned further into him, her heartbeat booming through her chest. "It's been a while since I kissed a man."

"Really?" he asked. "But you just got divorced this summer."

Alice's mouth suddenly felt sticky. "My ex-husband cheated on me a lot," she said, the words just flowing from her. "I didn't let him touch me for about the last oh, three or four years of our marriage."

Her insides burned because of that, and she desperately wanted to kiss Will and see if the things she'd been feeling had any merit at all.

"Alice, I'm so sorry," Will said. "My wife didn't cheat on me; she just didn't want to be with me anymore. She 'fell out of love with me,' whatever that means."

Alice knew what it felt like to fall out of love with someone. "It means she'd had enough," Alice said.

"Enough of what?"

"I don't know. Whatever it was that she thought she could handle forever. Turns out, she couldn't. For me, it was the cheating. I thought I could handle it. I knew Frank slept with whoever he could find in the city. I knew he had serious girlfriends. I thought I could handle him only coming home on weekends, because we had a lot of money. Big houses and fancy cars. Two perfect children, and I was the PTA president, on the HOA board, the whole nine yards."

All of those things had been so important to her once. Now, she counted herself lucky she didn't have to attend meetings where they literally discussed if Mrs. Webb could have eight rose bushes in her yard when she clearly could only take care of seven.

"I can see that about you," Will said with a smile. "You're smart and ambitious. I like that."

"You like smart and ambitious?" she asked.

"You sound so surprised." He looked at her openly, a measure of vulnerability in his eyes that spoke to Alice's soul.

"I mean, a little," she said. "After our summer together, you started going with Eden Brooks, and she was gorgeous. I thought you liked her more than me because of that."

Will gaped at her. "Alice, I didn't like her at all."

"What?" Alice asked. "Yes, you did. You guys held hands, and you snuck off with her during every football game that fall."

Will looked at her, his eyes crinkling in the corners as he smiled. "You were watching me."

She nudged his shoulder. "Stop flattering yourself." She couldn't help thinking how different her life would've been had she dated Billy Bridge her senior year. Would she have married him? Would she have left for college and never come back?

She'd had some pretty lofty goals back then, and she'd achieved every one of them.

Will chuckled and Alice pressed further into him. He'd asked to kiss her, but he wasn't taking any of the hints.

"Will," she said. "Are you going to kiss me?"

A strangled sound came out of his mouth. "I..."

"You asked, and I've been using body language to say yes for the past five minutes." She grinned at him, pleased when he returned the gesture.

"When I snuck off with Eden," he said. "The only way I could get myself to kiss her was if I imagined it was you." With that, he took her fully into his arms, leaned down, and kissed her.

Alice's blood turned to lava in her veins, and she pushed her hands through his hair, her eagerness to be close to him explosive and almost embarrassing.

He slowed her kiss, but Alice wanted to go fast. She was burning up from the inside out, and oh, she liked kissing him. He moved slower than he had as a teenager, and he knew exactly where to put his hands now.

He pulled away and said, "No instructions from you this time. I'm impressed with myself." He grinned as widely as the sea and kissed her again.

Alice couldn't get her brain to work, so she simply wrapped her arms around his neck and kissed him back.

CHAPTER THIRTY

Robin handed Duke a cup of coffee, and he grinned up at her as she stepped over his legs and feet and curled into the couch. "All right, Mandie," she said. "Go ahead." She lifted her own mug to her lips and sipped. The feeling of contentment spreading through her couldn't be described.

No, she hadn't heard from the loan officer at the credit union, and she wouldn't for another couple of days as tomorrow was Christmas Day.

No, Duke wouldn't be out on the water until after the New Year. He would likely drive Robin crazy before her wedding in only four days, but she was going to put him to work to help her with that event. After that, she had a long list of things he could do around the house to keep him out of her hair.

She barely recognized herself inside such calm thoughts.

"Okay," Mandie said. "This one's for Alice." She got up and handed a small package to Alice. Robin smiled at her best friend, glad she and the twins had agreed to come spend Christmas Eve at Robin's. Kristen had joined them too, because she was going to stay with Robin until she found somewhere to live.

Kelli was on Bell Island with her family, and AJ had taken Matt to Pearl to spend the holidays at her sister's house. Eloise and Aaron were at the inn, and Eloise's texts that afternoon had been full of all-cap messages and scads of exclamation points.

The first check-in of the new Cliffside Inn had gone really well, and Robin almost teared up again just thinking about it.

"How did you know I'd even be here?" Alice asked, looking at Robin.

"It's just something I pulled out of my cupboard," Robin said. "Low expectations, Alice."

Alice grinned and untied the blue bow on top of the package. The lid came off easily after that, and she lifted out a bag of butter mints shaped like lobsters. She started to laugh, her fingers already working to untwist the tie holding the mints captive.

"I love these." She plucked out a blue lobster and put it in her mouth. She handed the bag to Will, who sat next to her, but he declined.

"I don't like those."

"You're kidding," Alice said, looking at him with wide eyes.

"Oh, this might be a deal-breaker," Robin joked, grinning at the two of them. Alice had been especially tight-lipped about her budding relationship with Will, but Robin wasn't blind. She was a mother of two teenage girls, and she knew Alice had done something with Will.

His daughter was out of town, and while he had family in the cove, he'd opted to come here tonight for a couple of hours just to spend some time with Alice. Her kids didn't seem super happy about it, but they were minding their manners.

Charlie sat on the hearth alone, close to the tree and Mandie, his eyes watching her as she picked up another gift. She handed it to Charlie, who looked at it. "Duke." He got up and handed the present to him.

"Thanks," Duke said, smiling at Charlie. Mandie and Charlie didn't spend a ton of time together around Duke, but he hadn't made anything too awkward yet.

He ripped through the paper and unwrapped a boxed brownie mix. "Yes," he said, laughing. "Can you make this tonight, baby?" He handed the box to Robin, who shook her head.

"No." She pushed the box back at him. "Ask Mandie."

"Not it," Mandie said.

"Come on," Duke said. "It's my Christmas Eve gift."

"Maybe you should make it, Dad," Jamie said, and

everyone paused to look at her. She said so little that when she did, Robin listened.

"Maybe you should," he quipped, picking up a pillow from the floor and tossing it toward his youngest daughter.

She caught it and laughed, and Robin grinned at everyone in the room. The scent of the pine-scented candle filled the air, but the oyster stew was quickly taking over. There was nothing better than the scent of butter, milk, and seafood, and Robin got up to go check on the stew on the stovetop.

She'd toast the rolls and brush them with garlic butter once they finished their Christmas Eve gift opening.

"This one's for Jamie," Mandie said as Robin lifted the lid, and Jamie opened a pair of pajamas. Mandie, Charlie, and Ginny did as well, and Mandie gave a box to Will next.

"I can't believe there's one for me," he said, looking at Robin.

"You obviously don't remember Robin very well," Alice said. "She can cover any base, usually in a moment's notice."

"Again," Robin said. "Low expectations."

"It's heavy." Will's voice carried surprise, and he glanced at Alice. When he opened the package, he lifted out a box of Monster drinks.

"Charlie said you like those," Robin said.

"I do." Will said, grinning. "This is breakfast for the next week."

"Gross," Alice said, while Charlie said, "See, Mom? I told you those Monster drinks were appropriate for breakfast."

"No," Alice said, shooting her son a dark look. "Not for fifteen-year-olds." She slid a look of disgust toward Will. "I'm not so sure it's appropriate for you, even."

"It's orange-flavored," he said. "It's practically a fruit."

"I guarantee there's not a single ounce of fruit juice in that thing." She reached for it, but Will lifted the cans away from her before she get close.

"Two percent," he said. "Wanna bet?"

"I'm not betting you," Alice said with a grin.

"You guys are grossing me out," Ginny said, getting up. "Can you stop flirting for like, ten seconds?" She threw Alice a disgruntled look and settled onto the bean bag with Jamie.

"Sorry," Alice murmured, her eyes focused on the tree.

Will studied the cans of energy drinks. "Two percent," he murmured, and Robin caught Alice give him a small smile.

"That just leaves you, Mom," Mandie said, getting up and handing Robin the gift.

"Thanks, sweetie." Robin didn't know what was in the package. She'd told Duke the first year they were married that she wanted to have a holiday tradition where they opened one gift on Christmas Eve, and his job was to make sure she had one. When the girls had come along, Robin took care of them. She took care of anyone who came to the house, including her mother, siblings, and this year, Alice and her family, Kristen and Will.

"Wait," Robin said. "What about Kristen?"

"She opened hers," Mandie said, settling onto the hearth and taking Charlie's hand in hers.

"I missed it," Robin said, leaning forward to see Kristen.

She held up the bag of Snickers. "I'm like a ninja."

"You've already opened those," Duke said with a chuckle.

"I'm starving." Kristen smiled at Duke. "I won't ruin my appetite, Duke. Don't worry." With that, she unwrapped another mini candy bar and popped it into her mouth. Jamie snickered, and so did Ginny, and Robin took the opportunity to start opening her gift.

Treats and soda pop were the easiest gifts to give for this Christmas Eve tradition, and the girls always got pajamas. Today, though, Robin peeled back the final layer of paper and saw a long jewelry box.

"Duke," she said, the name mostly made of disbelief. They couldn't afford jewelry, especially right now. She didn't dare open the box, and she lifted her eyes to her husband's. "We can't—"

"I bought this months ago," he said with a soft smile and those sparkling, dark eyes. "Open it, baby."

Robin looked at the dark velvet and cracked the lid. A string of pearls sat there, and she sucked in a breath. "Oh."

"They're from the oysters I've collected this year," he

said. "I took them to Mark, and he made the necklace for me."

Robin heard all the time that had gone into this string, and she fell in love with her husband all over again. "They're wonderful."

"They're not all perfect," he said, reaching for the string. It wasn't long enough to be a necklace, but it would circle her wrist easily. "And they're not all the same size. They're from the wild, and Mark polished them and arranged them the best he could."

"I love them," she said, her voice slightly pinched.

"I love you, Robin," he said. "Our life isn't perfect either, and sometimes we're not very shiny and we're not all in the same place at the same time." He unclasped the bracelet, and she held out her arm. "But our family belongs together." He secured the bracelet and smiled at it, then her.

"We do belong together," Robin whispered, tilting her head back to kiss him. "Thank you, baby."

"Are they being gross?" Alice asked, and Robin broke her kiss with Duke and tucked herself into his chest instead.

"It's different, Mom," Ginny said. "They're married."

"That was really sweet," Mandie said, smiling at Duke and Robin.

"So it's only gross because it's me," Alice said.

"Yes," Charlie said. "You haven't flirted in a while,

Mom. You should let me and Ginny give you some pointers."

Alice looked back and forth between her son and daughter, and Robin laughed at the confused look on her face. "Time to eat," she said, getting up.

"I flirt just fine," Alice said, but all four teens in the room started shaking their heads.

Alice folded her arms and frowned. Robin gestured to her. "Come help me, Alice."

"I'm even more useless in the kitchen," Alice grumbled. "But it'll be better than being told I can't flirt."

Robin had a hard time stifling her laughter, but she'd been consciously trying to get along better with Alice, so she only said, "Put that butter in the microwave."

Alice did, and with both of them turned away from the group in the living room, Robin whispered, "You're doing fine with Will, by the way. He doesn't have a problem with your flirting, and that's all that matters."

Alice closed the microwave and said, "One minute?"

"Yep."

Their eyes met, and Alice nodded. "You're right. I don't want to flirt like a fifteen-year-old. I'm forty-five years old."

Robin grinned at her and handed her a mini-whisk. "Did you kiss him last night?"

Alice's grin said it all, and if it hadn't, the long, wistful sigh certainly did.

Robin giggled and said, “When are you seeing him again?”

“Like a formal date?”

“Yes, without the twins.” Robin turned on the broiler to toast up the rolls. “Grab that garlic powder and put a healthy amount in the butter.” She mimed whisking. “Mix it up.”

“Mix it up,” she repeated. “And we’re going out Friday. There’s a silent auction he wants to go to.”

“Fancy,” Robin said with a grin. “Can’t wait to hear about it.” She slid the rolls in the oven and set the timer for two minutes.

Five minutes later, she called, “Dinner, everyone. Come eat.”

CHAPTER THIRTY-ONE

AJ woke on Christmas morning with a perfect sense of calmness in her soul. Beside her, Matt breathed in softly, comforting her further. She didn't want to get up and disturb the peace, so she rolled over and slid her hand across Matt's stomach.

His breathing changed, and he moved to wrap her in an embrace. "Morning, AvaJane," he whispered. His lips touched her forehead, and AJ kept her eyes closed as she basked in this good man's love.

"I love you, Matt," she whispered.

He tensed, but AJ didn't move at all.

"I want to marry you," she said. "You mentioned it a few days ago, and we haven't talked about it again."

"No, we haven't." He ran his hand up and down her arm slowly. "I love you too, my beautiful AvaJane. You tell me when you want to get married, and I'll be there."

"I want us to plan something together," she said. "It's not just for me."

"I've been married before," he said as if she didn't know. "I want the wedding to be whatever you want."

"I want to get married before the baby comes."

"Okay."

AJ pulled away and looked into his eyes. "I want to wear a white, flowing gown and get married on the beach."

Matt smiled at her, and he was so handsome in the softness of morning. AJ loved this time of day, because the heaviness of life hadn't descended onto her shoulders yet. Her mind woke clear, and she felt like her authentic self first thing in the morning.

"What will I wear?" he asked, leaning his head closer to touch his lips to her cheek.

"You'll wear a pair of loose white pants too," she said, seeing the perfect wedding in her mind. "And a light blue shirt, open at the throat. No shoes. Neither of us will wear shoes."

"Sounds nice," he said, kissing her neck now.

"So maybe May." AJ pressed into his touch, enjoying his kiss in a whole new way. A less frantic way of making love. One where she wasn't trying to escape but to be present with the man she loved.

As he made love to her, AJ stayed right there in the moment, enjoying every kiss, every touch, and every breath she took with Matt.

As she lay in his arms later, she asked, "Are you ready to meet my dad?"

"I did okay with Amy," he whispered, his lips right at her ear. "Didn't I?"

"You did great with Amy," she said. "But you knew her from before. I don't think my father knows you used to sneak into my bedroom when we were in high school." She smiled at the memories, because she now recognized the feelings Matt had always awakened inside her. He'd been telling her for decades that she was good enough just as she was, and she'd been too numb to hear him.

"We're not going to tell him that." Matt chuckled and rolled away from AJ. "We better get up and get going. The girls won't be patient."

Just then, AJ heard squealing, and she slid to the edge of the bed too. She dressed quickly, and she and Matt went downstairs to the living room, where Amy and Donovan had their tree set up.

Mary danced around the tree, her eyes wide and filled with childlike wonder. "Look, Aunt AJ! There's this *huge* present with my name on it." She tiptoed over to the big green and white package AJ had put in the corner.

"You're kidding," she said. "How in the world did Santa get that in here? You don't even have a fireplace."

Mary looked at her with pure joy in her face. "I don't know. Mom! Mama, come look!"

"She's coming," Darcy said as she entered the living

room from the hallway that led into the master suite. "She said to put some coffee on, and Daddy wants toast."

"I can do the toast," Mary said, skipping into the kitchen.

AJ smiled at them, and Matt slid his hand along her waist. She leaned into him and said, "I don't want to exclude myself from my family anymore."

"You won't have to," he said. "My parents would love to see us today, but if we don't make it, we don't make it."

"We'll make it," AJ said. "I want to be part of your family too."

"What about my kids?" Matt asked. "Do you want to meet them?"

A tremor of fear ran through AJ. She'd almost forgotten that Matt had three other children with his previous wife. "Of course," she said. "Whenever you want me to meet them."

"I need to tell them about us," he said. "I haven't done that yet, AJ."

"I know."

"I was afraid they'd think it was too soon."

"It's definitely too soon to be out of bed," Amy complained as she entered the living room. Her hair looked like she'd rubbed a balloon on her head, and AJ grinned at her. She wore a pair of sweat pants and a bathrobe over that, and she looked so Suburban Housewife that AJ couldn't help laughing.

"Too loud," Amy complained.

"It's already after seven," AJ said, thinking of her morning and all she'd done already. "We went to bed at ten-thirty."

"Lucky you," Amy grumbled on her way into the kitchen. "Thank you, Darce. You're my favorite eight-year-old." She dropped a kiss on her daughter's head.

"Why were you up so late?" AJ asked, following her sister into the kitchen. The coffee had just started to drip, but AJ didn't want coffee anyway. She got out the electric kettle and asked Mary, "We get to have hot chocolate on Christmas morning, right?"

"Yeah!"

AJ grinned at her, noting that her sister hadn't said what had kept her awake. Her husband came into the kitchen, and he was barely dressed. He wrapped his arms around Amy and growled, which caused her to shrink into his chest and giggle.

AJ stared at the two of them, not because she didn't want to see them acting like they were in love, but simply because she'd never seen Amy act like this with a man. Even at Amy's wedding, she and Donovan had been very proper.

"Ho ho ho!" someone called from the front door, and Mary shrieked.

"Grandpa!" She ran down the hall toward the door, and AJ had a brief out-of-body moment. Grandpa. Her father would be the grandfather to her child, and she suddenly couldn't wait to see him in that role.

Darcy followed her sister, and Dad came into the living room with both girls in his arms a few seconds later. AJ hardly recognized him, though the eyes were the same. He was simply...different too.

"Morning, girls," he said, and AJ got thrown back in time. Before he'd started drinking heavily, he'd come into AJ and Amy's room and say those two words to them. She'd appreciated that, because it made a completely abnormal situation normal again.

"Merry Christmas, Dad," AJ said, stepping over to hug him. He put down Darcy and Mary and took AJ into his embrace.

"How are you, AJ?"

"Good," she said, taking a deep breath of his cologne, which hadn't changed in forty years. "I'm so sorry, Dad."

"It's okay," he said. "You don't need to keep apologizing. We're just going to move forward." He stepped back and smiled at her. "Okay?"

"Okay." AJ smiled and ducked her head. "I want you to meet Matt. We're going to be married in May or June."

Matt touched her back, and AJ glanced at him. "Matt, this is my father, Wayne Proctor. Dad, this is Matt Hymas, my fiancé, and the father of my baby."

Dad smiled at Matt and extended his hand. "Nice to meet you, Matt."

"You too, sir."

"Oh, no." Dad shook his head. "I'm not a sir."

"He's really not," Donovan said, handing Dad a cup of

coffee. "Come on, everyone. Mary's about to stage a riot if she can't open that big present." He smiled at his youngest, who stood right on the edge of the circle of presents.

He went to join her, and Dad did too. Matt started to follow, and when AJ didn't, he turned back. "You go," she said. "Save me a spot. I'm going to make some hot chocolate."

Amy still loitered in the kitchen too, nibbling on a piece of toast as she surveyed the situation in the family room.

"Thank you for having me and Matt," she said.

"Of course," Amy said. "You're always welcome here."

"Just not late at night," she whispered so no one would overhear her. "You know, you should try waking up early to make love to your husband. Then you won't be so cranky in the morning."

Amy's eyes widened, but AJ knew exactly why she hadn't gone to bed at ten-thirty when they'd all retired.

AJ grinned and poured the now boiling water into a mug. She added the powdered hot chocolate mix and stirred it all into a delicious drink. "I'm just saying, you're rested *and* you're off to a really great start to the day."

She left her sister standing at the island and went to sit next to Matt as Mary ripped into the big green and white package.

CHAPTER THIRTY-TWO

Eloise glanced at her phone, knowing she was already late. She'd had a hard time getting out of the inn that morning, because she'd been conducting interviews for a live-in manager. She found herself enjoying the chats with those who'd applied, and she'd fallen behind in her schedule.

She'd texted the group, so they knew she was still coming to lunch, but she wasn't surprised to find the table full when she finally got to the restaurant.

"I'm so sorry," she said, taking the last spot between Kristen and Laurel. She glanced around at everyone. "Look at all of us here, at a Wednesday lunch." Pure happiness filled her, especially when Kelli pushed a tall glass toward her.

"We got you the virgin strawberry daiquiri."

"Thank you." Eloise reached for a straw and

unwrapped it. "Should we do something like a Good News Minute?"

"Good News Minute?" Alice asked.

"Yeah, remember they used to do those our senior year? They'd highlight all the good things that had happened the previous week. Sixty seconds." Eloise stuck her straw in her drink. "We could do that. Sixty seconds each. Only good news."

"I feel like this is a new tradition," Robin said. "New Year's Eve lunch. Only good news can be discussed."

"I'm down," Alice said.

"Me too," AJ added.

"I'll go first," Kelli said. "The twinhome is *amazing*. It's so clean, and Parker and I had a great Christmas with my mom, and Devon." She smiled around at everyone. "I'd love to have a dinner there with everyone at some point. Nothing big or special. Pizza and bagged salad."

"I will take pizza and bagged salad any day of the week," AJ said with a grin.

Kelli laughed, and Eloise noted how happy she was now. She'd been through a lot in the past eight months, and she seemed more like the Kelli Eloise had grown up with. "I wish I could come to the Wednesday lunch every week," she said. "But some of us have to work, so I'm thinking we should do a Sunday dinner or something where we can all attend."

Several people nodded, Eloise included.

"One more thing," Kelli said. "I hope my time isn't up."

She looked at Eloise, who said, "You have ten seconds," as if she'd been timing her. She giggled, and Kelli grinned at her.

"I filed for divorce yesterday." She took a deep breath and blew it out. "I'm in control of my life for maybe the first time."

A beat of silence covered the table. Then Robin said, "Good for you, Kel."

"Proud of you," AJ said.

"Let me know if I can help," Eloise said. "In any way." She meant it too, because she'd do anything for these women. Anything at all.

"Okay, my turn," AJ said. "Matt and I are planning a late May or early June beach wedding." She beamed like she'd swallowed a ray of sunshine. "That's it. Good news second." She laughed, and Eloise joined her.

"That's it?" Kelli asked. "What about your Christmas with your family?"

"Yes, that was a lot of fun too," AJ said. "It's been really great to include myself with them again. They've been so accommodating and accepting." She actually looked like she might cry, and Eloise didn't know how to make the two halves of AJ line up. She was more emotional and hormonal now that she was pregnant, and Eloise was still adjusting to her new personality.

"And your mother?" Robin asked.

"Uh...that's to be determined," AJ said. "She came to the party, and it was awkward. She says she wants to be in my life, but I honestly don't know if that'll happen. Maybe if I reach out to her, but you know what? I don't want to. I want her to reach out to me. If she does, I'll accept it. If she doesn't...I think I'm in a place where I can accept that too."

"Wow," Kristen said. "That's quite different from what I saw in the pavilion a week ago."

"Yes, a lot has changed in a week," AJ said. "*I've* changed a lot in the past three weeks."

"You're still you," Robin said. "Just a more fabulous version." She grinned at AJ, who smiled back.

"Yes," AJ said. "A more fabulous version." She sipped her soda. "I'm done."

"I'll go," Alice said. "Will and I are getting along really great."

"That's it?" Robin asked, giving Alice a side glance as they sat directly beside one another. Eloise felt a brief flash of being left out of the trio she normally fit inside so well. She had to remind herself that she'd created and lived a life of her own with Aaron and the girls, and she couldn't expect to be inside everything.

"We've kissed a few times," Alice said, grinning. "It's all new and exciting, and he's definitely my boyfriend."

"Wow, straight to the labels," AJ said. "Look at you, Alice."

"Right?" Alice laughed too, and Eloise couldn't help feeling like she barely recognized her friend. She was so different from the waif of a woman who'd come for Joel Shields' funeral, and the complete opposite of the woman who'd brought her children to Rocky Ridge after filing for divorce.

She weighed more, and she laughed quicker. She seemed alive, and Eloise hadn't even realized she wasn't before.

"Robin?" Kristen prompted.

"Duke and I got approved for the loan for the boat," Robin said, grinning. "My mother returned home safely from her cruise, and the wedding went off without a hitch on Sunday." She picked up her soda pop glass and raised it slightly. "To a great holiday season."

Eloise shook her head, because she didn't want to toast to a holiday season that had started with a tsunami. She rolled her eyes at Laurel, but they both raised their glasses anyway. Eloise took a long drink of her fruity concoction, and she loved the tart sweetness of strawberries and lime.

"I talked to Billie about sex," Eloise said. "And I think I did a pretty good job too."

Another beat of silence.

"Wow," Robin said, her eyebrows high. "I thought you were going to say something about the inn."

"The inn is *amazing*," Eloise said. "I'm having so much fun with it. I was late, because I'm doing interviews today for my live-in manager. I've got some great candidates, and while I'd like to keep the apartment for myself, I'm going to be moving in with Aaron, and it's just not feasible for me to keep the apartment just because I like it."

Almost everyone nodded as she spoke, and Eloise was glad they agreed with her. Sometimes she just needed confirmation from people she trusted, and she grinned around at her friends.

"How's your mom?" Kelli asked.

"She's healing up nicely," Eloise said. "She hasn't had any problems with the insurance either, so she's going to be back to new in no time."

"That's great, Eloise," Laurel said, and Eloise smiled at her, so glad she was there.

"Your turn, Laurel."

"Oh, I don't have anything," she said.

"You don't have anything good that's happened?" AJ asked. "Everyone has something good, don't they?"

"You're still dating Paul," Robin said.

"Yes," Laurel said with a duck of her head, a brand-new kind of smile forming on her face.

"Oh, look at her," Alice said, clearly teasing Laurel.

"That smile is very revealing," Kristen said.

"It is not," Laurel said, and she straightened her mouth with relative ease as she lifted her eyes back to the group. "My house is almost all the way fixed too, and I'll be back there by the weekend."

"Where have you been staying?" Robin asked. "It better not be a hotel. I have plenty of rooms if you need a bed."

Laurel took a long drink of her lemon water. Eloise needed to be more like her—someone who drank water and ate salads. She probably ran too, and lifted weights, the same way Aaron did. Sometimes, Eloise still experienced a bit of doubt and jealousy when it came to Laurel, but she knew she didn't have anything to worry about.

"I know that look," AJ said, grinning. "She's been staying with Paul, of course."

"Nothing's happened," Laurel said quickly. "I'm...I'm sure he's frustrated with me, but I just need a little more time before I can do...that."

The women silenced again, and Eloise reached over and covered Laurel's hand with hers. "You've never really said what happened."

"It's Good News Minute," Kelli said. "This doesn't seem like a happy story, and Laurel...you don't have to tell any of us anything you're uncomfortable with."

"Yes, she does," Alice said, shooting a glance at Kelli. "That's *literally* what we do. We force each other to say things that are uncomfortable, and then we work to fix them." She looked at Laurel. "She's been around us enough now. She'll have to decide if she wants to stay in our group or if she wants to find other friends who don't want to help her."

"Okay, Alice," Robin said.

"I'm just saying, we tell each other things that are hard so we don't feel all alone." She looked around at everyone.

"We choose what to share, and when, but everything comes out eventually."

Laurel looked around at everyone, and the restaurant seemed to hold its breath. "I really like all of you," she said. "And I don't have many people I'm very close to. I'm a little...closed off, though. It's going to take some time for me to open up."

"One uncomfortable thing," Alice pressed, causing Kelli and Eloise to shoot her daggered looks. "What?" she asked. "You guys grew up with Robin, and she made us admit to so much. I'm just giving her a break as the pushy one of the group."

"Thanks so much, Alice," Robin said dryly.

"You're so welcome." Alice grinned at her, and the two of them laughed together.

"I was in a very abusive relationship," Laurel said. "He forced me to marry him, and he forced himself on me several times. I'm just—I really like Paul a lot. So much. I like kissing him, and I have very real feelings for him. I know he wants more, and I'm...getting there."

"You take the time you need," Eloise said.

"Yes," Alice agreed. "And now I feel like a jerk for making you talk. I'm sorry, Laurel." She looked at Robin. "How do you do this? It's terrible."

That caused the whole table to burst out laughing, even Laurel. She was definitely quieter than most of the other women, but she reminded Eloise of herself at a younger age, and she felt oddly protective of the woman.

Kristen obviously did too, because she leaned past Eloise and said, "You come eat cookies with me anytime, Laurel. I won't make you tell me anything unless you want to."

Laurel nodded, her smile beautiful and lighting up her whole face. "Thanks, Kristen." She met Eloise's eye, and understanding and compassion streamed between them.

"You're always welcome at Aaron's too," Eloise said almost under her breath. "Okay, Laurel? I hope I didn't make things so awkward that you can't go to him for help."

"You didn't, Eloise," Laurel assured her. "Besides, it was him who made things awkward."

"You're so right." Eloise grinned at Laurel. "Who's next?"

"Just Kristen," Alice said, and everyone looked at her.

Kristen gazed around at everyone. "When Joel died, I thought I'd be so lonely. I thought I'd be alone, and everyone would forget about me."

Eloise sobered, her heart going out to the woman who'd literally made her teenage years bearable.

"But you girls have been exactly who I thought you were. I'm so lucky that you're mine, and that I get to be in your lives."

Alice touched her hand to her heart and reached across the table to squeeze Kristen's fingers. "We love you, Kristen."

"I love all of you." She drew in a breath. "I'm staying with Robin and Duke right now, but I'm going to look at a house on Saturday, and if it's decent at all, I'll have my own place again soon."

"I hope it's decent," Kelli said.

"Me too," AJ said. "And Kristen, I know you miss Joel, but if he hadn't died, we wouldn't be here right now. I would've never come back to the cove."

Eloise didn't think she would have either. She certainly wouldn't have been on that stretch of beach where Aaron had been running with his dog. Her whole life had been steered down an entirely new path when Robin had called and said Eloise needed to come to the cove for Joel's funeral.

Others agreed, but Eloise just listened to them all talk. With the Good News Minute over, regular conversations started to resume.

"Wait," AJ said. "Wait, wait a second, guys."

Everyone quieted down, and Eloise knew what AJ was going to say. "We need to gather every year for the holidays. I want a firm confirmation of that." She looked around at everyone. When no one jumped to commit to such a thing, AJ asked, "Robin?"

"Yes," Robin said. "I'm in for that. I liked what we did this year—a little gathering before Christmas Eve, so we can still do our own individual family traditions."

"I'll pay for the inn," Kristen said. "Four nights, three days, just before Christmas."

"Kristen," Eloise said. "You don't need to do that."

"No, you don't," Alice said. "We can all chip in."

"I own the inn," Eloise said. "No one needs to pay for it."

"It's four nights you can't book your rooms," Robin said. "Of course we'll pay for it."

"So it's settled then," AJ said with authority. "Every year, for the few days before Christmas Eve, we'll meet at the inn for Christmas in the Cove."

"Yes," they all said together, and Eloise watched as a smile spread across each of their faces, none bigger than AJ's.

"All right," a waitress said. "Here's the fried calamari and oysters." She set a couple of platters of food on the table, and it was like none of them had eaten for days. The noise level increased with the food, and Eloise thoroughly enjoyed herself at this New Year's Eve lunch, and she had high hopes for the next twelve months that lay in front of all of them.

Read on for the first couple chapters of **The House on Seabreeze Shore, the next book in the Five Island Cove women's fiction series**.

SNEAK PEEK! THE HOUSE ON SEABREEZE SHORE, CHAPTER ONE:

Kelli Thompson looked at the house she'd owned for decades now, her heartbeat giving her an extra thump she didn't quite understand. She'd been coming here for a few months, and she'd brought Parker several times.

"Thanks, Rich," she said to the RideShare driver. "Could you help me with the boxes in the back?"

"Of course," Rich said, grinning at her over the console. "When are you gonna move in, Miss Kelli?" He was an older gentleman with rich, dark skin and a quick smile every time he saw Kelli. She'd gotten into his SUV many times for a ride from the ferry to this house, and they'd become friends over the past few months.

"Soon," Kelli said, reaching to unbuckle her seatbelt. Getting items for the house from Diamond to Bell Island wasn't easy, and she'd left Parker with Jean Shields today to get some things done.

The springtime ocean breeze met her as she got out of the car, and Kelli took a moment to breathe in the scent of flowers mixed with sea salt. She loved springtime in the cove, and it felt like it was coming early this year, as it wasn't even April yet.

The sky held a shade of blue rarely seen by the human eye, and Kelli looked up into it and felt the magnificence of life pressing down on her. Gratitude for the life she now lived streamed through her, because a year ago, she hadn't even known how unhappy she was.

She'd been through some trials in the past twelve months, that was for sure, and her mind flashed past Zach Watkins, Tiffany Mueller, Julian, hard work in a moldy, greasy kitchen at The Cliffside Inn, a tsunami, getting up at five-thirty to go to work every day, and losing everything she owned to water damage.

She'd also attended a court hearing to finalize her divorce, learned to let go of her tight grip on her son, and spent a lot of time with her mother and her boyfriend.

"Just in the garage, Miss Kelli?" Rich asked, and Kelli snapped out of her memories. She had plenty of others, and in fact, this house was stuffed full of them. She wanted to make even more here with her son, and she once again had the thought that she had more to do before she could move into this house.

And it wasn't moving in several small appliances, new

bedding, and a box of cleaning supplies. That all needed to be done too, of course, and she shivered as the breeze turned into a wind.

She stepped to the back of the SUV and picked up the new coffee maker, stacked a toaster on top of it, and then grabbed the basket where she'd put all the kitchen utensils. She was stocking the house one purchase at a time, using some money from every paycheck.

The house had hardly any furniture, but those were bigger purchases Kelli hadn't been able to afford yet. She'd been saving a little bit from every check as well, and she had four big items on her list before she and Parker could move into this house on Seabreeze Shore.

Two beds—one for her and Parker. A couch. A new dining room table and chairs, one that wouldn't break when she sat down to breakfast.

If she could somehow get those pieces, she could envision herself living in this house.

"Right there is fine," she said to Rich, and he set down the blender and the laundry basket filled with new sheets and pillows. "Thank you so much, Rich."

"You're welcome, Miss Kelli," he said. "You text me when you're ready to go back. I'll come get you."

"Yes, sir." She put down her boxed appliances too and stepped into him to give him a hug. "You say hello to Miss Everly for me, okay?"

"Oh, that reminds me." He stepped away and snapped his fingers. "She sent a buttermilk pie for you."

"She did?" Kelli turned as Rich hustled back to the SUV. "How did she know you'd see me today?'

"It's a weekend," he said as he opened the passenger door and bent inside the vehicle. "I've had the pie since yesterday, but it'll still be good." He lifted it from the glove box, and Kelli gaped at the personal-sized pie. He grinned as handed it to her, and Kelli felt more love from him and his wife—a woman she had never met—than she had from anyone but her best friends.

"Thank you." Her voice choked slightly, and Rich held her tightly.

"She loves to bake," he said, stepping back. "So you're doin' something good for her."

"I hope she feels better quickly," Kelli said, as Everly seemed to have a multitude of health problems Rich had told Kelli about over the months.

"I'll tell her you said so," Rich said. "I best be going. Lots of people coming to Bell today."

"Yes, go." Kelli smiled at him as he got behind the wheel, and she stood in the carport until he left. She started hauling in the appliances and things she'd brought to the house that day, and nothing gave her greater joy than unpacking things she'd worked hard to afford. She put them in cabinets and closets that made sense to her, and Kelli enjoyed the progress she'd made over the weeks.

The kitchen sat clean and ready for her to use. She'd bought curtains and hung them on the windows, one over the sink and a huge one that overlooked the small back yard. The old table and chairs sat pushed into the corner, and Kelli needed to haul it away.

She wasn't paying for any services here yet, though, so she couldn't just put it on the curb and have the garbage truck haul it away.

The pantry held bottled water, fruit snacks for Parker, the popcorn she and AJ shared when they came to the house for their private chats, and a box of protein shakes. Kelli needed to start thinking about stocking the house with more to eat, as well as all the home goods people needed to live.

Toilet paper, paper towels, towels, wash cloths, oven mitts. The list went on and on.

Kelli had lost everything in the tsunami that had hit Five Island Cove just before Christmas, and she'd been renting a fully furnished twinhome on Bell Island since then. Everything she'd been able to replace, she'd bring here, like her own silverware, clothing, and a few blankets.

All in all, she wanted to be ready to move into this house by summertime, but she still wasn't sure she'd make it. She worked as a teacher's assistant at the junior high on Diamond Island, and she managed to pay her bills with that income. There wasn't much leftover, and Julian had been sending her money for Parker before the divorce was final, and now that it was, she was receiving alimony too. The money she got from her ex-husband paid for all of Parker's school expenses, their groceries every month, and as she unboxed the toaster, she realized he'd paid for that too.

"You're getting closer," she said to herself.

After putting away all of the items she'd bought that weekend, she wandered from the back of the house to the front, where a large room spanned the width of the house. The front door sat squarely in the middle of the room, and a large staircase went up to the second floor directly across from the entrance.

The hall beside the stairs led back to the kitchen and dining room, which took up the back of the house. Her father had kept an office in the space to the right of the front door, and the family had enjoyed their movie nights and family meetings in the room to the left.

All the bedrooms were upstairs, including the master suite, and Kelli turned to go that way. She'd shared a bedroom with her younger sister, Heather, while her older one, Sabrina, had always had her own room.

Once Sabrina had graduated and left the cove, Kelli and Heather had their own rooms. She'd always had to share a bathroom, and her parents were the type that didn't keep their bedroom door open.

Kelli still hesitated before going into the master suite, as she was never allowed in there as a child. She wasn't sure why. She'd started Parker's life with him in a bassinet right beside her in the master suite she and Julian had shared once upon a time.

When he couldn't sleep, she brought him into their

bedroom. The door was hardly ever closed or locked, and Parker came into her bedroom at-will, even now.

Memories of the house flooded Kelli's mind as she stood in the large room that had once housed her mother and father's bed. She could see the hulking, dark-wood dresser that had sat next to the door, and the lacy, cream-colored curtains her mom had put over the bay window that looked over the back yard.

Kelli went to the window and looked out, the view of the yard, the cliffs, and the ocean beyond the most beautiful thing she'd ever seen. She did love the cove, though she'd always been afraid of the water. She wasn't as much anymore, but a hint of trepidation still stole through her from time to time when she thought about swimming in the ocean or getting on a boat.

She had to ride a ferry to work every weekday, and she'd had to do the same as a child and teenager growing up. Somehow, a ferry wasn't the same as any other boat, and especially if she stayed inside on the ferry, she didn't worry about sinking.

Her parents had forced her to join the Seafaring Girls, and Kelli hadn't been happy about it. She was now, though, and she thought about the women she loved so dearly.

"You need to tell them all about this house," she said to her partial reflection in the glass. Only AJ knew she owned this house, and Kelli wasn't sure why she wanted to keep it a secret.

"You need to tell your mother."

She wasn't sure how her mom would take the news that Kelli had bought this house and had owned it all of these years. Her mother hadn't wanted it, not after everything that had happened here.

The walls started to whisper, little hisses of sound in Kelli's ears.

She turned quickly and left the master bedroom, skipped going into the one she'd once used, and hurried downstairs instead. She burst out the front door, as she'd done many times before, one instance of when she had fresh in her mind.

When her father had lost the Glassworks, it had felt like everything in Kelli's life stopped making sense. That was the beginning of the end for her family as she'd previously known it, and she remembered keenly listening to her parents argue in loud voices that only increased in volume. She remembered the feeling of unrest, the worry which writhed way down deep in her soul, and the fear that if her family fell apart, she'd crumble too.

She remembered jumping to her feet and leaving Heather and Sabrina huddled together in the hallway outside their parents' bedroom and racing down those steps. Two long strides, and she reached the door.

A twist, a pull, and she burst onto the front porch.

She stood there now, letting the fear and doubt and worry wash through her. Accepting how she felt was the only way she'd been able to rid herself of it. If she didn't allow herself to feel the feelings, they built up to dangerous amounts, infecting her thoughts and influencing her actions.

She didn't want to live like that anymore. She wasn't afraid of what might happen anymore. She'd learned that she could take a situation and work through it. She could think, and she was smart enough to come up with solutions. She could help others, because she wasn't drowning the way she'd once been.

She drew in a deep breath and found her center. "You're okay," she said out loud. She had no idea how to start a conversation with her mom about this house, and she hoped all the progress they'd made over the past year wouldn't be undone when Kelli finally confessed she was the owner of the house.

Her friends could help her, and she took out her phone to send a few texts. Number one, she needed to get this Wednesday off of work. Her friends met for lunch every Wednesday. Kelli could never go, and she tried not to let it bother her. In her quiet moments, though, it definitely bothered her that everyone had a job that allowed them the freedom and flexibility to lunch together every week.

Kelli didn't have that luxury, and her ideas of starting a yoga studio in the right part of the house where her father had once kept his office entered her mind again. That would have to wait though, as she needed money for furniture, food, and the necessities of life before she could even think about starting her own business.

A business that may fail.

Kelli was still mighty afraid of failing. Failing herself. Her son. Her friends.

Her principal said, *I'll call Miriam, and if she can come in on Wednesday, you can have it off.*

Thanks, Kelli typed out.

Before she got confirmation from her boss, Kelli sent a message to the group string that housed Alice, Robin, AJ, Eloise, Kristen, and Laurel.

I have something to tell everyone on Wednesday for lunch. Will everyone be there?

They'd talked about getting together for Sunday dinners, but it had only happened a couple of times. Alice and Robin loved to entertain, and without them, the dinners probably wouldn't have happened at all.

Messages started to pour in, and before another sixty seconds had passed, everyone had confirmed that they'd be there on Wednesday, even Laurel.

Kelli's lungs tightened, but she pushed through the pressure on her chest. This was okay. She could tell her friends about the house, and when she asked for their help with how to break the news to her mother, they'd all have solutions and suggestions she hadn't thought of.

That honestly wouldn't be that hard, because every time Kelli thought about telling her mother about this house, she pushed the idea away. She didn't even entertain it, and keeping the house on Seabreeze Shore a secret was second-nature to her now.

She took another breath and released the tight grip her fingers had on the railing. She looked down at her fingers as the tension released, a plan coming together. Kelli loved plans, and once she had one, she could execute it. Her friends would help her come up with a plan to tell her mother about this house.

"Kelli?"

She looked up from where she'd been staring at the porch railing, her pulse pounding at the familiar voice.

Her mother stood next to her car in the driveway, pure confusion on her face. "What are you doing here?"

SNEAK PEEK! THE HOUSE ON SEABREEZE SHORE, CHAPTER TWO:

AJ Proctor finished her third freelance article for the week and sent it to her four biggest contacts. They all knew to check their emails on Sunday evenings, because AJ tended to work in spurts, and she liked taking the beginning of the week off from researching, interviewing, and writing as she negotiated contracts and sniffed out new stories.

She worked a lot from Wednesday to Sunday, and she put the finishing touches on her articles so they'd land in inboxes first thing on Monday morning. Some people over the months had learned to check their messages on Sunday evening, and she'd gotten exclusive contracts offered before the new week started from big papers out of New York and LA, Miami and Dallas, and she'd just submitted a story that would blow away the baseball world once it went to press.

"Done?" Matthew Hymas asked as he came into the little office they shared. He pressed a kiss to AJ's neck, and she grinned in his direction.

"Just finished," she said.

He moved away from her and sat at his desk with a groan. "Sounds good." He barely looked at her as he woke his laptop. "My dad wants me at the course by six, because Greg Sherman is going to be there for a press release at seven."

"Oh, right." AJ leaned back in her chair, grateful for her fiancé for making room for her in his life. He'd moved in the desk where she worked, and he'd been sharing his bed with her since a week or two before Christmas.

Matt shared his family with her, and he came along with her to spend time with her friends. She still hadn't met his children yet, as none of them had come to the cove in the past three months.

A blip of anxiety moved through her, but AJ had tactics to tame it before it grew into full-blown panic. She'd been seeing a counselor here in Five Island Cove every week since the new year had begun, because she couldn't be on her anti-depressants and anti-anxiety medication during her pregnancy.

She put her palm against her belly, trying to feel the life within her. She'd been told at her last doctor's appointment that she should start to feel the baby move at any point now, but she still hadn't felt anything except sharp disappointment.

In the beginning, Matt had asked her questions about her health every day. He doted on her constantly, and he was so good and so kind to her. He still was, but now that the morning sickness had ebbed away, all that was happening to AJ was an increased midsection.

She definitely had a little baby bump now, but she didn't have to leave the house for anything she didn't want to, and she had covered up her pregnancy with sweaters and bulky winter jackets for the past few months.

Matt still hadn't told his parents about AJ's pregnancy, and she knew he hadn't told his kids. He hadn't been divorced for a year yet—that anniversary wouldn't happen until July. Their baby was due in August, and AJ had been trying to see things from his perspective.

She tried not to worry about what his silence might mean or not mean, but she wondered what his end-game was.

Their wedding was slated for May twenty-eighth, and as AJ clicked to open the calendar on her laptop to see they were exactly sixty-eight days away.

"Are your children coming to the wedding?" AJ asked. The only time she ever brought up his kids first was when speaking about the wedding.

"Justin is," Matt said. "He'll be here in three weeks, remember?"

"Yes," AJ said. His youngest son was finishing his first year at NYU, and he'd asked if he could come live in Five Island Cove with Matt. He'd taken a job at the family golf course in order to save money for his sophomore year of studying civil engineering. "I'll have the room ready for him."

"It's ready already, sweets," Matt said, wearing a smile in his tone.

AJ turned her chair to look at him, and she found that handsome smile on his face. He kept his beard neat and trimmed, and when he'd asked her if he should dye his hair to keep the gray away, she'd steadfastly protested. She loved the silver in his beard and sideburns, and she got up to kiss him.

"Mm," he said, grinning to break the kiss.

"Have you told Derrick or Lisa?" AJ asked, settling herself on his lap, though he clearly had work to do for tomorrow's press conference at the golf course. Gregory Sherman was running for major of the cove this year, and AJ didn't doubt for a moment that he'd win.

His son was the Chief of Police, and everyone on all five islands loved Aaron Sherman. He was marrying one of AJ's best friends in only a few weeks, and the Cove Chronicles had called it the wedding of the year.

Robin had been thrilled, of course, as she'd been working on Eloise and Aaron's wedding for the past eight months. Eloise had finally embraced having the wedding of her dreams, and AJ couldn't wait to see it.

She and Matt had been planning something similar, and with Robin's help, AJ was sure she'd get the wedding she'd always wanted too.

"I'm going to tell them about it this week," Matt said.

AJ's eyebrows went up. He'd never committed to a timeframe before. He'd always said, *I'll tell them soon, AJ.* Or, *I'm just waiting for the right time, Ava.*

He'd never said, *Try to understand, AvaJane,* but that was the message she'd gotten.

She had been trying.

"This week?" she asked.

"Yes." He finally looked away from his computer and wrapped his arms around her. She directed one of his hands to her belly, and he grinned as he put his palm against their baby.

He hadn't wanted another baby; he'd told her that in precise words. They'd used protection when they'd been intimate, even though AJ believed herself to be past the age when she could successfully carry a baby.

Yet AJ had missed her period, taken a test, and found herself pregnant, all within four months of reconnecting with Matt. She knew it was fast, and unexpected. She had no idea how she'd feel if her ex-husband got himself a new wife and a new baby only a year after his divorce was final, and she had no idea how she'd have reacted if her father had met and married another woman at the same time she'd moved out to go to college.

"Lisa wants to come to the cove for her summer vacation before she starts medical school, and she needs to know what she's going to find here."

AJ bit back the question that popped into her mind.

Would he tell his daughter if she wasn't planning to come to the cove this summer?

She hated the poisonous thoughts, but she didn't want to be naïve either. She'd spent plenty of years with men unwilling to commit to her, and she couldn't stand the thought of Matt being one of them.

Perhaps it was time to say something. *Be brave,* she told herself. She didn't want to raise a baby alone, not at her age. At the same time, she absolutely would not marry a man who didn't want to marry her, who was embarrassed to be with her, or who couldn't tell his family about her and his life with her.

"Matty," she said, covering his hand on her belly with both of hers. "Be honest with me. Just be honest. I feel like you're hiding me and our baby from your family." She'd told him several times since Christmas that she wanted to talk to his parents, and he'd put her off.

"I want to talk to your parents about us and our baby. I want them to know they're going to be grandparents again. I want your children to know they're going to have a half-brother or sister." She stopped, because her heartbeat reverberated in her own ears and made her chest vibrate in a strange way.

"I don't care if you tell Melanie or not, because she doesn't really have to be part of our lives. But your kids do, and your parents are."

Matt didn't say anything for a few seconds. "I might have been hiding you and the baby from my family," he finally admitted. "I'm sorry, AvaJane. I'm not embarrassed about it."

"They're going to know," she said. "The baby is due August eleventh, Matt. They can do math. They'll know we've been sleeping together since November." Sooner than that, but that was one thing they didn't have to disclose.

"I know," he said. "You're right. I know you're right. I have this...mental block I can't seem to get past."

"Do you really think Justin hasn't told his siblings?"

"I asked him not to," Matt said practically under his breath. "I shouldn't have done that."

AJ cinched her bravery tight, because she didn't want any secrets between her and Matt. "If you don't want to be with me, it's really okay."

"Don't even say that," he said instantly. "It's not true, AvaJane. I've wanted to be with you since I met you way back in high school." He'd told her that several times, but she needed his actions to start to match up with his words.

"I need you to tell your family," she said.

"I know you do." He shifted, and AJ stood up. "Let's call my parents right now."

"Really?"

"Yes." Matt stood too and took her into his arms. "I love you, AvaJane. Please do not doubt that for even a moment."

"You didn't want another baby," she whispered, watching him.

"A baby is a blessing," he said, his dark eyes serious and genuine. "Especially for you, and I'm thrilled you get to have the things you've wanted. I'm just worried about raising another child. I'm *old*, AJ." He grinned at her, and AJ couldn't help smiling back up at him.

"So am I," she said. "We can do it. Together, Matty. We can do anything together."

"We sure can." He kissed her temple and reached for his phone. "Let's get them both on the speaker." He tapped and a moment later, the line started to ring.

"Matthew," his father said, as he always used Matt's full name.

"Can you get Mom?" Matt asked. "I need to tell you both something."

"Sure," Yancey said. "Give me a minute. She went into the storage room to find some chocolate chips."

Barbie Hymas made cookies as easily as breathing, and AJ wasn't surprised to hear she'd gone to find an ingredient to satisfy her husband's sweet tooth. The time passed between her and Matt in silence, and then his dad said, "We're both here, Matthew."

"We're both here too," Matt said. "AvaJane and I. Mom. Dad. We're going to have a baby."

"Oh, my goodness," Barbie said, her voice mostly made of shock.

Matt cleared his throat, his gaze seeking and finding AJ's. She reached out and cradled his face, a physical reminder that they could do anything together. "The baby is due in August, and we're getting married at the end of May. We want you there for all of it."

"Of course we'll be there for all of it," Barbie said. "Congratulations, you two."

His father said nothing, AJ noted, but his mother carried the conversation with her excitement and the call ended when Matt promised his father he'd be at the golf course on time in the morning.

AJ released the breath she hadn't realized she'd been holding in the bottom half of her lungs. "Thank you, Matt."

"We're not done yet," he said, still tapping on his phone. "Let's call Derrick first. Once Lisa knows, she'll want to call the boys and talk it all through." He smiled at AJ, and she marveled that he didn't harbor any apprehension in his expression. She only knew he was nervous about telling his kids about his new relationship and the new baby because he'd told her he was.

They made the call to Derrick, who said he suspected something, because Matt had been posting pictures of him and AJ on social media. He didn't seem terribly upset, and he said he'd come to the cove for the wedding in May.

"One left," Matt said with a sigh. AJ gave him a smile, because she knew this wasn't easy for him. It wasn't easy for her either and meeting his children would be worse. She'd only meet Justin before the actual wedding as things stood right now, and she wondered if she should suggest she and Matt go visit his other children where they lived so she could at least meet them once before she married their dad.

"Hey, Dad," Lisa said, and AJ hadn't even realized he'd dialed. "What's up?"

"Lisa," Matt said. "I have AvaJane Proctor on speaker with me."

"AvaJane Proctor?" Lisa asked.

"She's my girlfriend," Matt said as he sat down in his desk chair. "Wow, there's so much to tell. She's not just my girlfriend, Lise. She's my fiancée, and we're going to be married at the end of May. I'm not sure what your schedule is like, but we'd love to have you there."

He looked up at AJ, who nodded.

"Hello, Lisa," AJ said. "It's AJ. I'd love to include you in whatever you're comfortable doing for the wedding. Bridesmaid or...something."

His daughter said nothing, and she must've gotten that trait from her grandfather.

Matt just held up his palm, and AJ remembered that he'd told her once that Lisa needed a few minutes to absorb information. AJ's pulse ricocheted through her body, because he hadn't even mentioned the baby yet.

By the end of May, she wouldn't be able to hide the pregnancy, and she didn't want to. If she'd wanted to marry Matt in a skinny dress, she'd have done it months ago.

"Wow, Dad," Lisa finally said. "Okay, yeah. When? What day in May?"

"The twenty-eighth," AJ said. "It's a Sunday."

"Just a sec," Lisa said. "Yes, I can be there by then." She cleared her throat. "I'd like to be in the wedding, AJ. Thank you for offering."

Warmth filled AJ, and she beamed at Matt's phone. "Of course," she said. "I'm glad you want to participate. I can start to send you details, if you'd like."

"Sure." They exchanged numbers and email addresses, and AJ climbed back into Matt's lap while he chatted with his daughter about her upcoming finals, and her plans for moving to Colorado for veterinary school.

He then surprised AJ with the words, "AJ and I will be in Maryland for your graduation, Lise. Love you, baby."

"I love you too, Dad," his daughter said, and the call ended.

He sighed and pressed his face to AJ's chest. "You'll go to Maryland with me, right, AvaJane?"

"Of course," she said, still somewhat surprised. "I didn't realize you were going."

"I'm going," he said. "She's my oldest, and my only daughter. She's been at Johns Hopkins for four years on a scholarship." He wore the pride right in his eyes. "Of course I'm going."

"Then I'll go too," she said. Her stomach clenched, and AJ winced slightly. She was used to having different aches and pains in her abdomen since she'd learned she was pregnant, but this felt different.

She let out a cry and put her hand on her stomach.

"Hey, what's wrong?" Matt asked, covering her hand with his. "Are you okay?" Concern filled his voice and face, and AJ wanted to tell him she was fine.

But pain ripped through her core, moving from front to back, and all she could do was suck in a breath and then let out a scream. The piercing pain sliced through her with white-hot precision she didn't understand, and all AJ could think was, *Please don't let me lose the baby now.*

Not after Matt had just called his parents and told them. Not after he'd called his children and told them about her and the wedding. He hadn't mentioned the baby, but now that his parents knew, the word would spread quickly.

"Matt," she whimpered as the pain subsided. "There's something wrong."

"Let's go to the ER," he said, moving so that AJ had to stand up from his lap. She couldn't quite feel her legs though, and she leaned heavily against the desk in front of her.

"I can't move," she said, fear taking over in such a way that AJ couldn't name where she was or what was happened.

"Then I'll carry you." Matt scooped her into his arms, and AJ wrapped her hands around his neck as she started to cry.

"Hurry, Matty," she said as he hustled toward the front door. He set her delicately in the front seat of his SUV, and AJ's fingers trembled as she pulled her phone from her pocket. She needed all the help she could get, and she put her sister and Robin in a text together before sending a message to both of them.

On my way to the hospital. Having pain in my abdomen. Tell everyone to pray.

Tears streamed down her face as Matt got behind the wheel. She tapped to send the text, and then she dropped her phone as another wave of agony threatened to rip her apart cell by individual cell.

The House on Seabreeze Shore is coming soon!

BOOKS IN THE FIVE ISLAND COVE SERIES

The Lighthouse, Book 1: As these 5 best friends work together to find the truth, they learn to let go of what doesn't matter and cling to what does: faith, family, and most of all, friendship.

Secrets, safety, and sisterhood...it all happens at the lighthouse on Five Island Cove.

The Summer Sand Pact, Book 2: These five best friends made a Summer Sand Pact as teens and have only kept it once or twice—until they reunite decades later and renew their agreement to meet in Five Island Cove every summer.

BOOKS IN THE FIVE ISLAND COVE SERIES

The Cliffside Inn, Book 3: Spend another month in Five Island Cove and experience an amazing adventure between five best friends, the challenges they face, the secrets threatening to come between them, and their undying support of each other.

Christmas at the Cove, Book 4: Secrets are never discovered during the holidays, right? That's what these five best friends are banking on as they gather once again to Five Island Cove for what they hope will be a Christmas to remember.

BOOKS IN THE FIVE ISLAND COVE SERIES

The House on Seabreeze Shore, Book 5: Your next trip to Five Island Cove...this time to face a fresh future and leave all the secrets and fears in the past. Join best friends, old and new, as they learn about themselves, strengthen their bonds of friendship, and learn what it truly means to thrive.

Four Weddings and a Baby, Book 6: When disaster strikes, whose wedding will be postponed? Whose dreams will be underwater?

And there's a baby coming too... Best friends, old and new, must learn to work together to clean up after a natural disaster that leaves bouquets and altars, bassinets and baby blankets, in a soggy heap.

ABOUT JESSIE

Jessie Newton is a saleswoman during the day and escapes into romance and women's fiction in the evening, usually with a cat and a cup of tea nearby. The Lighthouse is her first women's fiction novel, but she writes as Elana Johnson and Liz Isaacson as well, with over 150 books to all of her names. Find out more at www.authorjessienewton.com.

Made in the USA
Middletown, DE
24 August 2021

46763781R00250